TO KILL OR NOT TO KILL

ALSO BY JOHNNY GUNN

Brookside, Oregon Territory Series

Ezekiel's Journey Series

Jack Slater Series

Slim Calhoun, Bull Morrison Series

Snake and the Dog-Man Series

Terrence Corcoran Series

TO KILL OR NOT TO KILL

A Terrence Corcoran Western

JOHNNY GUNN

WOLFPACK
PUBLISHING
— EST 2013 —

Wolfpack Publishing
701 S. Howard Ave. 106-324
Tampa, Florida 33609

wolfpackpublishing.com

Paperback ISBN 978-1-63977-365-7
eBook ISBN 978-1-63977-364-0
LCCN 2024932147

TO KILL OR NOT TO KILL

CHAPTER ONE

"MY FAVORITE TIME of the year, Sean," the tall man with the long and deep red curls waving in the chill air said. His bright green eyes swept across the open face of a hillside still alive with summer's lush green, yet showing the first signs of old age. The lush green, that was, certainly not the man.

He was wearing a bearskin coat to fight off the chill one finds at about eight thousand feet above sea level. Under the warm coat was a large tin badge that read, "Chief Deputy, Eureka County Sheriff." Terrence Corcoran was in his mid thirties, in excellent health, and doing what he loved, roaming the mountains of northern Nevada.

"Just a few days and we celebrate Thanksgiving." Corcoran said.

"First snow coming our way right now, Terrence. Your carrying on is bringing it sure as I'm standing here freezing my manhood off. The only thing good about this time of the year is what we're doing right now. Hunting elk, Terrence. Bringing home sage hen, Terrence. Being able to sit in front of a raging fire all winter, Terrence."

His rolling laughter came from deep in his chest and his eyes sparkled the more he laughed. Sean O'Keefe was a happy man, happy in his work, happy with his life. While Terrence Corcoran had to deal with the gutter-snipes of life, Sean O'Keefe went out of his way to deal with happy, vividly alive, and honest folks.

Sean Gaston O'Keefe, like his hunting companion, was about as Irish as one could get, loved his whiskey, loved the ladies, they returned the effort, and was a splendid hunting companion. He spread his arms wide, looked out across the vast Diamond Valley stretched out far below, and howled like a wolf at moonrise. "It is a fair time of the year at that."

Both men had been raised in Irish immigrant families on the East Coast, but neither had put a foot on the old sod. Corcoran was born four days out at sea when the family emigrated while O'Keefe was born in Boston. Corcoran had to laugh watching O'Keefe howling as well as any alpha dog in the pack.

"And we'll not find any elk if you keep that up." Terrence Corcoran lived in Eureka, the county seat of Eureka County, in the heart of north central Nevada. He had a rugged face, bright eyes, and a natural smile that could turn ugly and mean in a flash of witnessing wrong-doing. He relished these few opportunities to get away from those sometimes difficult duties. He sat down on a broken piece of scrub cedar and rubbed three days of stubble on his chin.

"We've done well, Sean. The elk have cooperated,

too." Corcoran chuckled at his little joke. "Ever wanted to just not go back? Smoke the meat we have, build a rock hut, and just stay?"

O'Keefe looked at him and smiled. The man was a master wheel-wright and learned the trade as a youngster growing up along the docks in Boston. He built wheels for the heaviest freight wagons to the slightest of carriages and had orders pinned to the wall to keep him busy for at least another two years.

"Aye, laddie buck, that I have." He had caught Corcoran spending some time all morning looking at the ground they were covering.

"Have you been looking for man prints, Terrence or are we still hunting elk?"

"Sometimes it feels like no one has ever been where we are, never seen vistas roll out like this, never breathed in cold, thin, energizing air like this. There are no law-breakers up here, Sean. It's forbidden, you know."

"Ha, you say, Terrence, but you're right. The birds and bees and the leaves on the trees but no, not outlaws, ne'er-do-wells, or failures at life. It is a wonder then why more people don't live at these high altitudes, these cold climes."

"I'm glad it is they don't, Sean. Let's go find another elk so some of those having a hard time of it might have a pleasant Thanksgiving. I could spend weeks at a time up here instead of days." Terrance immediately remembered old Gustaf, the kindliest old man he had ever known. Gustaf was a meat cutter and built a stone cabin high in the Diamond Mountains, well above the eight thousand foot level, and he would live there for two months every year.

Gustaf used to say his two months in the high mountains gave him the energy to spend ten months among people. He had more animal friends than people friends, I think. Old age finally caught up with the bugger. Corcoran had a hard time getting back on his feet, not from a physical problem, more from simply not wanting to.

It's a hard and ugly mind that can't hear the poetry one finds deep in the mountains, peaks soaring, grasping for the higher yet clouds scudding along. Winds making the tall pines dance with an erotic cadence, and wildlife plying their trade of staying alive fill a canvas that changes second to second. *At some point,* Corcoran thought to himself while watching a golden eagle scramble to fight off a playful raven, *I'm going to set aside this tin badge I wear and find a mountain of my own.* "Ah, Sean, it's not a dream you know."

His Irish companion gave Corcoran a strange look since he'd not been privy to the first part of the conversation.

CHAPTER TWO

"ARE YOU SURE OF THESE NUMBERS?" An angry William Sherman snarled, shaking the paper in his hand. "If you're right, it indicates something I don't want to think about. Someone in a position of trust may not be trustworthy and that's worse than a slap in the face."

William turned on his company's treasurer/accountant, Gerald McKinnon, with rage in his eyes. The penciled numbers on the note paper meant someone was a thief and that was a hanging offense in Sherman's eyes. He ran the Eureka Mine and Mill as a third-world dictator might, and the thought of an employee stealing from the company was reason for a killing. "I want your full audit on my desk in an hour, McKinnon, and not a word of this is to be spread about. Got it?"

"You'll have it, Bill. We have to keep this quiet until a full investigation can be held." McKinnon got out of the office as quickly as he could knowing that Sherman's volatile anger would light the place up in seconds. Like

Sherman, McKinnon had been with the mine from its beginnings, held a portion of ownership, and the idea of a thief on the payroll was cause for alarm.

Every mine manager was aware of the lust for gold in many men's hearts and that often actual nuggets of gold would be found in the mining process. There were mining men who would take the chance and steal from the company. High grading was an art form with some while others didn't consider it a crime, rather, just an opportunity to take from those who had.

Controls on the product were strong. Ore in, processed, and gold and silver out, and the left over waste accounted for. The mill was efficient, operating at full capacity most of the time, and there had never been a discrepancy of any kind in the last five years or more. McKinnon had gone over his figures more than ten times and they came out the same every time.

Someone somewhere along the line has figured out how to take almost ten thousand dollars out of the pipeline and it isn't ore, isn't final product. It's actual cash and Sherman won't stop looking until whoever it is is found and probably thrashed if not hung. This really needs to be known by the sheriff but Sherman would never allow that.

McKinnon, while working at the mine was not a miner, in stature or ability. A small, balding man nearing fifty, he might have been the typical visualization of an accountant and he was proud of being one. *Money seems to be slipping out of more than one of our accounts. We have purchasing accounts for each of the departments; mine, mill, assay, crushing, and final recovery. No one person has access to all those accounts except Bill Sherman.* It dawned immediately that he, too, had such access. *Oh, my.*

McKinnon shook his bald head and narrowed his eyes knowing what he had just thought could get him killed in a heartbeat. He eased himself into his desk chair and looked at his notes. "Only two people in this entire operation are in a position to create this kind of shortage. The assay office could possibly alter their reports enough to hide a deficit and of course the manager himself could simply forge some papers. I would have little problem creating a special account." McKinnon enjoyed these discussions with himself knowing no one could hear them.

"So, how would the assay office do it? They could falsify reports then simply take the gold but none of that would show in my reports, so, no, maybe not them. It's not that kind of shortage."

This was an interesting dilemma, a theft, for sure, but not as a gun-in-the-face robbery. No...items—expensive things—were ordered, delivered, and paid for, but none of them seemed to exist. No one has seen oak desks, fine linen, silk drapes, or wool carpet on the property, yet it had been ordered and paid for.

"Fraud of this kind is almost an art form in itself and someone understands planning. They received checks from us made out to fictitious companies. Those had to be cashed somehow." The accountant was amazed at just how easy this fraud came together in his mind. *There has to be two, maybe three people here at the mine, a shyster to handle the checks, and somewhere in the neighborhood of twenty thousand dollars was distributed.*

He was looking at paperwork that indicated purchases from several departments but no receipts or indications that orders were delivered. They were paid for but didn't exist as far as he could tell.

His mind was quick; numbers, he believed, didn't lie, but people did. "Twenty thousand dollars is a lot of money, and it wasn't taken as gold bullion or raw ore. These were mine funds that were taken through false orders." His mumbling comments continued as he went over his figures one more time.

McKinnon spent the next several hours writing the full report and he thought that he was beginning to see how these funds were moved from the mine's coffers to someone else's. "Gonna be damned hard to prove," he muttered, putting the report in a manila envelope to deliver to William Sherman.

"That man's gonna be hard to live with until we clear this up." He saw money flowing to several different companies for a variety of products that would have little use on a mine and mill property. "This would be far more interesting if my job didn't hang in the balance." He looked at the envelope and shook his head.

He wondered how he would get out of Sherman's office alive after telling the man that he, Sherman himself, had signed for a considerable amount of the merchandise and that Sherman's good friend, Assayer Sam Tankersley signed for most of the rest." *Thank the gods of time that my signature isn't on anything.*

Sam Tankersley was a big, ribald man, known as one of the finest assayers in Nevada, and had worked with Bill

Sherman at two other mines. He was married to a lovely woman who had been killed just a year ago. They had two children, Barbara, nineteen, and Sam Junior, coming on seventeen.

Barbara was vivacious, outgoing, and headstrong, giving Sam headaches by the dozen. She wanted to be a singer and dancer, wanted to have her own theater troupe, and there were some that said some of her dancing was far too suggestive.

Her current man friend was a loser in Sam's mind. A gambler, not the ranch owner he said he was. John Nichols was taking advantage of his daughter and Sam was furious about the matter, intending to finally put his foot down and demand Barbara not see him again.

Tankersley had a deep baritone voice and was a fine signer. He and Barbara often sat at the piano singing traditional songs, even ditties Barbara wrote for them. She was a talented young lady, just not very smart in her choices in life.

Junior on the other hand had been troublesome in a different way. He was a big boy, rough in his dress, his actions, and his manners. The boy, like his sister and their mother, was good looking to a fault and knew it. He was arrogant, intelligent, and a born troublemaker. Sam wanted the boy to follow him in one of the fine trades associated with the mining industry but the boy had no desire. Learning a mining trade was not something he had any use for. He was learning a better one in his mind.

"Pa, you slave all day at that mine and don't got much to show for it," he said at supper just a few weeks ago. "I want to work with Slim Caldwell and make more money than you."

"Caldwell's a sneak thief and gambler, Sam. He doesn't have a trade, he has an invitation to a life in prison. You wouldn't do well in prison, Sam, and you aren't doing well by your family, either. We've had this conversation before, and I'm not pleased by your decisions. You're far too bright to see your life as a gambler and crook being the best you can do."

"Bah," Junior said, and left the table, grabbed his coat, stormed out the door.

"He'll be fine, Papa," Barbara said. "He's just trying to grow up."

"He's not growing up, Barbara, he's growing away. Your mother would be crying at what just happened. Talk to him." He remembered a conversation he had with Emmet Taylor just a day or so ago. "You know Emmet Taylot?" She nodded. "Well, he's looking for someone to learn his cabinet making trade. Was thinking of Junior becoming his apprentice. You two were always close. He'll end up in serious trouble if he doesn't change his ways and he isn't interested in listening to an old fudge like me."

Barbara laughed. "Old fudge, is it? I'll put that in one of the skits I'm writing. Mr. Taylor is an artist with wood and Sam has always had time to do some woodwork. I'll talk to him, Papa."

Tankersley sat back and watched his daughter walk out of the room. "One day she's a sweet, charming daughter wanting to help her brother and the next you'd think she was a tart or something." He muttered to himself for another couple of short conversations and gave it up. "One can't solve other people's problems when the other people aren't aware they might have a problem."

CHAPTER THREE

"Looks like you and the mad man had a fine time roaming around in the high peaks," Sheriff Ed Connor said when Corcoran walked into the office. He, along with many others often called O'Keefe the "mad man" but not to his face. It was a Monday morning, just a few days before Thanksgiving and the wind had picked up. It was blowing the clouds through at a high rate, boiling across a gray sky. Corcoran smiled remembering that O'Keefe had predicted the storm.

"I saw the two of you coming through town yesterday. Those mules looked to be carrying a big load. How long have you been doing this, providing meat for those who need help?"

"Oh, my, Ed, I'm not sure. Five years at least. I get my full share, too, you know." Corcoran chuckled, giving the boss a wink and a nod as he poured some coffee. "I'd love to be able to eat elk and deer every day if I could. I'd love to live in those high mountains the rest of my life."

"Ain't nothing holding you back," Connor said. He

poured the two some coffee. "You ain't welded to that badge; ain't got a contract with the county keeping you here."

"It's just a dream, Ed. I am married to this damn badge, you know. Got too many thoughts about people who need help, and people who need some corral work." He sat down across the desk from the sheriff and stared at him for a couple of moments.

"There are a couple of families that will eat well this winter. Ain't easy trying to raise a family on what some of these people are able to earn. Got no profession, not a craftsman, it ain't easy for some. I ain't the only one that helps out, you know." He winked at the sheriff. "You've been known to take in a soul or two during these winters of ours."

Connor looked away, took a sip of coffee, even coughed slightly. And, he changed the subject quickly. "Too many of those out of work become crooks, too," Connor said. "It's a nice quiet morning. What say we go across the street and get some breakfast."

The Bonanza Club featured a café along with its saloon and hotel facilities and the two found a table near a window where they could look out on the main street of Eureka. The town was settled in a long gulch. Some preferred calling it a canyon, and there were mountains crowding in on the north and south. To the west the Diamond Valley's southern end spread out for miles, and continued north all the way to Palisades, Carlin, and the Humboldt River.

The valley was lush, home to many fine herds of cattle along with herds of mule deer and antelope.

Water from the high Diamond Range was plentiful most years. To the north, south, and east of the little town, bands of elk were found in the high country always coming down to the valley floor in the winter. Desert big horn sheep along with mountain goats frolicked in the high peaks.

Often when the fresh snow has fallen and early risers greet the town about the same time as the sun, prints of wild animals will be seen, including mountain lion and bobcat. Wolves and coyotes had been known to hunt right in town during the fiercest of winters.

The village was the county seat for Eureka County, featured a well constructed rock and brick courthouse, and was home to several successful mining operations. The community was served by the Eureka and Palisades Railroad as well as the Wells Fargo stage line, and the citizens enjoyed the services of the Eureka National Bank and the *Eureka Sentinel* daily newspaper.

"Anything exciting happen while me and Sean were gone?"

"Just the regular," Connor said. "We're hosting a couple of drunks who tried to start a war and we have Andy Jorgenson locked up again. Can't keep his hands to himself, that old boy can't. Slapped little Peggy Newsom hard enough to loosen a couple of teeth. This is the third time we've hauled him in. Judge might send him away this time."

"He's mighty lucky I wasn't here," Corcoran said. "Damn it is, but the idea of a grown man hitting a woman raises my blood temperature to the boiling point. Maybe we shouldn't wait for the judge, Ed. Maybe I should just go back in that cell and beat the daylights out of the man."

"He needs it, Corcoran, but you know I wouldn't allow it, and I know you wouldn't do it. Let's think about breakfast, the rest of the day, and a better conversation."

The sheriff's discussion was broken up when little Cindy Cook came flying out of the kitchen and landed squarely in Terrence Corcoran's lap. She flung her arms around the big guy and planted a whopper of kiss on his mug. Corcoran just sat still, enjoying all the frivolity.

"About time you got back, Terrence. My heart has been so cold and lonely. Whatcha gonna have for breakfast? Of course you can have me anytime you want, you know." Cindy didn't quite make the five-foot mark and weighed ninety pounds at the most. She wanted to be Mrs. Corcoran in the worst way and never let Terrence forget that.

Sheriff Connor chuckled watching the show, enjoying the look of helplessness on his chief deputy's face. "If I'm not interrupting anything, I'd like a nice venison steak and a few scrambled eggs, Cindy. Maybe a biscuit or two, also."

Cindy jumped up and almost curtsied to the sheriff, smiled, and said, "And, you, Terrence?"

Corcoran straightened up, a little kid's smile on his face and said, "That sounds good to me." The sheriff just chuckled at what he saw.

"Have you seen Jimmy this morning?" Corcoran asked her with a straight face. Jimmy Henderson was one of the first men in the old camp to start a business. He put up a tent, laid some planks between a couple of barrels, and called the place the Bonanza Club. As the camp blossomed, Henderson built a building, then added a second floor, and eventually added the kitchen and café. It became the social center of the town's activities.

"He's in the counting room," Cindy said. "I'll tell him you're here." She grabbed a quick kiss and danced off toward the kitchen.

"Ain't had that level of energy for nye on to a decade," Sheriff Connor said. "You got plans for the Thanksgiving weekend? Ain't got no family so I'm plannin' on cookin' up a big pot of chilies. Grew some fine peppers this year." His eyes glazed over, and a kind of softness spread across his mug. "I'll let them simmer with onions, chunks of elk and pork, and I'll give thanks to a fine harvest."

Corcoran caught himself chuckling right along with the sheriff. "I might just have to be payin' you a visit. I'll bring a bottle." He had a few more things to say, but Jimmy Henderson picked that moment to make his appearance. "Mornin', Jimmy. Join us."

"Glad to," Henderson said. He grabbed a chair from a neighboring table and settled in. "Saw you riding through town. Nice to have you back. What do you know about Sam Tankersley?"

"At the mine?"

Henderson nodded.

"Heard he's one of the better at assaying. Got a nice family. Neither one of the kids, almost grown now, ever got in much trouble. Understand his daughter, Barbara, is putting together some kind of theater group. Why the interest?" Corcoran asked.

"His daughter, I guess, more than Sam. She's a good

singer, loves to dance, maybe a little risqué at times, but fun to watch. Young and impressionable. Been hanging around some dude who is trying to pass himself off as a rancher north of Palisades. Looks and acts much more like a big-city type gambler."

"Wouldn't happen to have a name, would you?" Sheriff Conner asked.

"Don't think I ever heard it."

"Tell me about this theater thing," Corcoran said.

"She came to me about helping to fund this theater group. They want to rent a building to put on shows and they're looking for sponsors."

"I can almost hear your reaction," Corcoran said. "Something about pulling paying customers out of the Bonanza Club?" Corcoran chuckled seeing Jimmy's face cloud over some. Henderson added the second floor as a hotel when he heard someone else was planning to build one. He added the restaurant when Jasper Collins started building his successful little café.

"Humph," Henderson chortled. "You're right, of course."

"So what did you actually say?" Sheriff Ed Connor asked.

"We'll be adding a music and dance hall this winter and hiring the Barbara Tankersley Players to perform," Henderson said. His eyes were bright and he gave Corcoran an evil look. "See? I'm not always a bad guy, Mr. Corcoran, sir." He sat back and got serious again. "I'm just worried about something that ain't none of my business."

"The young Tankersley girl and the gambler,"

Corcoran said. "That story has been played out many times, Jimmy. Ain't your problem, surely ain't mine or Ed's. It's between Sam and his daughter, and I think Sam's done a fine job raising those kids so far."

Henderson shook his head as if to say, you're right, of course, and headed back to his counting room. "Catch you fellers later."

Corcoran and the sheriff applauded as Cindy Cook arrived with the first of several platters of breakfast. Henderson stuck his head back in the dining room. "It'll be built right on to the back of the saloon but as a separate entity," Henderson said. He laughed. "Don't want my customers to have to leave the building, you know."

"You are the one," Corcoran said. "What would Eureka be without you?"

CHAPTER FOUR

MINE MANAGER BILL SHERMAN was quietly sitting at his desk after going over the paperwork that McKinnon brought him. His brow was knotted and his face showed considerable anger, but what was missing was the physical end of that anger. Sherman was a big, powerful man and his anger often was demonstrated with broken doors, smashed glassware, and thumped heads. Introspection was not in the man's make up, on the one hand, but an understanding of a problem was.

Everything he saw in the audit McKinnon just brought him indicated that he and one other person had been stealing large amounts of money from the company. It did make sense in a way for whoever the thief was to make it look like someone else was responsible, but the manager himself?

"There's something very wrong with these figures, McKinnon." The accountant sat quiet, looked into Sherman's angry eyes, and waited for the explosion he knew might cost him his job. Sherman had fired people for far less than this. He remembered the phrase, "kill the messenger."

"Are you sure of this?"

"The numbers have been checked and double checked, Bill. They are not wrong. Considerable merchandise has been purchased, high-cost items, but none of it is in inventory. I'm in no way suggesting you are behind this, sir, but you signed for the majority of the merchandise." McKinnon, as Sherman himself, realized the fingers were pointed at the manager.

"No, Gerald, I did not, but someone did and that someone is capable of signing my name correctly. Who else's names were used for receiving this stuff?" Sherman was actually almost proud that his accountant would bring such a set of papers to him. "You're a brave man to bring these in here."

Sherman could almost see McKinnon take a deep breath and let it out ever so slowly. "Besides what appears to be your signature, most of the other items were signed for by Sam Tankersley, the assayer."

"Why weren't these purchases questioned? Irish linen? Wool carpeting?"

"Because it appears you did most of the ordering. People aren't in the habit of questioning you, Bill."

"Hmmm." Sherman had to grin, just a bit, looked out the high window in his office in the mine's office building. Clouds had been building for a couple of days, rain or snow was predicted, and Sherman had his own storm to worry about. "I, of course and Sam Tankersley's department along with maintenance are always making considerable purchases."

"Yes, but most of Tankersley's are chemicals and crucibles, some hefty equipment, but not these expensive items that are listed but non-existent. According to the paperwork I've put together, you and Tankersley appear to have signed for just about everything that's been ordered but is missing."

Bill Sherman walked back to his desk and sat down. He looked around the sparse office. A couple of old, ratty chairs for visitors, a large table covered in paperwork acting as a desk, and the hard-backed chair he was sitting in made up the furniture. "So, I'm supposed to be sitting in a comfortable armchair before an oak desk with numerous drawers, eh? There is supposed to be plush carpeting under my dirty work boots? Oh, and elegant drapes over those crusty windows, too?"

McKinnon didn't want to, but had to chuckle at the descriptions. "That's what the mine paid for, yes sir."

Sherman took another look around and frowned some more. *So, Tank and I supposedly signed for all this but I wonder who might be behind it? Tankersley is not, neither am I. So, who? At the mine only a few of us are authorized to sign for or order supplies and equipment and it isn't any of them. This is a well put together scam and probably by someone who knows his way around our operation.*

Sherman had a couple of questions he wanted to ask, but McKinnon was only the delivery man, the bearer of bad news, not the man who might have some answers about people who might know something. Tankersley on the other hand had his nose in every aspect of the mine's operation. Not as the company assayer, but as one who has plans on being a mine and mill manager himself one day.

Sherman chuckled softly. *Tank knows more about this operation than I do, I think. If someone at the mine is behind this he might just be able to tell me who. If this is an outside operation, we might be up the creek.*

"Best ask Mr. Tankersley to come see me. Keep all this to yourself, Gerald. Twenty thousand dollars? Somebody created all this and got paid for it. Amazing," Sherman said. "An artful deception, eh?" He thumped his desk. *I wonder if we have any new people in the office? This didn't start underground or at the mill. This started somewhere in the office complex. I'll take a dull knife to the man when we find him.*

Sherman's anger was still evident but it was mixed with awe and frustration, and Gerald McKinnon slipped out of the office, unscathed. *That man's anger won't be kept inside for much longer and I won't be there.* A smile worked its way across his mug but he was still going to be wary around Bill Sherman for a while.

Sherman watched his accountant leave and sat down to go over the papers one more time, letting his mind calm down. "This is more than an intricate con-job," he muttered putting it together in his mind. Sherman was an engineer and a geologist, had worked underground even during his college years, and had a quick mind.

He stood up and started walking around the less than tidy office. There were a few rock picks, a muck stick, often called a shovel outside the industry, and a few carbide lamps, even underground candle holders stuck in the wall planking. He was talking to himself as he walked, slowly letting this broad and audacious plan work itself out.

"There appears to be three or four companies where purchases were made and payment authorized. Checks were then issued to them. How would someone set that up? The companies have to be fake, so where did the checks go? Who was at the reception line? These were not one time purchases so somebody had to have a way to receive mail and had to have a way to cash those checks."

Banks weren't the answer, Sherman knew that. They were mighty fussy about who could cash a check unless they had accounts with the bank. Since these companies didn't exist in the first place it was highly unlikely someone would take all the time and bother to try and create fake bank accounts.

The deeper he got into it the more complex the fraud became, and the more complex it became the angrier he became. "Someone put an extraordinary amount of time and effort into this scheme. The time and effort paid off to the tune of at least twenty thousand dollars and if I'm reading this correctly, we are open to ordering even more non-existent merchandise. Someone is going to die." He almost crumpled the papers McKinnon provided and carefully laid them back on his desk, a wry, maybe ironic look on his face. "How many people working at this company would have to be involved?"

It wouldn't take that many, he thought. Someone to make up the order and authorize it. Someone to accept the authorization and write the checks. "We're talking two or three people," Sherman said, right out. "I've got to get with McKinnon and change the way we do business."

Oak desks, fine carpet, silk drapes, English walking sticks, Kentucky bourbon, Irish linen, Italian silk. My god-a-mighty, of course mines buy these things. But all of this over just a six-month period? I think I'll instruct Mr. McKinnon to do these in-depth audits a little more often.

He sat back in his chair and stared at the ceiling, trying to put the theft together. He believed that someone at the bank might have some answers for him. Was there anyone else who might either be involved or have some answers? Yes, he thought, maybe someone at the post office. He was interrupted by Sam Tankersley's knock on the door.

"So, Tank, what makes you think you have need of several bolts of Italian silk?"

The heavy-set assayer stood at the open door looking around, wondering what Sherman was talking about. "Silk? What would I do with silk? What the hell are you talking about?"

Sherman indicated a chair and walked back to his. "You authorized payment for several thousand dollars worth of imported Italian silk, Sam. You signed for the delivery and authorized payment. I want to know where that silk is and why you bought it."

"I've never bought silk in my life, Bill. What the hell are you talking about?" Tankersley was tall, like Sherman, and heavy. Unlike Sherman, his heavy was centered around his waist, not his shoulders and chest. His jowls quivered as he looked at the angry mine manager, and his eyes seemed to beg for an answer.

Sherman's anger subsided quickly looking at the forlorn figure slumped in the chair. *I've known this man for many years and I've never met a more honest man. How many hunting trips, how many fish have we caught? He isn't going to take this easily, I'm sure. With his mind, he might even come up with the answers we need.*

"Look at these papers, Sam. Take your time and read every line." He handed the audit across his desk and reached down to open the bottom right drawer of the beat-up desk. A flask of Kentucky's finest was pulled out and Sherman's tin cup was filled to the halfway mark. The flask was returned to the drawer. Tankersley didn't drink.

Tankersley had a fine reputation in the mining and milling world, read through the audit quickly, took a few quick glances up at Sherman, and when he finished pulled a handkerchief out and wiped his balding head. "In all my years working in assay offices in California and Nevada, I've never seen anything like this." He shook his jowly head slowly back and forth, wiped sweat away again.

"Somebody has a fair game of steal the money going here, Bill. I see you've been buying things, too. We've run up quite a bill here. Lordy, lordy, lordy. What do you make of it?"

"That was my question to you, Sam. Recognize anything there?"

"Only one thing," Tankersley said. He sat forward in his chair and laid out the sheets of paper. Pointing at two or three items for Sherman to look at, he began slowly. "Notice that there are two companies involved. One seems to be focused on furniture and hardware while the other sells fabrics, such as carpet, drapes, and bolts of linen and silk. I've never heard of either company before."

"Nor I," Sherman said. "Somebody here on this property is able to sign our names to bills of lading and to authorize payment. It isn't me."

"I hope you don't think I had anything to do with this. I have not, Bill. I have never ordered or signed for anything listed on these pages."

"I believe you, Tank. Don't think otherwise. We've worked together a long time and I've always trusted you. But somebody did sign for all this and the company did pay for all this. Who, Sam?"

"Mighty big question, Bill. My first thought would be to bring in the sheriff. He and

Corcoran could ferret out the culprit."

"And ruin the fine name of our mine and mill. I don't think the group that owns this property would be happy to see those headlines. They'll be unhappy enough getting my report." Sherman showed that he was a politician as well as a mining man and Tankersley hadn't seen that side of him before.

"Really, Bill, I don't think you have any choice. Can't sweep a loss of twenty thousand dollars behind the lagging. We're not talking high-grading here."

Bill Sherman laughed for the first time since receiving the audit and looked at the old assayer, knowing that, underground, a high-grader stole small amounts of gold and hid it behind the lagging along the tunnel walls, to be picked up at the end of shift. "No, Sam, these aren't high-graders we're talking about."

He didn't come right out and say it, but Tankersley got the message that Sherman would be paying the Eureka County Sheriff a visit soon. "I'd be more than happy to be alongside if you want."

"I haven't had lunch in town for a long time, Sam. Let's you and me have lunch at the Bonanza Club, talk this over some, and then visit the sheriff. I'll bring the report. We'll take my carriage."

Gerald McKinnon was looking out the window later that morning and saw Sherman and Tankersley leave the property just before the noon whistle blew. *Maybe they are co-conspirators.*

"Drop me off at the house, Bill, and I'll meet you in just a few minutes. I'd rather not eat in these clothes. Acids and other nasty things that don't taste good are the things I work with." The two gave each other knowing glances as Sherman drove off.

CHAPTER FIVE

BILL SHERMAN WAS STANDING at the bar in the Bonanza Club waiting for the assayer and having a glass of cold beer. "How long does it take to change clothes?" he muttered. "Fastidious bastard." It didn't take a lot to get Bill Sherman upset. First a bunch of mine money missing, a storm brewing, and now, the man couldn't simply put on clean clothes. He signaled Jimmy Henderson working behind the bar for another beer.

It was a cold November day but the predicted storm seemed to have blown itself out. There were still gusty winds blowing a few dried leaves about but no rain or snow. Was it the weather or was it the theft of a considerable amount of mine company funds driving Sherman's mood.

He'd been in the mining business for fifteen years and had never run into a situation like this. "People steal from you, Henderson? Your own people, I mean."

"Only once," Henderson replied with a hint of a

smile. "Got problems out at the mine? If I find someone filching money or material I don't bother going to the sheriff."

"No?"

"Hell no. I take 'em out back, beat the daylights out of 'em and send 'em on their way. Doesn't take long for the word to spread. Don't be stealing from Jimmy Henderson."

Sherman smiled at the thought. He'd done that with more than one high-grader, but this situation was a little different. Trusted people in his office were behind the heist. "Thanks Jimmy. Good idea."

The weather was simply something one had to put up with, whether it be good or bad. The theft however was a different deal. The more Sherman thought about it the more upset he became. *Somebody in my employ knows how to sign my name. Somebody knows how to order merchandise and pay for it with mine funds under my authority. This is more than just running off with twenty thousand dollars. They have taken our money and are thumbing their noses at me.*

"To hell with lunch, maybe I'll just stay here at the bar."

"I haven't seen you here this time of the day in a long time," Jimmy Henderson said, wiping glasses.

"Having lunch with Sam Tankersley. He should have been here by now. He needed to change out of his work clothes. But, he is a little slower than some of us. Better give me one more beer, Jimmy. What's all the building back there?"

"Putting in a small theater. In fact, it's Sam Tankersley's daughter who will be running the place. Having live shows, music, dancers. Eureka's growing up, Bill." He poured the big man another glass of beer.

Sherman blew off the foam and took a long drink. "That Barbara's a go-getter ain't she? Tank thinks she's grown up too fast. She don't mind showing it off some. I wonder how he feels about all this?"

"I know he wouldn't give her any money to try to get her theater group started. That's why she came to me. She ain't no little girl anymore, Bill. She is one fine looking young woman."

Sherman finished his beer and took a long look out the front windows of the Bonanza Club. "Where the hell is that man? He's usually the one hurrying people along. Maybe I'd better go check. Heavy as he's gotten, his heart might have gone out on him."

"Good luck," Henderson said and watched Sherman stride out the door. The mine manager drove his buggy the two blocks to Tankersley's large home and tied the horses off. *Can't possibly take this long to change clothes,* Sherman fumed. He mounted the porch and slammed his fisted hand onto the door three times.

The front door wasn't latched and swung open at the attack and Sherman stepped into the welcoming foyer. "What the hell you doing, Tank? Damn, let's get moving." There was no one in the spacious living room but Sherman couldn't help notice the fine carpet and elegant furniture. Drapes of high quality hung near the windows and a grandfather clock was standing near the fireplace.

"Rather elegant," he muttered. There was no answer

to his call and Sherman moved into the front parlor to the stairs leading to bedrooms upstairs. "Come on, man," he hollered out. Still no answer and Sherman stormed up the stairs, figured the room at the end of the hall was the largest and threw that door open.

"Oh, my god," he said, stepping into the dimly lighted bedroom. The shades were drawn but with the door open, Tankersley's naked and very dead body stood out. The knife was still sticking in the man's chest, clear to the hilt, and blood had spurted well out from the body. He turned and bolted down the hallway and took the stairs two and three at a time.

He pulled the horses to a sliding stop in front of the sheriff's office and jumped from the carriage, running into the office. "Tankersley's been murdered," he said, panting from all the effort.

Corcoran was seated across the desk from the sheriff, both of them with tin cups of coffee in hand. "Sam Tankersley?" Corcoran said, getting quickly to his feet. "Here, Bill, sit down. You look like hell. What happened. Coffee?"

"Anything stronger? Tank and I were going to have lunch and then come see you," Sherman said. "He needed to change clothes and I went on to the café to wait for him. When he didn't show up, I went to find him. He's naked, in his bedroom with a big damn knife shoved in his chest."

Ed Connor pulled a bottle from a desk drawer and poured the three of them a healthy draught. "You were coming to see me? Why?"

"Our bookkeeper found that we have been suffering a

series of thefts." Sherman reached inside his coat and pulled the folded report. "This is what brought us to town."

"Interesting," Corcoran said. "You're saying you would not have been coming to town if you hadn't been told about the thefts?" He took a quick glance at the sheriff.

"We rarely come to town in the middle of the day. No, Corcoran, we would not have been coming."

Connor gave Corcoran a sideways look, almost smiled, and handed the sheaf of papers to his chief deputy. "Looks like your head accountant thinks maybe you and Tankersley were involved in this."

"Somebody placed those orders in our names and knew how to sign the requests and checks. None of the merchandise is in inventory according to McKinnon. Can't imagine what we'd be doing with Irish linen in a mine anyway." He looked at the sheriff. "No, Ed, I didn't have anything to do with this."

Corcoran emptied his tin cup and slipped into his coat. "Send Lou for Doc Whidby, Ed. I'll be at Tankersley's." Corcoran gave Bill Sherman a long look. "We'll need a signed statement, Bill. I think it would be best if we kept that audit from your accountant as well." Sherman nodded and Corcoran walked out.

"How long have you and Tankersley worked together?" Ed Connor asked.

"This is the second mine we've worked. The two of us came to Eureka from Placerville, in California. He's one of the finest assayers I've ever known. We're both geologists, too. This is the worst day I've ever had. We've hunted and fished together, worked together for years. I've watched his kids grow up, was with the family when Emily, his wife, died."

The sheriff motioned for Sherman to sit at the desk and handed him some paper and a quill. "Write down what you saw when you found him, Bill and make yourself available for Corcoran, he's sure to have questions."

"Of course," Sherman said. It took just a few minutes for him to write his report and he headed back to the mine not caring that he never did have lunch.

———

CONNOR SLIPPED into the cell area to find Deputy Lou Foster.

"Been a killing, Lou. Go find Dr. Whidby and take him to Sam Tankersley's home. Corcoran is there now. You'll need to work with Terrence on this." Connor went back to his desk to go over the mine audit one more time. His mind was already full of questions.

Did Tankersley interrupt a robbery? Probably not if Sherman found his naked body. If they came to town without anyone knowing they were coming, how did someone know Tankersley would be at his home changing clothes? And why does the accountant seem to think that both Sherman and the assayer were the ones stealing the money?

Connor sat back in his chair, looking up at the ceiling, and smiled. "Corcoran's gonna have fun with this little mystery."

———

SHERMAN WALKED into the offices and called everyone together. Four men handled the day-to-day office work which included daily reports on mine production, mill production, and individual shift production.

Jake Pardee was the office manager. "You don't look well, Mr. Sherman. Can I get you something?"

"Anybody missing today, Pardee?"

"One man, Mr. Samuels, had to leave early. Ate something that made him mighty sick."

"When did he take out of here?" Sherman asked.

"Sometime around ten o'clock, I think. Everyone else is here right now." Pardee answered the question as it was asked. "Anybody missing today?" He didn't mention that Duane Holloway had quit his job two weeks ago.

"Good. Spread the word that we'll be doing a full mine and mill inventory in the coming days." Sherman asked Pardee to come into his office and sent everyone else back to work.

"Tell me about this Jonah Samuels, Mr. Pardee. I'm not sure I've met him."

"He's a big man, worked in the freight business, actually warehouse business in Chicago before coming west. He's a good worker, good with numbers, good with inventory control, not that easy to get along with. Has a nasty temper. I've had to reprimand him more than once about that. He's not married, no family that I know of, but has friends in Palisades that he visits often."

"Thanks. Anybody else giving you problems?"

Pardee chuckled. No, sir. And Samuels doesn't give me much."

So, Samuels has friends in Palisades. Doesn't mean much to me. But the fact that he left before Sam and I left could mean something to the sheriff. I'll get that word to him. All of this has to be centered right in that office. Connor is going to want to know more about Samuels.

CHAPTER SIX

CORCORAN WAS KNEELED close to Tankersley's body, looking at the knife protruding in a most ugly manner from the overweight man's chest when Doc Whidby and Deputy Foster arrived. "A nasty business," Whidby said. "I've known Sam for almost five years, Terrence. I wonder what led up to this?"

"That's what Mr. Foster and I will be trying to find out, Doc. Ever seen a knife like this?" Corcoran nodded to the ornate handle, a gem-encrusted animal horn laced liberally with inlaid strands of what appeared to be gold and silver.

"European, I believe. Eastern Europe, maybe even Russian. Expensive. Interesting that the killer would leave it behind." Doc Whidby opened his valise to begin his quick study of the corpse.

"My thoughts exactly. Those stones buried in the handle are not fake. The gold and silver in the mountings are heavy, too. This is a showpiece," Corcoran said. "An expensive showpiece."

"I wouldn't leave something like that behind," Foster said. "Shouldn't be hard to find out who owned it. Got to be one of a kind in Eureka."

Corcoran nodded. "When you're through with the remains, I want that knife, Doc." He looked at Foster. "Let's not mention the knife when we first start talking to people, Lou, and Doc, please don't mention it either." *Maybe we can get somebody to hang themselves,* Corcoran thought. "Strong person to drive that blade that deep?"

"Knife slipped between a couple of ribs. Average person could do it."

"Even a woman?" Foster asked and Dr. Whidby smiled and nodded in the affirmative.

"What do you know about Sam, Doc? He's not been active in town goings on, not a hunter that I know of."

"He used to hunt and fish regularly. He's been pretty much a homebody since his wife was killed, Terrence. Hunter? Yes, and fisherman. He's a good fisherman. He has been seen talking with Betty Johansen, the lady who raises goats." Dr. Whidby stood up from the body and wiped his hands on a clean cloth. "She's a looker, Terrence."

Corcoran caught a quick smile from Whidby and wondered if maybe he might be calling on the goat lady as well.

"Remember that, Mr. Foster. Might want to pay a visit. Thank you, Doctor." Corcoran started slowly walking around the rather large bedroom, careful not to touch anything. He stopped by the window and found it closed tight, stood next to a high bureau of drawers, eased himself into a chair in front of a table backed by a mirror, and returned to where Tankersley's body was.

"Whoever did this didn't touch or move anything as far as I can tell," Corcoran said. "How did they get in the house, although Sherman said the door wasn't latched when he got here? How did they know Tankersley was even going to be here?"

Corcoran looked at Lou Foster who just shook his head. Dr. Whidby did the same, and he continued asking questions. "I wonder where Sam Junior is? Or his sister?"

"Young Sam just started his apprenticeship with Emmet Taylor, the cabinetmaker," Foster said. "He's been there for a couple of weeks. His first job since he left school. You want me to talk with him?"

"Good idea. Break the news as gently as you can and be easy on the questions until you have an idea of how the answers are coming." Corcoran watched the young deputy head out and had even more questions for himself.

Is the death of the assayer tied to the thefts at the mine? The audit seemed to indicate Tankersley and Sherman were involved but Sherman obviously had nothing to do with the murder. "When you wrap up here, Doc, make sure I get that knife. I've got to find his daughter. Lock up tight when you leave."

"Wait another minute or two and I'll give you the knife. I've no more use for it. This wound is obvious as far as cause of death goes."

Corcoran watched as Whidby eased the knife from deep in Tankersley's chest. He wiped it clean, admired the keenness of the blade and handed it to Corcoran.

"Three men will be here with the wagon shortly, Terrence. I'll examine the body in my operating room and the children can make the burial arrangements. You can come by anytime this afternoon and I'll have a full report on the death. It's a thin blade and quite sharp. It looks more hefty than it is, but slipped easily between the ribs. I'll have more for you later."

Whidby shook his head and looked at Corcoran. "How can a man this size with this strength, let someone with a knife get that close? Not a single bruise, Terrence. No scratches, no busted knuckles, no bruises."

"I'm afraid I've got my work cut out for me, Doc." Terrence Corcoran went over to the bedroom again, looking at the distance between the door and the body in particular. Could someone rush through the doorway and stab the man before the man could respond? Maybe, Corcoran thought, if Sam had his back to the door and spun around in time to get stabbed in the middle of the chest.

"Unlikely," he muttered. Was he well enough acquainted with the killer that he welcomed him in his bedroom even if he was naked? "Unlikely," he muttered again. Whidby watched the action until Corcoran just shook his head and walked out.

————

CORCORAN FOUND nineteen-year-old Barbara Tankersley standing with Harold Baker, Eureka's well-known carpenter. "Well, Terrence Corcoran," Baker said, "Are you here to tell me how to do my job, too? Seems like the elegant

Miss Tankersley knows more about pounding nails than I do. This will be my last day. Henderson can find someone else to finish this job."

"Hello, Hal. No, you're the expert," Corcoran said. "Doesn't look like your regular crew, here."

"Isn't. Seems as though Jimmy Henderson, who is paying for all this, brought in a crew. I did some drawings of what Henderson and the filly want and turned them over to a guy named Lefty. I'll let them figure it out. I'm outta here."

Baker turned to Barbara and smiled his goodbye. She was not smiling, Corcoran noted and saw that the petite young lady even had her fists balled up. "We need to talk, Miss Tankersley," Corcoran said. "Let's find someplace nice and quiet." He took her elbow and eased her away from the men busy at work.

The young Tankersley stood about five and a half feet tall and was well put together. She wore a close-fitting yellow dress that showed off her nineteen-year-old body very well. While the fashion of the day would have had the hem of the dress scraping the floor, this one ended at about Barbara's knees, giving Corcoran a good look at lovely legs. The scoop neck of the dress made her breasts more than obvious as well.

"This isn't a good time, Deputy. That man isn't building this theater the way it needs to be built. Please, let go of my arm." She stood defiant, her hands on her hips, her chin jutting a bit.

Just like her father, Corcoran thought. *This is what I would have expected from Sam if someone came at him with a knife. Damn.*

"Not just yet, Miss Tankersley." Corcoran had a firm grip on the young lady's elbow and she fought back for another moment or two. They were standing more inside the Bonanza Club than in the new theater addition and Corcoran led them to a table.

"Please, sit down. This is important." There's nothing more difficult for a lawman than to bring this kind of horrible news to relatives, and when the relative is as close as a daughter or son, it's even worse.

"There is no kind way to say this," Corcoran said. "Your father was attacked by someone with a knife early this afternoon. I'm afraid he didn't live."

"Oh, no," Barbara cried out, her hands flying to her face. In less than a second, the tears were flowing and the sobbing began. Corcoran wanted to reach out, draw the young woman close, say all the things that can't be said, do all the things that can't be done. Instead, he sat straight in the chair and reached out to softly take her hand. "I'm terribly sorry to have to bring news to you like this."

At nineteen, Barbara Tankersley was a nicely developed young woman and Corcoran noticed immediately that, as Jimmy Henderson had pointed out, she wasn't backward in letting people know just how mature she had become. *I can understand how a big-city gambler type would zero in on her. I'll have to be careful and try to get more information on the man.*

"Oh," she cried, over and over, gripping Corcoran's hand tightly. "No. Who did it? Deputy? Why would someone kill Daddy? Why?" Corcoran offered her his handkerchief and she dabbed her eyes and blew her nose.

"I'm working on answers for you. You're the oldest and I'm afraid you're going to be called on to be a lot more grown up than you want to be." He was as gentle as he could be but this was the right time to get as many answers as he could. "Can you think of anyone who might want to harm your father? Anyone who might have a grudge or a serious problem? Does your father play at the gaming tables?"

"No. Daddy didn't have any enemies that I can think of. Since Mother died, he's been staying home most of the time. He doesn't even go fishing anymore." She looked at him with the saddest eyes Corcoran had ever seen, tears cascading down her young, soft cheeks.

"There was that one woman. Daddy told her to leave and never talk to him again. That was just in the last couple of weeks."

"Do you know who she was?" Corcoran wondered if Tankersley had a falling out with Betty Johansen, the goat lady of Eureka.

"No. I wasn't there and Daddy didn't mention her name." Barbara Tankersley was trying to stop her sobbing but not doing a good job of it. She was almost wailing her answers at him. Corcoran took the handkerchief from the table and handed it to her. *She's still just a child. How did she get tangled up with this gambler type we've heard about? Naive? Probably, and led like a lamb by a bastard of a man.*

"What was your father's relationship with Betty Johansen? Did they see each other regularly?"

"She's so nice," Barbara said. "She's so sweet. I don't know how she can kill those young goats like she does. Since she and Daddy have been seeing each other it seems like we have roasted goat for supper every other night. I think it's as good as lamb, myself. Do you like it?"

Corcoran saw an immediate change in Barbara's attitude. No longer sobbing but not quite smiling either. "I'll take elk over everything," he said. "Tell me about Miss Johansen." He couldn't get the thought of Tankersley in some kind of difficulty with a woman that his daughter knew nothing about yet is enamored of Eureka's goat lady.

Betty Johansen was Aunt Betty to almost every child in the village, supplied meat and cheese to many of the poor families, and had a bright, engaging personality.

"She's fun to be around, tells off-color stories that make Daddy blush, and can actually dance what she calls a jig. Do you know what a jig is?"

"I know of Irish jigs." Corcoran smiled. He knew how to jig. Get him just slightly in the bag, bring out the fiddle, and watch that man dance. He had half a smile on his face, Barbara's sobbing had toned down to simple sniffles and she continued to talk about Betty Johansen.

"I'm going to ask Betty to be one of the dancers when I get my theater operating. How can I even think about the theater with Daddy being dead. Oh, damn it all," she said, turned almost scarlet at the comment, threw her hands to her face and tried to look away. "I'm so sorry."

"It's quite all right," Corcoran said, doing his best to hide a smile. "You said your father had words with a woman and told her to leave and never come back. What can you tell me about this woman? It might be important."

"I only heard part of what was happening and didn't see her," Barbara said.

Was there more? Corcoran wanted to press the issue but worried, the girl being so young.

Barbara was nineteen with a lovely face and dark but not quite black hair. She had long attractive legs, the legs of a dancer, Corcoran thought, and she wasn't afraid of letting the deputy get a good look. *Give her another five years and I might come calling,* he thought. *So young and so innocent. A big-city gambling man would zero in on this mark.*

Her eyes were brown and dull at the moment but Corcoran could imagine how they might sparkle under the right conditions. *She's a bit of a flirt, uses strong language, and is used to getting her own way. I wonder if she was the reason for the dispute between her father and that other woman? There appears to be a strong bond between father and daughter.*

"I couldn't place her voice either," Barbara said. "She was gone by the time I walked into the room and Daddy didn't say anything about the woman. Daddy didn't have many visitors, except for Betty of course. Mr. Sherman would drop by once in a while but that's about all."

Corcoran wondered if that was when Sherman and Tankersley concocted the plan to rip off the mine, if it was their doing. "What did your father and Bill Sherman talk about, do you remember?"

"Fishing," she said. "That's all they talked about. Fishing and hunting. Bill chided Daddy about not going fishing with him any more, and not hunting. They used to go all the time but Daddy quit doing anything when Mother died."

Corcoran had mixed feelings about the thefts at the

Eureka Mine and Mill. At the moment he was thinking that Sherman and Tankersley were probably involved in the mine's financial shortage, but again, it also seemed their names and signatures were used without their knowledge. *I wonder, though if this unknown woman might be a part of this? Maybe, if she was planning on blackmail, it didn't work, so murder the man? Interesting.*

"Why is Jimmy Henderson fronting your theater troop? I'd think your father would." Corcoran figured that question might raise some hackles and was surprised by the answer.

"Daddy has worked hard all his life and has sunk just about every dime he had into our home. We have, I believe, just about the best of everything as far as furniture, and what makes for fine living. He said he just didn't have any money to spare."

That wasn't the answer Corcoran expected, and he gave the girl another long look. *She's right about the furnishings and her answer sure changes my thoughts about Sam being a part of the plot to defraud the mine. I need to find out about that unknown woman.*

"Thank you, Barbara. Doc Whidby will need to talk about a proper burial. If you remember anything about the unknown woman, let me know." He smiled as he stood up. "Good luck with your theater project." He started to walk away.

"Oh, one more thing." He reached into his coat pocket and brought out the knife, wrapped in a clean cloth. He unwrapped it and held it out for her to see. "Ever seen this before?"

"Where did you get that? I've been searching for it for days now. Why do you have it?"

"Then you have seen it?"

"Of course," Barbara said. "It's part of one of my dance acts. I found it when Daddy took us to Denver last year and knew it had to be a part of an act. It's Persian, according to the man who sold it to me. Dangerously sharp. I don't understand. Why do you have it?"

"I'm afraid this was what killed your father." She gasped and the tears flowed again. Corcoran continued. "You say it's been missing?"

"Yes." She tried to straighten up, wiped her nose, whimpered a little, and shook her head slowly back and forth. "It has always been with my theater props and costumes and it disappeared sometime last week." She reached out for it but Corcoran held on.

"I'll see to it that you get it back but for right now I need it as evidence. I'm sure I'll have more questions as my investigation continues," he said. She continued staring at the knife and he knew he had to ask more questions.

"You said it came up missing. Where did you keep it?"

"In my bedroom at home, with my dance stuff. I don't understand."

"Neither do I," Corcoran said. "Who besides you would have access to the knife."

Barbara took in a deep breath and almost collapsed. "John," she muttered and tried to look away from the almost boring eyes of Terrence Corcoran.

"John?" he asked.

"We were seeing each other. Father told him to leave. He's a rancher but Papa didn't believe that."

Is this the big-city gambler we've heard about? "Where would I find this John feller?"

"He's gone back to his ranch somewhere around Palisades," Barbara said. "He and Papa didn't get along and Papa thought I was too young for him. Oh, this is terrible."

"I'll find out who's responsible, Barbara, and I'm sure I'll have more questions for you." He wrapped the knife and put it back in his pocket. "Again, Miss Tankersley, my deepest condolences. We'll find whoever did this. Is there anything at all you can remember about this woman who upset your father?"

"I don't know why, but I think she was from Palisades, or somewhere north of here. Maybe I'm mixing her up with John."

"John? The rancher?"

She nodded.

"John left for his ranch late last night, I think. Maybe this morning. He's just a friend who owns a big ranch north of Palisades. I thought he was a nice man but I won't be seeing him again." She started to say something else but stopped, shook her head again, and wiped some tears away. "It's not important."

"Thank you, Barbara. If you remember anything, let me know." They shook hands and he watched her walk back to where the carpenters were working. *A mighty fine specimen indeed,* he thought as he made his way across the large open floor to the bar.

Interesting that the man Tankersley didn't want his daughter seeing might be from the same place that the woman Tankersley threw out was from. Partners in a fraud? Might be time for a trip to Palisades.

Jordy Lane was taking care of business and had a cold beer waiting for the tall deputy. "That girl's a pretty one, Corcoran, but just a bit young for you, ain't she?"

"Ain't my type, Jordy, young or not. Her father come in for drinks?"

"Not since his wife died. Used to be a regular. He and some of the hands from the mine would come in after shift for a couple of snorts, but not since the tragedy. He's a recluse anymore." Jordy Lane paused and then started up again. "Well, there has been a time or two with that woman from up near Palisades. She only comes to town once a month or so."

A woman from Palisades? This John character, a gambler or a rancher, from near Palisades? Am I looking at something important or just coincidence?

"Know her name, by chance?"

"Sam called her Lacy. Don't know if that's first or last name. Not much to look at. Kind of dumpy, really, and a high, almost screechy voice. Distracting to say the least."

"Thanks, Jordy. Where's Jimmy?" Maybe, Corcoran thought, Jimmy Henderson might know more about this Lacy woman.

"He's down at the train station. His brother's coming in for a visit. Lives in San Francisco."

"Didn't even know Jimmy had a brother. I'll catch him later. Thanks, Jordy." Corcoran drained the glass and headed out the door. *A woman named Lacy from Palisades meets Sam Tankersley at the Bonanza Club then gets thrown out of Sam's house and told never to return. And the mine finds that twenty thousand dollars' worth of merchandise has been purchased but doesn't exist. Sam dies a terrible death. Are any of these tied together?*

Corcoran was a thinking man, always had been, and with what he'd learned in the last few hours, that head was going to hurt before long. He decided to head back to the office and get some of what he's learned down on paper before it got lost in the shuffle.

And Barbara's been seeing a man described as a big-city gambler type who is passing himself off as a rancher from near Palisades. I think it's coming time for me to make a little trip to Palisades.

Corcoran was almost chuckling as he walked down the main street. "Dumb question, eh? Of course they are connected. It's all the little loops in the knots that have to be undone before I get any answers."

A couple of ladies walking down the boardwalk gave the deputy a strange look, but he just kept right on talking to himself. "I need to know who that woman is. That's the key."

CHAPTER SEVEN

"HELLO, EMMET," Deputy Lou Foster said. He took a step inside the large open doors to Emmet Taylor's cabinet shop where some fine woodwork was produced. Taylor's chairs, tables, chests, and cabinets were known throughout eastern Nevada. "Is young Sam around?"

"Sent him home, Lou. Feller came in just a few minutes ago, said Sam's father was killed, and the boy almost fell to the ground. Should have taken him myself but didn't think about it soon enough." Taylor shook his head and motioned Foster to come all the way in.

"That boy was closer to his father than any boy I've ever known. Worshipped the man, Lou. What happened, anyway."

"Bad thing, Emmet. Tankersley was murdered in his own bedroom. I came down bearing the bad news. Better get back up to their house. Don't want that boy walking in on that scene. Thanks."

It was a quick walk up the hill on the south side of town even though the wind had picked up some. Leaves and dust were blowing around, clouds were building to the northwest and there was a definite chill to the air. As he walked up to the Tankersley home Foster noted that Dr. Whidby's wagon was gone, which meant the body would be, too. He hurried up the front porch stairs, found the door standing open and stepped inside, yelling out for Sam Junior.

"I'm up here," young Sam hollered back. "Who is it?"

"Eureka County Deputy Foster, Sam. I'll be right up." He took the stairs two at a time and found Junior slumped in a chair next to the bloody bed. "I'm so sorry, Sam. I just left Taylor's. Came to see you. Can we talk some?"

"I suppose," the young man said. Junior was what most called him, was seventeen, soon to be eighteen, just out of high school, and apprenticed to Emmet Taylor for maybe lifelong work in cabinetry. His face was etched in iron, Foster thought as he sat in a chair near the bed. The boy's face was frozen in grief, his lips were quivering, but the tears hadn't spilled over yet. Loss was clearly evident.

Junior's eyes were as dark as his hair, sad and dull, lacking the brightness of youth. His mouth, so often in a grin or wide smile was turned down and grim. Foster saw the boy's jaw muscles working hard, teeth set, hischin jutted out. The boy was smacked hard by the realities of maturity.

Where Sam Senior was tall and heavy, Sam Junior was tall and lanky, almost thin, but strong. He had long arms and large hands with long tapered fingers. His shoulders, slumped at the news of his father's death, were normally held high and straight.

"Emmet tells me you and your father were very close. This is a horrible time for you but it's important that we find out who did this. Was your father having problems with anyone that you know of?"

"I don't know. He's never talked about something like that. We've had our problems but they're behind me now." He wiped his nose, tried to turn his face away. "Tell me what happened. There wasn't anyone here when I got home. Why would someone kill my father?"

"We'll find out, Sam," Foster said. He looked at the boy and remembered it had only been a year ago that his mother was killed. That death, despite a vigorous investigation still hadn't been solved.

"Someone knew your father was going to be here. He was murdered but we do have some evidence to work from. Tell me about any problems your father was having. Somebody clearly didn't like him."

"I can't imagine anyone not liking Papa. He was a big, jolly man, loved life, loved his work. I didn't think he had an enemy in the world. He and Mama were very close and it almost killed him when she was killed. He hasn't been the same even though it's been more than a year now."

Tankersley's wife, Gretchen, a lovely lady of German descent, was riding one of her prized English hunters when a stray bullet slammed into the horse's neck. The horse threw a fit of course, blood was flying, and although Gretchen was a fine rider, when the horse collapsed, she was unable to fall free and was crushed under its weight. No one ever claimed responsibility and despite all the efforts of Terrence Corcoran and Sheriff

Ed Connor, the shooter was never discovered. In Corcoran's mind, it was still an open case.

"Did your father have any interests outside the mine? Business interests?"

"There was a woman, a mean old hag if you ask me, who wanted Papa to go into business with her. Some kind of venture that wouldn't take him away from the mine and his work in the assay office. He was vague in trying to describe what this business was, but he told me numerous times that he didn't think it was legal and he didn't want anything to do with it. He didn't like the idea and when she kept hounding him about it, he told her to leave and not come back."

"Do you know what the venture was?" Lou Foster asked. *I wonder if this has anything to do with the loss of funds reported by the accountant? Wouldn't that be nice, to find out this woman is behind that.* "Do you know the woman's name?"

"I think she was from north of here. Up around Palisades, I think. Papa was interested at first but something changed and he turned the whole thing down. She was loud and angry and Papa told her to leave and not come back. Couldn't tell you her name. Don't think I ever heard it." Foster saw the tears begin, knew the boy was going to have a hard time of the loss.

"There's something else, Mr. Foster. Somebody has to tell Betty Johansen about this. She and Papa have been awfully close and she's so nice. She's added a sparkle to our lives and she'll be devastated. I've called her Aunt Betty since I was a kid."

"I know," Foster said. "All us kids called her Aunt Betty. I know where she lives," Foster said. "I'll ride out there now and tell her the bad news. Thank you, Junior. If you think of something, let me or Corcoran know." Foster stood up and was surprised when Junior stood up and offered his hand.

"You've been very kind, Mr. Foster. Thank you. Find out who did this. I wish I was more help."

He's only a few years younger than I am, Lou Foster thought, walking down the stairs. Foster was just a year or two out of school when Ed Connor hired him as a deputy. Deputy Sheriff Lou Foster lost his parents in a horrible fire just a few years ago and could feel that loss again when he was talking with Junior Tankersley. *Aunt Betty. the sweetest person in the whole world. We all teased her, calling her the Goat Lady of Eureka, and she took it as a compliment.*

It was going to be a long ride, those short five miles out of town. Lou contemplating the loss the Tankersley children and Betty Johansen were facing, knowing how his loss had affected his life. "If I know Aunt Betty, she'll take those children under her wings and they'll be loved and safe," he said, almost in a whisper.

———

FOSTER RODE EAST, down out of the Eureka Canyon into a broad valley and found the small Johansen ranch off to the south. Betty had a herd of goats for meat, milk, and cheese along with a small herd of cattle. Johansen Ranch Cheeses were found in many markets in central and eastern Nevada, and the lady had three hands working for her along with two large, aggressive Alsatian guard dogs tending the goats.

The dogs were growling and threatening as Deputy Sheriff Lou Foster rode toward the house. His body language told the world he was not going to step down off that horse unless someone was there to hold those dogs. If he could he would get his feet even higher off the ground. He could plainly hear the snapping teeth and evil growls, and the dogs' eyes were on fire is all Lou Foster could think he saw.

Deputy Sheriff Foster knew the dogs, snarling and snapping their jaws, could very well have taken a leg off while he was still in the saddle. They didn't need for him to step down. But that wasn't their job. They were there to chase the threat away and would only attack if they or their goats were attacked first. In the saddle, Lou was as safe as a baby wrapped in loving arms.

Twenty or more goats were milling about, chickens were trying to get out of harm's way, and dust filled the chilly fall air. One of the Mexican hands ran out from a barn to call the dogs off as Betty Johansen came out onto the porch of the small ranch house tp see what all the noise was about. Chaos slowly became an autumn's calm day.

"Lou Foster," she said. "My goodness, how you've grown, boy. And just look at that big old badge you're wearing. I wouldn't want to be an outlaw in this county knowing you and Terrence Corcoran might be after me. Come in, boy, come in."

Betty Johansen knew every child in the county by

name, had a hand, if she could, in getting them all grown and strong, and had the most lively personality of anyone Lou Foster had ever met. Every kid in the county called the Eureka goat lady Aunt Betty. How many times had he sat at that kitchen table getting first, a taste of fresh cheese, or a glass of cold goat's milk and fresh baked cookies? He smiled at the thought as he rode up to the kitchen fence.

Foster eyed the big white dogs who had calmed down after a talk from the Mexican and stepped down to tie off his horse. "I'm not bringing good news, Aunt Betty," he said, gathering the thin lady in his long, strong arms. "You'd best sit down," he said as they walked into her generous kitchen.

She bustled about, pouring a glass of milk, finding some fresh bread and a tub of sweet butter. "Here, Lou, gotta keep your strength up now that you're one of our protectors. It's been too long since you've been here."

"I know, Aunt Betty. Please, sit down. There's been trouble in town," he said. He dreaded what he had to say, didn't know how to ease the news out. "Someone broke into Sam Tankersley's home and the man, that is, Sam, was killed. I'm sorry to just blurt it out like that, but there's just no other way."

Betty Johansen's face froze, her body almost fell into the chair, and tears coursed their way across high cheekbones and sunken cheeks. "No," she cried softly. "No. Not Sam." She looked up into Lou Foster's soft brown eyes and reached out. He slid his arms around the lady and she held on tight, rocking back and forth, both of them sobbing.

It must have been a close relationship, he thought.

Betty Johansen had never married, wasn't known to even have a close friendship with any one particular man except for this new closeness with Sam Tankersley.

He looked around the old kitchen, saw the crockery that seemed ageless, the beautiful lamps that had been brought from Europe, a cookstove with two full ovens, and the split wood and kindling in boxes alongside. Good memories being sundered by the news he was forced to bring to the lady.

"I'm so sorry, Aunt Betty. How close were you and Sam? Do you know of any enemies he might have had?" He didn't mention the woman from Palisades nor did he mention the losses at the mine.

"I can't imagine anyone not liking Sam," she said. She took a swipe at her eyes with the tag end of her apron, blew her nose, and straightened up in her chair. She reached out and swept some breadcrumbs from the table. Foster saw the softness in her eyes and the hardness in her muscles and wondered about what that relationship might have been like.

The only thing Lou knew about Sam Tankersley was that he was the mine's chief assayer, was overweight, lost his wife in a tragic accident, and had two mostly grown children. What would draw him to Aunt Betty, he wondered and smiled thinking, what would draw the Eureka goat lady to Sam?

"Sam was a teddy bear, Lou. A great big old huggie bear, full of laughter, ready to dance at a moment's notice. Did you ever hear him sing? A most beautiful full baritone that could rattle windows."

She stopped talking suddenly and looked right into

Lou Foster's eyes. "Damn me, Lou, but I really loved that man." It was as if the thought had come, sudden like. Tears flowed and the terribly thin lady was racked with sobs. Foster sat, frozen in place. He had never imagined that Betty Johansen was anything but the strongest woman he had ever known. She did the work of two men around her property, helped deliver goats, helped slaughter goats, milked the does twice a day, and churned her own cheese.

She was still staring into his eyes. "There was someone, a woman who seemed to come into his life not long after his wife was killed. Wanted something from him and he wouldn't talk about whatever it was or the woman. It wasn't a friendly relationship."

"Did he ever mention a name? Or where the woman was from?" This was the second time Foster had heard about a woman who was bothering Sam Tankersley in some way. Was this woman also tied to the death of Mrs. Tankersley? "It might be important, Aunt Betty."

"Someplace north of here. She would come to town once in a while, always on the train. Her visits usually left Sam in a dark mood, an almost angry mood. I don't think I ever heard her name."

"If you can remember anything, get in touch with either me or Terrence. I better be getting back. I'm so sorry, Aunt Betty."

She hugged him tight, tears still wet on her sunbronzed cheeks. "You need some good cheese," she said. She opened a half barrel and pulled part of a wheel of cheese out, cut a large, maybe half a pound chunk of hard cheese, and wrapped it in a dishcloth. "Good for your muscles, Lou. Please come by anytime. You'll always be welcome."

He kissed her lightly on the forehead, tucked the cheese in his saddlebags, mounted up, waved, and rode off back to town. She waved back but there was no smile on the lady's face. Betty Johansen slipped back into the kitchen and plopped down in her chair at the head of the table.

Dear, dear Sam. We were close and I guess I really do love you, old man. Her eyes misted over again as she recalled so many times they sat at this table, so many times he helped her milk the goats, and how many times he took her in those big heavy arms and spoke soft and endearing words that penetrated what had been a bit of a hard heart.

You taught me how to love, Sam. My love had always been directed toward children even though I've never had one of my own. She sat up straight in her chair, blew her nose one more time and glared at the wall across from her. "I ain't no crybaby," she said right out loud. "This isn't what you'd want to see, is it, Sam? I've got animals to take care of, and a ranch that needs work done.

"No sir, Sam Tankersley, you could have had a wife and ranch, even though we never talked about it. But I did think about that. Goodbye Sam," she whispered. "I really did love you." The Mexicans out in the barnyard weren't sure they heard sobs, probably thought it was the goats. She hoped Sam heard.

CHAPTER EIGHT

"You're gonna wear a rut in them boards if you keep that up, Terrence." Sheriff Ed Connor was behind his desk watching Terrence Corcoran pace around the small office. "I hope your mind is working as hard as your legs."

Terrence Corcoran was a big man, broad shoulders, narrow hips, and long legs, a body and head more used to hard work and fast action, and was instead pondering the murder of a man in his own bedroom, a man who might be involved in the pilfering of some twenty thousand dollars from the mine where he was employed.

Corcoran didn't stop but did slow his pace a bit. "Working this Tankersley death around the old head bone, Ed. More than one thing wrong with what I see. There was no fight before he was stabbed. Someone he knew was in his bedroom with a big knife and there was no fight. Worse, he was naked."

"Bill Sherman said he went home to change his clothes so they could have lunch. Who ever killed him must have walked in after he took his clothes off," the sheriff said.

"Makes sense." Corcoran nodded. The pacing kept up. "Had to be someone he knew well enough to not get upset about being caught naked like that. Can't get it out of my mind that he never fought the killer off. Tankersley was a big man, overweight, maybe, but still strong."

Corcoran shook his head and picked up the pacing. "Either someone was already in the house and it didn't bother the man, or someone came into the house and he didn't get upset. A longtime friend? A relative? A neighbor?"

"What do we know about that knife?"

"Learned some," Corcoran said. "On first look it's beautiful, I thought it was a fake, a showpiece for display, not use, although it is sharp as a razor. It belongs to Barbara Tankersley and she had it for one of her dance routines, she said. It's supposed to look like a knife from an eastern European royalty or something like that. Persian, that's what she said." Corcoran stopped pacing and sat across from the sheriff.

"Barbara said the knife disappeared about a week ago. She said she searched for it and was surprised when I pulled it from my pocket. I asked Jimmy Henderson if he'd seen it before and he said he hadn't. Neither had anyone else at the bar or in the restaurant." He shook his head again, tried to smile, and poured a cup of coffee.

"Heard about a woman from Palisades named Lacy who's been having trouble with Tankersley for some time. Don't know if Lacy is a first or last name. Ring a bell?"

"Nope," Ed said. "What did you hear?"

"Barbara told me about her. Said this woman had been pushing hard for Sam to work with her on some kind of project that would make a lot of money. Said Sam at first was in favor but changed his mind when it appeared the project would be illegal. A big argument followed and Sam told her to leave and not come back."

"Interesting. Speaking of Barbara," the sheriff said, "she's involved in theater. Did you ask her about any of that?"

"Only after we talked about the knife. Didn't get into any detail. We'll have more conversations, I'm sure," Corcoran said.

"Did Miss Tankersley know what the project was that got Sam so upset?"

"No, and when I brought it up at the bar, Jordy said that Sam met the woman from time to time at the Bonanza. She would come in on the train from Palisades. Both Jordy and Henderson said that Sam called her Lacy."

"Did you gat anything else?"

"Yup" Corcoran smiled. "Henderson said she was not his type. Short, heavy, gray hair, and just dumpy looking. Never smiled, he said, and had a quick temper. With Sam Tankersley's quick temper, the two must have been fun to watch."

Ed Connor got up and started his own pacing around the small office. "Barbara have anything else to say?"

"Sam's been seeing Betty Johansen, the goat lady. Both Barbara and Junior are pleased with that, too. She's a stick of dynamite that lady is. She even taught Sam how to milk the goats." Both men chuckled at the thought of the slightly rotund Sam Tankersley milking a goat. "Did you know Sam could sing? Barbara wanted him to be in the show she's putting together. He and Betty."

"You've been busy. Let's find out what we can about this Lacy woman," Connor said. "Right now, it's time for the sheriff and his chief deputy to make a quick walk to the Bonanza for a cold beer."

"A cold beer and time to put together a pack, eh? I'd like to take young Foster with me, Ed. He's going to make a fine lawman and a day or two in Palisades will do him good."

"Can't do, Terrence. Nope, that would leave our town open to problems. Take the train out this evening, spend as much time as you need, and get back. I'll send a wire to Resident Deputy Holloway that you're coming. He's a bit headstrong and you might have to remind him that *you're* Chief Deputy Sheriff."

Corcoran chuckled. "Last time I had to remind him he ended up taking some time off to heal up. He'll remember who I am. Holloway worked in the office at the mine before he left. I wonder if he might know something about these fraudulent transactions? He's a little rooster, Ed. I'm still not sure we should have hired him."

"Take it easy on him. Find out what you can. He might have some ideas about some of the people who work at the mine."

Corcoran held the door for Connor and saw Lou Foster at the bar talking with Jimmy Henderson. "Glad you're here. Find anything out?"

"Let's take a table," Sheriff Connor said. "We all have

plenty to say and don't need to make our thoughts the talk of the town." He looked right at Henderson as he spoke. Henderson paid no attention and the men walked off.

Jimmy Henderson brought mugs of beer over and Connor nodded his thanks and waited for the barkeep to make his way back before starting to talk. "You've been busy, Mr. Foster. Bring us up to date."

"Talked with Junior. He was close to his father since he's become an apprentice at the cabinet shop. He's straightened up his act. He told me about some woman who might have been trying to get Mr. Tankersley involved in something illegal. When I visited Betty Johansen, she told me the same story. They were very close as well. Neither Junior nor Aunt Betty knew the woman's name but thought she might be from some-where north of here."

"Good work," Corcoran said. "We think the woman's name is Lacy. Either something Lacy or Lacy something. She might be from Palisades. I'm leaving on the evening train and see if I can find her." He looked at Sheriff Connor. "Right now, she's as close to a suspect as we have."

"'Fraid so," Connor said. "Going back to what you said in the office, Corcoran, about no fight, about Sam being naked. What we've heard about Tankersley's rela-tionship with this Lacy woman is he threw her out, remember? He told her to never come back. He wouldn't welcome her in his bedroom, and him being naked to boot."

Corcoran had to chuckle at the thought. "No, Ed, he most certainly would not. There, see? Damn it, somebody that Sam fully trusted was in that room with him, and him being naked, drove a knife deep into his chest. It would not have been Lacy."

"I agree but we still need to know more about Lacy. What was she wanting to get Tankersley involved in? Why did he throw her out?" Connor looked at his two deputies and took a long sip of beer. "Do we know of anyone closer to town who had problems with Sam? And, gentlemen, what about that big scam and loss at the mine? Was Sam involved as the paperwork seems to indicate?"

"I'm thinking they're all connected," Corcoran said. "What if this Lacy woman came to Sam with this idea of the mine buying considerable amounts of stuff and faking the paperwork and Sam throwing her out, but the woman going ahead with the plan?"

"Might be plausible but somebody at that mine had to be involved." Connor again looked at the two.

"Yeah," Corcoran drawled it out. "Somebody at the mine who might be involved but Sam didn't know that. And that somebody shows up in his home unexpectedly, finds the man naked, and kills him? One person setting up fake companies to accept checks and one person to create fake accounts to be paid by the mine."

"Where were those checks sent?" Lou Foster asked. "Not which company but what town?"

"We have that answer at the office," Connor said. "All the names of the companies and their addresses." Connor looked at Corcoran. "You can check them out while you're there. Also, who at the mine other than Tankersley, Sherman, or McKinnon would be able to manipulate those signed vouchers? Remember, all three of the companies that received money have post office addresses in Palisades."

"I'll find that out," Corcoran said, "And Lou, you find out who it might be at the mine who would have the right to sign off on those purchases. Talk with McKinnon and Sherman and maybe some of the people who work in the business office."

"All of this could very well be connected while it is also possible that we're looking at three completely different situations," Corcoran said. "Simply because Sam didn't want anything to do with Lacy doesn't mean Lacy is a killer, so let's tread a bit lightly until we know more." He shook his head slowly back and forth, his eyes not landing on anyone or anything in particular.

"I can't let go of the fact there was no fight. Lou, your time at the mine could prove dangerous if, as I believe, someone from the mine killed Sam Tankersley. Just walked up to the man and drove that knife hilt deep."

Corcoran wouldn't let go of the idea of no fight at Tankersley's death. The rest of the early afternoon, while preparing for his journey north, he put together half a dozen ways the scene could have played out. *One of the men in the mine office at the helm of the scam finds out that Tankersley knows something. Sam might not look for a fight. So many people at the mine who might be in a position to sign off, using Sam's or Sherman's names on purchases would not raise a fear in Tankersley.*

Corcoran finally just set it aside and prepared for the trip to Palisades. "We'll find Lacy and maybe find other answers as well. One thing I'm certain of," he was talking to himself again. "The theft of money at the mine and the killing of Sam Tankersley are connected."

CHAPTER NINE

"YA CAN'T JUST DRAG an old man from his dedicated work, now, Terrence me lad. I've got people waiting for me to finish their work."

Sean O'Keefe stood in the middle of his carriage and wheel-wright shop, covered in sawdust, wood chips, and sweating from the heat of a forge. Building wood spoked wheels was an art and O'Keefe was a master at the craft. His lathe was turned by his foot pressing a pedal up and down, he was able to fit the iron tires on the wooden wheels while they were red hot. As they cooled, the iron contracted and the assembly was rock solid.

The fact that his carriages were driven by some of the most successful people in Nevada added to his popularity. "Remember now, Terrence, these people pay me for this. Real cash money, bucko."

O'Keefe had two boys in their midteens learning the trade. The boys lived on the property and went home to their parents on the weekends. "What am I going to do with my boys, Terrence? I have responsibilities, you know. Can't just be traipsing off on a whim."

Corcoran chuckled but continued his almost demand that O'Keefe join him on the trip to Palisades. "We'll only be gone for two, maybe three days, Sean, and it's good work you'll be doing. I've got questions that need answers and I need the likes of someone like you to be with me. I'll even see to it that the county pays you a dollar or two for your help."

O'Keefe was a big man, strong shoulders and arms, hands wide and strong, and a chest equal to a large keg. Corcoran and O'Keefe had stood back-to-back in more than one saloon melee, had fought hand-to-hand battles with Paiute and Shoshone bad men, and Corcoran was determined to have O'Keefe on this trip.

"Don't want the county's money, laddie buck, but I will enjoy your company." He had a smile on his well-worn face, thinking about a few days away from a hot forge or a drawknife. "Palisades, is it? Town's grown some. Railroads have put a small dent in my wheel making business, I'm sure you're aware, but Palisades wouldn't even exist if it weren't for the Western Pacific. When do we leave?"

O'Keefe was right about the town's existence. As the Western Pacific made its way east to join up with the Union Pacific, little towns were developed along the right of way. First as a place for staging the work, and then as a stop on the line. It didn't take long for prospectors to move out and discover gold and silver almost close-by. Palisades was a railhead and mining camp, all grown-up in to a full sized town. Ranches had grown up around it as it sits close to the north end of Diamond Valley.

"Train pulls out at six and I've arranged for our tickets. Bring a basket of food for us."

"I've already got the bottle chilling some," Sean laughed, and Corcoran frowned, but only for a moment.

"You're the kind of man who makes a fine travel companion. We need to find a woman named Lacy, need to find out who owns these companies that get their mail at Palisades, and solve Sam Tankersley's murder. Then we can come home."

"Aye, well, if it's just that, let's get moving." Sean O'Keefe was still laughing as Corcoran mounted his horse and rode off to pack.

He grew up as a copper's grandson in Boston, Corcoran remembered. *Hope he remembers some of the things he was taught. Regardless, he's the kind of man I want with me.*

O'Keefe stood in the wide doorway watching. "Finest man I've ever known," he muttered. "All we have to do is solve a murder, solve a large fraud, and find a woman who might have committed both. Sure, and I'm with you, bucko."

———

THE EUREKA and Palisades Railroad evening express north pulled out at 6:03 in a cloud of black smoke and white steam with two boxcars, one of which also served as a baggage car, one flat bed, and two coaches between the engine and caboose, with Corcoran and O'Keefe settled in the rear most coach. Corcoran gave the passengers a quick looking-over and spotted a young buckaroo he'd had problems with recently.

The last time Spider Watson had come to town he picked a fight with one of the miners at the Bonanza Club and got the daylights beat out of him. He was run out of the club, bleeding and bruised and came back an hour later, far more inebriated than when he left. Spider was armed with a shotgun and rifle, threatening to blow half of Eureka's population to Hades.

O'Keefe caught the look that came back from the bushy-haired passenger. "What's that all about, Terrence?"

"That's Spider Watson, Sean. A drunkard at best, a poor example of a horseman, and more than likely on the prod now that he's seen me. You can bet he'll make some kind of fool of himself before the night's over. I took his guns away, slapped him across the side of the head with his own rifle, and stuffed him in the hoose-gow for a night or two. He don't much care for me."

"Humph," Sean O'Keefe said. He didn't give the cowboy a second glance. "I brought some sliced buffalo hump that I smoked last week. Falls apart it's so tender." O'Keefe laughed and reached into his knapsack. "And a bottle of what Jimmy Henderson passes off as fine bourbon. Ain't up to Irish standards, laddie buck, but it's tasty." He produced two tin cups and handed one to Corcoran.

"What's with this Lacy woman we're looking for?"

Corcoran and O'Keefe spent the next hour eating smoked buffalo and drinking good whiskey while Terrence outlined the criminal plot that took some twenty thousand dollars from the mine's coffers, the killing of Sam Tankersley, and how the woman known as Lacy might fit in to it all.

"Somebody went to a lot of trouble for twenty thousand dollars. Robbing a bank might be easier," O'Keefe said. "You say Sam Tankersley was changing clothes when someone barged in and knifed him? And Sam didn't fight back? That's not like him. He was a joyful man, Terrence, could sing like an angel, but was known to stand his ground when pushed."

"Somebody pushed harder," Corcoran said. "Whoever it was had to be well known by Sam. Standing naked in his own bedroom and a visitor pops in? And no fight comes from the visit?"

"Wouldn't happen at my cabin." O'Keefe snorted.

———

SPIDER WATSON SPOTTED Corcoran as soon as the tall lawman boarded the coach and gave him the big stare. His head still hurt but not as much as his feelings. He'd been humiliated twice in the same day, first by the burly hard-rock miner who whopped him a good one, and then by Terrence Corcoran who slammed him across the side of the head with his own rifle.

Gonna take me a chunk of that bastard's hide, I am. Ripping that rifle right out of my hands in front of all those men? Damn me if I ain't gonna kick him in the head and shoot him too. The anger had been building from the moment Corcoran grabbed Spider's rifle, through the two days in jail and now finding the man just twenty feet away.

He watched Corcoran and O'Keefe talk and laugh, eat and drink, knowing Corcoran was telling lies about him. *He's telling him all about beating me up and throwing me in jail. I ain't gonna let him tell no more lies about me.* Spider Watson had to sell his horse to pay the fine that Justice of the Peace Rimfire Gallagher demanded, but he was able to save his saddle, bridle, and saddlebags.

Spider reached in the saddlebag and pulled a bottle of whiskey out and took a long snort of the hot liquid. It burned as hot as his hate had grown, and it only took another two long snorts for the foul stuff to start working. His anger was explosive and he couldn't hold it in another second.

"You're gonna die, Corcoran," he yelled, jumping to his feet with a large Remington six-shooter in hand. Was it luck or did Terrence Corcoran actually see it coming? Regardless, he was on his feet, heavy Colt in hand when Spider jumped up. Two shots sounded like one, but only one man fell to the floor of the rambling rail coach. The only sound for a second or two was the clickety-clack of wheels on rails.

Then there was chaos in the coach, with women shrieking, men growling, and one large lawman standing with a smoking revolver in his hand. "It's all over, folks. Take it easy. There won't be any more trouble." Corcoran kneeled down beside Spider, noted that the man was still breathing, and worked to stem the blood flowing from high on Spider's left shoulder.

The conductor appeared quickly following the shots and helped Corcoran get Watson moved into the baggage compartment. "Ain't had a shooting on one of our runs for more than a year, Corcoran."

"Couldn't be helped, old man. He ain't gonna die but he won't be giving us any more trouble. Spider's had it coming for some time." Corcoran stood up alongside Sparky Mulroon and patted the conductor on the shoulder. "When we get to Palisades, run and find the resident deputy and a doctor, will you? I'll take care of the boy until then."

Sean stepped in as Mulroon stepped out. "Help with anything?"

"Got a handle on it, Sean. Sit and be comfortable and when we get to Palisades, after you get our stuff onto the platform, you might help me get Spider off the train. Sparky's going to find Duane Holloway and a doctor."

Keeping Spider Watson alive was the easy part because when the man awakened, he wanted to fight. Corcoran had the bleeding under control, felt the train begin to slow down and gave Watson an ultimatum. "Make one more stupid move and die, fool. All I gotta do is release the pressure on my left hand and you'll bleed out in one minute or less."

Spider Watson quieted down considerably, and Corcoran did what he could to tie off the wound. "You didn't much care for our facilities in Eureka, Spider, so I'm pretty sure you won't like the ones in Palisades." Corcoran needled the boy just a little bit more. He could feel the boy's anger building and knew, also, that there was nothing Spider could do about it.

"You'll be moved out of there, though. Moved west into the wonderful Carson City Prison. It ain't nice to shoot at deputies, son. Don't do it again, hear?" Corcoran had to chuckle at the flaming language that came from the young outlaw.

"Somewhere along the line, Spider. Somebody forgot to teach you manners, how to behave in public and all that. You ain't much of a buckaroo and you've failed miserably at being an outlaw. You need to get your act together, boy. You're too young to die."

It was one of Terrence Corcoran's calling cards even if he wasn't aware of it. He would arrest if possible, shoot only if he had to, and offer help in some way at every opportunity. The words just spoken to Spider may have not hit their intended mark but they were offered.

CHAPTER TEN

IT WAS LATE when the train pulled into Palisades and the conductor, Sparky Mulroon, spotted the resident deputy already at the station. "Corcoran's in the baggage car. Where would I find Dr. Costello this late?"

"Corcoran start trouble, did he? Should have known that would be happening. What happened?"

"Some young cowhand tried to shoot him. Where's the doc?"

"His office is down that street," he said, pointing north. "You'll see the sign," Holloway said.

Mulroon had some interesting thoughts about the deputy, along the lines of, thanks for offering to help, thanks for being an arrogant, egotistical bastard, and others. *I live here you ass. I know where the office is. That wasn't the question.* He hurried down the street, talking to himself the whole way.

Resident deputy Holloway walked off toward the baggage coach as train station employees were getting the sliding door opened. "Stand back," Holloway said.

"Sheriff's business. Stand back now." He elbowed his way through those who were already trying to help.

He clambered up into the coach and found Corcoran easing the wounded Watson into a sitting position. "Deputy Holloway," Corcoran said. "Glad you're here. Give me a hand here, will you? Need to keep pressure on the wound. Bullet hit a vein. Don't want the fool to bleed out."

"You just gotta shoot people, doncha?" Holloway said. Sarcasm spilled out covered in shards of hate.

"Don't start, Holloway." Corcoran gave the resident deputy a grand scowl and spat out his next word. "Give me a hand now. The doctor will be here shortly and we need to make this fool somewhat comfortable. Since you're here, I assume Ed Connor sent you a wire that I was coming. You know anything about this Lacy person?"

"The only thing I know is that you shot a man on the train coming from Eureka to Palisades. I'll need a full written report on that from you."

"Don't mess with me, Holloway. We've been through this before. I'm chief deputy of this county and you're a resident deputy. Now either help me or get the hell away." He looked up and saw Sean O'Keefe climbing back into the coach.

"Doc is right behind me, Terrence. I'll help him in." O'Keefe bumped Holloway out of the way. "Give me some room, bucko."

"Who is this man?" Holloway snarled and Corcoran came up to his full height towering over the considerably smaller man.

"He's my special deputy on our investigation,

Holloway. Now get the hell out of the way." He shoved the smaller man aside and reached out the door and he and Sean helped the portly doctor into the coach. "He's got a bullet high in the shoulder Doc. He was bleeding pretty heavy there for a while."

"I've got a wagon right out there," Doc Costello said. "Let's ease him out of here and into the wagon. If one of you will drive it, I'll tend him."

"Be glad to, Doc," Sean said. "I'll meet you at the hotel, Terrence." He looked at Holloway and gave him a big smile. "Yup, special deputy. That's me," he said, and he chuckled as Holloway tried to scowl.

Corcoran and Holloway watched the wagon move off and Corcoran turned to the resident deputy. "Just couldn't bring yourself to help, eh? You'd best start helping, and I mean right now. What do you know about this Lacy person?"

"Never heard of anyone named Lacy, man or woman. This is my jurisdiction, Corcoran, and I don't appreciate you just barging in, more or less shooting people."

"All right, Holloway, you've used up your complaints. You are a Eureka County Deputy Sheriff, the resident deputy in Palisades. I am the Eureka County Chief Deputy Sheriff. Chief Deputy for the entire county. The whole damn county, Holloway. Take your sniveling and tuck it in somewhere. You will help me in my investigation or you will give up that badge. Got it?" He was right in Holloway's face, growling, demanding an answer.

Holloway shriveled from the assault, tried to turn away and Corcoran wouldn't let him. "Don't walk away from me when I'm talking to you. I work for Eureka

County Sheriff Ed Connor. You work for me. One more little piece of crap from you and you're out."

There was more than one man standing around waiting for Corcoran to rip the badge from the resident deputy. Holloway was a rooster, wearing flamboyant clothing, highly tooled leather gun belts, tall heeled gambler's boots, and a badge so highly polished it gleamed even when there was no sunlight. Besides all that, the man was arrogant and treated those who lived in Palisades as second-class citizens.

The sheriff had received more than one complaint from up north but settled for simple reprimands, which Holloway seemed to ignore. Corcoran wasn't in favor of hiring the man in the first place but understood how difficult it was to even get someone to hire on as a deputy, more or less be a resident deputy in Palisades.

Corcoran couldn't see it, but more than one man standing on the platform chuckled or smiled. Several nodded their heads in full agreement with the idea of taking Holloway's badge.

Holloway's shoulders sagged at the attack and he slowly let out his breath. He tried to fight Corcoran once and that was a bad decision. Wouldn't do that again. No way was he going to give up that badge. It got him time with some lovely ladies, was always worth an extra beer or two, maybe a meal at the café. No, as much as he detested Terrence Corcoran, he was not going to jeopardize that badge.

"The sheriff told me to work with you, Corcoran. Reminded me that you were the boss, and I will attempt to assist. You had no call to talk to me the way you just did. You had no call to threaten me, either."

Corcoran wanted to either laugh right out or punch the little rooster in the mouth. He remembered when the sheriff told him who was going to be appointed resident deputy in Palisades. Corcoran objected vehemently but to no success. "He's a worn-out miner, relegated to office duty at the Eureka Mine and Mill, Ed. Doesn't have a minute's time wearing a badge."

The argument went nowhere. "Change your attitude, Holloway. Change it right now. I'm going to find our rooms, have a fine supper, and get a good night's rest. I'll be in your office early and you better be prepared to help find answers to my questions." Corcoran turned and found where Sean had their gear placed on a wheeled buggy that could be drawn by a man.

He wheeled the buggy into the hotel lobby and got the two of them registered. With help from the hotel clerk and one other person, Corcoran got their gear into the room, handed the men each a quarter, and sat down on the edge of the bed. *Sean must have brought half of what he owns with him. Lordy, lordy, lordy.*

———

THE CATTLEMAN'S HOTEL was a simple clap-board building, two stories tall with a saloon and café dominating the first level. Their room looked out on the main street, all but empty on this late night. Corcoran went down to the saloon figuring Sean would look there first and of course he did.

"Dr. Costello seems to think you shot him high on the shoulder like that on purpose, Terrence. Apparently he's treated some of your victims before." O'Keefe drank half his glass of beer in one swallow, took a swipe at his massive walrus 'stache and finished the glass off. "Ahhh," he said, easing the empty mug to the bar top.

Corcoran chuckled and motioned for the barman to bring more. "Didn't want to kill the boy."

"Why not? He wanted to kill you."

"I suppose you're right." Corcoran felt the cold beer make its way down and smiled. "Spider was drunk and stupid. Ain't a killing offense, Sean. His attempt at killin' me was, but I ain't that kind of feller."

"What kind of feller are you?"

"I look at it this way, if it's at all possible. What would I gain, what would the fool lose in the shooting?"

"You actually think about it before you shoot?"

"It's an instant thing. To kill or not to kill, Sean. My first reaction was not to kill because I knew I didn't have to. With Spider, all drunked up, I didn't shoot to kill. Let's have us a fine supper, bucko, and get on this Lacy chase in the morning."

O'Keefe looked at Corcoran as if seeing the man for the first time. *I've seen him shoot varmints dressed like men before, and with deadly aim. He has a great dislike for those who break the law, and God help the man who raises a hand to a woman, but this is different somehow. I wonder what that boy means to him?*

The hotel café was almost empty at the late hour and the men had elk steaks, mashed potatoes, and apple pie for desert. "That's what's right about this time of the year, Sean. All the apple trees giving 'em up and all the best cooks proving their pies are the best. I do love the fall."

Sean chuckled. "Applejack barrels are filled, too. Meats are salted or brined or smoked, whiskey barrels and applejack barrels are filled. Better make sure the wood pile is ready for that long winter giving us the eye."

O'Keefe was having fun, turning his comments almost into a song. "Applejack on a cold frosty morning, and good whiskey later in the evening. That's what winter is for, Terrence. I might have to howl with the wolves some."

"You're a fine poet, Sean O'Keefe. Drink up, tomorrow's on its way."

One final nip of good whiskey and the men fell into their beds for a quick sleep. "Morning always comes early, Sean. Let's be ready for it."

It did come early and they were ready when bright rays splayed across the wide expanse of Nevada range and splashed through the open window to come up short hard against the walls of their room. "After we eat, I'll head over to the sheriff's office, Sean, and you nose around and see what you can find out about this Lacy woman."

"Meet you back at the hotel saloon. I think I'll start at the livery and maybe even go back to the train station. You said she comes to Eureka on the train."

"We'll save the post office for later," Corcoran said.

Corcoran found Resident Deputy Holloway at his desk when he walked into the small sheriff's office. He had a bright red shirt on covered by a buckskin vest, which was flavored with beautiful Indian beadwork, which did not take away from the shiny badge.

The office featured a desk, just a simple affair with drawers down one side, a potbelly stove, lit and hot on a cold morning, and wanted posters hanging from the walls. Corcoran was glad to see a coffeepot boiling away. A rack of rifles and shotguns stood behind Holloway's desk, and a spike driven into the wall had a ring of keys hanging from it.

Behind the office were two cells, and directly next door, a small cabin for Holloway. Palisades was half a railroad town, half a mining camp, and half a cattle ranching town. In the saloons one would find buckaroos talking business with miners and railmen, and of course, from time to time, good old brawls proving that one of the three means to a fine lively hood was best.

Holloway was an arrogant man, not quite five-foot nine, only about one-fifty in weight, and quick to anger. The cells were often filled with those getting into fights, but there was little major crime in the community. Corcoran had heard from more than one source that the resident deputy had a mean streak in him, and an ego of considerable size.

Corcoran grabbed a tin cup from a rack and poured coffee. "Hope you're feeling better. When the doctor releases Spider Watson book him on attempted murder of a lawman." He sat down in one of the chairs next to the desk and pulled some papers from his shirt pocket. "These are the companies that received payments for goods from the Eureka Mine and Mill." He handed the paper across the desk.

"I'm sure none of them really exist but checks were cut to pay for products that were not delivered. All of the companies have Palisades addresses." Corcoran watched Holloway look at the sheets of papers and waited for some kind of reaction. Holloway tensed up, looking at the list of names.

"Recognize any of the names?"

Holloway handed the sheets back. "Never heard of any of them." He took a long drink of coffee and looked up at the ceiling. He couldn't bring himself to look at Corcoran. "Why would an Irish linen company be in Palisades?"

Corcoran almost gagged on his coffee. *What the hell am I dealing with?* "We're talking about a major scam, Holloway. Of course there is no Irish linen company. There is no English cabinet maker, there is no velvet drapery company."

I wonder if maybe there just might be a little more crime in Palisades than we think. If this is his way of thinking, anyone could run a conspiracy game and he'd never know it. Is he this dense or is it a game for my benefit? Corcoran stood up and found his coat.

"If you hear anything about someone named Lacy make sure I know about it. What's the name of the bank manager here?"

"Dillon. Kenneth Dillon. He's a pretty straight old man, Corcoran. He wouldn't be involved, would he? I mean, he being a banker and all."

"Of course not." Corcoran snapped out the answer watching Holloway looking all around the office. "If you think of anything, let me know." *Dense. Not playing games. And then again...*Corcoran let the thought pass.

I could take him for a month's wages inside of one minute. Better keep Sean away from this mark. Corcoran was able to hold in his chuckles until he was out of the building and the door was closed.

CHAPTER ELEVEN

"I'M sure you're aware, Chief Deputy Corcoran, that the bank cannot release information about our clients without a court order."

"I am, of course, sir," Corcoran said. He was enjoying a comfortable seat in a plush, velvet-covered high-backed chair. The bank manager's office was carpeted in heavy wool, the high windows were draped in wool, velvet, and satin, and Dillon's desk was a massive example of overkill. White maple, brass ornaments, and carved in elegant Roman figures.

"I'm only asking if these particular companies are clients, not anything specific about them. Only, do any of them actually exist?" If they do exist, Corcoran thought, he would have to figure out how to get information about them. Getting a court order would alert any wrongdoers and send them running. Despite its growth, Palisades was still a small community and people loved to talk.

"Let me see the list," Kenneth Dillon said. The man was elderly, overweight, dressed in fine wool suit and silk-lined vest. He wore gold and silver jewelry. Corcoran figured the man's most exertion was counting the money every evening. "Hmmm. I don't believe I've even heard of these businesses, Corcoran. They do not do business with this bank."

Dillon handed the sheet back and sat back in his massive chair looking more like European royalty than a frontier banker. "These types of businesses would more likely be found on the East Coast than in Nevada."

"I would think so," Corcoran said. He debated for just a moment or two and decided to let the banker in on his investigation. Only to a point, though. "There has been a scam going on in which these companies have produced bills as if product had been delivered."

"Ah, yes. No product but paperwork indicating that the product was ordered and delivered and the bill must be paid. I've run into that type of conspiracy in the past, Corcoran. I'm sure the checks have not been cashed here but to make sure, I'll have one of my clerks investigate."

"Thank you." Corcoran smiled. "Where would someone running a con like this cash those checks?"

"There are criminal elements that would arrange such, I believe. I'm certain this bank wouldn't. I'll check back with you."

Corcoran nodded and turned to leave and held up. "By the way, do you know a woman named Lacy? It might be either first or last name."

"Yes, yes I do," the banker said. "Lacy Samuels owns a half interest in the livery stables. You might know her brother, Jonah in Eureka."

"I've met the man. Thank you, Mr. Dillon." Corcoran's mind was working hard to place Jonah Samuels, but he had definitely heard the name before. His stomach told him it was well past the lunch hour and he made his way the two blocks back to the hotel. He found Sean O'Keefe standing at the bar rather close to the free lunch spread, a cold mug of beer near his lunch platter.

"I found our Lacy person, Corcoran, or at least where she should be."

"Let's take a table, old man. We have lots to talk about."

———

LACY SAMUELS HEARD about Corcoran arriving in Palisades and made plans to be out of town for a few days. Along with part ownership in the livery, she had an interest in two cattle operations in the area. She had a few things packed and in the buggy early that morning and drove the carriage the several miles north, toward the Humboldt River and the YL ranch.

She and her brother Jonah ran several illegal scams in Chicago and came west when things got a little hot for them. They maintained contact with some of the organized outfits in the big city, particularly the ones who could transfer money from legal sources to their private accounts.

Jonah found work at the Eureka Mine and Mill because of his abilities at writing, filing, and general office procedures, and Lacy became close to railroad managers, cattlemen, and mining executives. The

Samuels siblings weren't interested in some small-time operations, they wanted a couple of big hits. They maintained fronts that raised no eyebrows.

It was a combination of Jonah's work and Lacy's meeting Sam Tankersley that got their current affair moving right along. It was always the third cog in the wheel that would bring down the game. Jonah kept up his part and Lacy hers, but that third cog, they called him Pretty Boy, should not have been in the game.

No matter how hard she tried, Lacy Samuels could not con Sam Tankersley into becoming involved and turned to one of the men who worked closely with the mine accountant, Gerald McKinnon. He was easily swayed, saw to it that merchandise appeared to have been delivered, and allowed for payments to be made. It was his sudden departure from the company that led McKinnon to run his audit.

The woman was not attractive, could not use so-called feminine wiles on Tankersley or any other man. Lacy Samuels stood just slightly more than five feet tall, and was overweight, stoop shouldered, and had never taken particular care of herself. Her hair, dull brown with strands of gray, simply hung with little life.

Lacy drove her buggy through the wide gates and up to a rambling ranch house tucked into a copse of cottonwood trees. As she was tying off the horse her ranch manager, John Nichols walked out to greet her. "Howdy, John. Hope the coffee's on."

"Always," Nichols said. He was a big man, heavy in the shoulders and chest but looked more like a big-city businessman than a frontier cowboy. He always wore a three-piece suit, often shoes rather than boots, and did not have a well-tanned and weathered face. "Trouble?"

The fact that Lacy rode out without letting him know she was coming gave him the first clue. As she pulled a leather case from the buggy he knew he was right. "Corcoran's scratching around our Eureka job. Need to get rid of a few things, John."

John Nichols had been able to turn all the checks from the Eureka Mine and Mill into cash money in a Chicago bank with very little loss. Money dealers often took as much as fifty percent but Nichols made the exchanges for as little as ten. "I take it we're burning some paper today?" he asked. Just a hint of sarcasm caught Lacy's attention.

"Damn right we are," she said. "This was a good job, John. Don't forget that. It was Pretty Boy who messed it up for us. Could have run this con for another twenty thousand if he hadn't been stupid." Pretty boy was afraid he was going to be found out and quit his job at the mine, which left Lacy with only her brother on the scene.

"Should have stuck with one of our own," Nichols said. "Well, that's water under the bridge. Tell me what you know and what we have to do."

She didn't tell Nichols everything, only that Terrence Corcoran was in town looking for her. "We have to make sure every single piece of paper we have is burned, John. If there's anything that might lead Corcoran toward Pretty Boy, we'll get it planted somewhere, otherwise, burn everything."

"My man in Chicago was hoping for some more from us. He's exchanged those notes three times now. We'll have bank transfers coming our way next week, Lacy. Our original con was for twenty thousand dollars but we'll end up with slightly less than fifty thousand. The mine's bookkeeper only knows about the first transaction, not these latest two."

"I'd love to see the look on Corcoran's face when he finds out," Lacy said. "I left word at the livery that I was going to Elko for some shopping. That should keep Corcoran busy for a day or two and we'll be more than clean by then."

"You haven't asked, so maybe you aren't aware. Sam Tankersley is dead," Nichols said.

"That's what brought Corcoran. Good," she said. "Did you set it up so one of the children might get blamed?"

"That cute little Barbara might get blamed," he said. "I enjoyed my time with her but she was a dumb as a turtle." He shook his head slowly back and forth. "I'm really sorry this is going to end, Lacy. You've put together a fine little operation."

"I like money," she said but there was no smile to go with the words. The two spent the afternoon burning anything and everything that had to do with the Eureka Mine and Mill Company. "That should do it," Lacy said. "If there is anything out there, it would be in Pretty Boy's hands."

"He needs to die, Lacy, and you know it." John Nichols had a mean look on his face. "We've talked about this before. You've been too soft with him. He can bring all this down on our heads and we should have eliminated him the day he left the mine."

"You're right, John and it is my fault. I'll take care of the bastard."

CHAPTER TWELVE

"If that's what you learned then we need to take a little ride, Sean. See what that ranch looks like but not get caught doing it. You never saw the lady?"

"No. Tiny, her partner, said she left yesterday. He thought she was going to Elko but told me about the ranch. Her partner is a wisp of a man, old as the rocks, and doesn't much care for his partner. I'd be willing to bet she's holding out on him."

He gave Corcoran a long look. "I almost had a partner once."

"Didn't know that. Almost? What happened."

"He was all for being a partner in the wheel and wagon industry until it came time to do the work it takes to make wheels and wagons. Brought him for a week before I let him invest and he didn't quite make two full days. Wanted to sit behind a desk and tell people what to do."

"Well, he never had a chance to steal from you,

anyway." Corcoran mulled the thought. "Partners stealing from each other is something I run into often, old man." The two men laughed a bit and Corcoran continued.

"We need to make Tiny our best friend, Sean. Let's go have a chat, shall we?" Corcoran had already determined that the Lacy woman was involved in criminal activities and knew from years of experience dealing with outlaws that they would take advantage of a partner just as fast as they would a stranger.

"Right now, Sean, all we have are our own thoughts on this. A twenty thousand dollar fraud at the mine and the head assayer murdered. That's it." Corcoran was frustrated, almost angry at the fact they were a long way from home chasing shadows.

"You think she murdered Sam Tankersley?" Sean O'Keefe asked. "What about this resident deputy here? You and he don't exactly come together in my mind. Didn't he work at the Eureka mine?"

The two were walking along the boardwalk toward the Palisades Livery and Blacksmith, and O'Keefe's question stopped Corcoran in his tracks. "Damn me, Sean," he said. "Holloway worked in the office, not the mine or mill, probably doing the same work as Jonah Samuels. That's how they got those accounts paid. I wonder if that's what led to Holloway quitting his job and wanting to be a deputy sheriff? Be here and able to protect the boss lady?"

"Why would he quit?"

"I don't think Holloway is much of a man, Sean. If he thought maybe he was getting in too deep, maybe afraid of being caught and sent to prison, maybe just he and

Jonah had a difference of opinion. Possibly Jonah threatened him. Like I say, Holloway has a hard time standing up for himself. And, then there's my first thought, being in a position to protect the firm."

O'Keefe looked at Corcoran and Terrence could see all the parts clicking into position. "If he helped Samuels and is now a deputy sheriff, he might still be helping," Corcoran said. "He said he'd never heard of this Lacy woman yet worked with her brother? This scam has been going on at the mine for several months. All those purchases weren't done in a week."

Corcoran tried to remember when Holloway came to Sheriff Connor looking for a job. How long ago did this mine fraud get underway? It would have been a perfect union but Holloway quit the mine. Why? Was he chased out? Or was he let go?

Corcoran turned around and headed back toward the sheriff's office. "Or did he quit because he knew too much?" Corcoran said, mixing up what he had been talking about with what he was thinking. "Holloway isn't very bright. There isn't a chance in hell that he did any of this on his own. He was probably enticed with thoughts of big money and helped Samuels until it finally dawned on him that he was involved in something illegal."

"How did he end up as resident deputy here? Moved right into their nest." O'Keefe laughed.

"I have some thoughts on that." Corcoran turned to O'Keefe. "Let's get to the office, Sean. Holloway came to the sheriff when he left the mine wanting to be a lawman."

O'Keefe laughed. "Maybe to purge his already committed criminal acts?"

Corcoran chuckled. "Ed and I had some interesting talks about the man. I was not in favor of Ed hiring him and was strongly against him being named resident deputy here. I'm afraid I might have been on the right side of the discussions."

Corcoran remembered the man wanting a new badge, not one worn. "He even bought a new gun belt and holster to show off. He's egotistical to a fault, and I'm betting right now that he's either looking to be the one to arrest Lacy Samuels or will try to bribe or threaten the woman and get more of that twenty thousand dollars for himself."

"You think he's in danger, don't you?" O'Keefe said. The two were walking fast along Palisade's main street. "If the Lacy woman is out of town, who are you thinking of?"

"We only think she's out of town. Neither one of us saw her leave, Sean. We think she's out of town because that's what you were told. Don't mean it's true."

"Learn something new every day," Sean muttered.

They turned up the next street to see a small crowd of people outside the sheriff's office. "Might be too late," Corcoran muttered and picked up the pace. He shoved his way inside the small office and found Duane Holloway sprawled across the floor, a large hunting knife protruding from low on his chest.

"Anybody see this take place?" He looked at those milling in the office. "If you did not witness this crime then kindly get the hell out of here. This is a murder scene, not a carnival," he said, and started easing people out the door. He looked at Sean O'Keefe and nodded, telling him to keep everyone out.

O'Keefe's heft was all it took and he stood in the middle of the doorway, effectively blocking any possible entry. "Don't look like your man put up much of a fight, Terrence."

"Sure don't." Corcoran looked at Holloway's hands for any sign of a fight, looked at his face, too, and then the furniture in the office. Desk hadn't been moved, all the chairs were standing upright, there were no skinned knuckles or split lips anywhere.

"He felt safe with whoever it was knifed the life out of him."

"Isn't that what you said about whoever killed Sam Tankersley?" O'Keefe asked.

"That's exactly what I said." Corcoran walked around behind the desk, pulled the chair out and sat down. Without touching anything he took a long look at the papers and items on top of the desk. *I don't remember him writing down any of the names of the businesses that were part of the mine fraud. Why is there a list here?* Other items like quill pens, ink, coffee cups were not scattered as if someone had taken a swipe at them.

That's it. Two coffee cups. He was discussing the fraud with someone who joined him for coffee. Was it Lacy Samuels herself who did this? He moved back over to the body and yelled up at Sean. "Send someone for the doc, will you?" *Just like with Sam Tankersley. A heavy and sharp knife, slammed into the chest, slipping between ribs, and doing plenty of damage. Somebody neither man felt any fear of and strong enough to drive the knife in deep.*

Corcoran walked back to the desk, and in turn sniffed at the coffee cups. "He didn't even offer his visitor a splash of whiskey. He knew whoever did this well enough not to have any fear but not well enough to have a drink with. This was purely a business meeting."

"Interesting, Corcoran. Was the deputy a fighter? You said there was no fight, but would there have been one if he was afraid of whoever came in?"

"Not much of one," Corcoran said. "Anybody say anything while you were at the door? Maybe about a visitor or someone seen hanging around?"

"The man who will bring the doctor said he wanted to talk to you. I'm almost sure it was the conductor from the train. I told him to bring the doc and you'd talk with him. Nobody else said anything. This Holloway wasn't much liked around town."

"Oh?" Corcoran said.

"Well, the general conversation was, maybe we'll get a real deputy next time and not somebody who pretends at the job. Their comments about showing off, about rousting people who couldn't or wouldn't fight back. No respect for the man." O'Keefe chuckled. "Not like you, that's for damn sure."

Dr. Costello made his way in followed closely by Sparky Mulroon, the conductor from the train trip the night before. "What have we got, Corcoran?"

"One dead deputy, I'm afraid, Doc. Hello, Sparky. You wanted to talk to me?"

"I do, Terrence. It might be important."

"Good, let's have a seat and stay out of the good doctor's way. Sean, keep that door closed." Corcoran slipped back behind the desk and sat down. "Grab a seat, Sparky and tell me what's on your mind."

"Well, I was on my way to the café when I saw a horse drawn buggy with a man and woman pull up in front here."

"Why would that be unusual?" Corcoran asked.

"By itself, it wouldn't be, but the man got out of the buggy and the woman drove off alone. The man didn't go straight into the office, and instead, walked up and down the street twice before going in. He was looking for something."

"Something or someone?" Corcoran said. "Did you recognize either one, Sparky?"

"I'm pretty sure that the woman was that mean, really nasty woman who is partnered with Tiny Lawson at the livery stables. She's a mean one. Drives off more business than she attracts."

"And you say whoever was with her got out and she drove off? Are you sure of that?"

"I am, Corcoran. I'm as sure as knowing the sun comes up every morning. The man walked up and down the street twice before going into the office."

"What did he look like, Sparky. Tall? Short? Heavy?"

"About medium, I guess. Average height and weight. Wore a full beard. Red," Sparky said, as if just remembering. "He had a full red beard and was wearing a green shirt under his brown coat. Yes, a full red beard."

"That's good, Sparky, that's good. Were you still around when he left the office?"

"No, I went into the café. I was hungry. I never saw him again." Sparky Mulroon sat back in his chair and took a quick glance at the body on the floor. "That's a nasty knife. Never did much care for the deputy but still, that's a nasty way to die. Nasty."

"Thank you, Sparky. If you remember anything, find me, will you?"

Sparky Mulroon made his way through the small crowd still arrayed around the front of the office and Corcoran looked again at the papers on the desk. "Full red beard mean anything to you, Sean?" He couldn't remember if Jonah Samuels had red hair or if he wore a full beard.

"Lots of men wear full beards, but I don't recall anyone recently having a red one."

"Neither can I. The Lacy woman has never been described as having red hair, only dull and dumpy, and I can't remember enough about her brother to tell you, either.

"Well, Doc, do you have anything to tell me?" Corcoran walked back around the desk and kneeled by the body.

"Obviously died by having a knife stuck deep in his chest but I don't see anything else. There apparently wasn't any kind of fight between the deputy and the killer. Must have welcomed your redheaded killer."

"Thanks, Doc. You'll see to the body?" Costello nodded. "How's our crowd doing, Sean? We need to get over to the livery."

"They're gone. Saw the doc and knew the show was over. Thinking Tiny might know who the man with the red beard might be?"

Corcoran chuckled, getting back to his feet.

"Indeed I do."

CHAPTER THIRTEEN

"I'VE HEARD ABOUT YOU, Corcoran. Our rooster of a deputy here don't much care for you." Tiny Lawson had a cackle of a laugh and let it all out. He was a thin man, short and wiry, and Corcoran took an immediate liking to him. Tiny was a fighter, whether to uphold a belief, to protect a friend, or support someone in trouble, and Corcoran seemed to read that in his wrinkled face and bright eyes.

Tiny looked over at Sean. "Didn't you tell him that Samuel's woman ain't here?"

"He did, Tiny. We just need to talk some. Got a few questions for you." Corcoran had no intentions of telling Tiny about Holloway's death.

"Well then, fire 'em off. I been standing in front of this fire all morning, beating the hell out of some chunks of iron. I could use a break." He pulled a bandanna from his trousers and wiped it across his face and wrapped it around his neck, tying it loosely.

Corcoran had a smile on his face. *I could get to like this old man. A week in the Diamond Mountains and we'd come out blood brothers.* "So, Tiny, when did she leave and did she have anyone with her?"

Lawson walked over to a barrel that sat off to the side of a table well back from the hot forge. He lifted the lid on the barrel and reached deep inside, pulling a jug out. "Grab a tin cup, gentlemen, and we'll snort some mule piss while we talk." He poured a healthy cup full for himself and handed the jug off to Sean O'Keefe. Been makin' this stuff for nigh on to twenty years now," the old man said.

Corcoran watched Sean pour a little and sniff at it and he took the jug and poured a little bit for himself. "Thank you, Tiny. Make your own, eh? Never tried that. Let's talk about the old lady."

"Let's see, now," he said. "That angry old lady left out of here very early this morning, by herself, but when she came back, she had a big ugly man with her. She called him Jonah but didn't introduce him." He took a long drink from his cup. Corcoran had to chuckle when Tiny cringed some as he swallowed. "She was like that. Better than everyone else. No manners, Corcoran. None."

"Jonah, eh?" Corcoran looked over at Sean who had taken a drink of Tiny's liquor and had a sour look on his face. *So, maybe I'm right in my thinking. Jonah got Holloway mixed up in their scheme and now had to get rid of him.* "What did this Jonah look like, Tiny?"

"He was younger than her but they could have been brother and sister. That is, except for the hair. That Jonah feller had red hair and a full beard. Where she was short and stumpy, he was about medium height and hefty, strong. Their eyes and the way they held their heads and their mouths is what made me think they were related."

"After Lacy and Jonah left, did she come back?" Sean had taken another couple of tastes from the tin cup and still had a strange look on his face.

"It's all confusing," Tiny said. "She left out early this morning for Elko, she said, but came back in just a few hours with this Jonah feller, left again, and came back again."

"With Jonah?" Corcoran asked.

"No, she was alone."

"And apparently left again," Corcoran said. "How long ago was this last time she left and did she say where she was going?"

"Hour ago, maybe. Didn't say where she was going. That horse and buggy belongs to the livery. Don't know where she'd be going. Ain't got a lot of friends here in Palisades. I know she lives here but I couldn't tell you where. She don't talk much to me and I don't talk much to her."

He looked around the livery, stared for a moment at the hot forge, and seemed to sigh. "Needed some money, I did. Needed to buy another couple of wagons, needed some tools for the smithy work, and she came in as a partner. Biggest mistake this old boy ever made, Corcoran. That rooster of a deputy might know. They was pretty close as strange as that might seem."

"You're right. He might know." Corcoran thinking that if he did it wouldn't matter much in his current condition. As resident deputy, it would not be out of line to know where many people lived, but Lacy Samuels? You bet he'd know.

"When that deputy first got to town they would meet late at night out behind the corrals back there," Tiny said, pointing toward the back of the stables. "As time wore on, they met far less often."

"Thank you, Tiny." Corcoran looked at Sean and then back to Tiny. "Other than our resident deputy, did Lacy Samuels have any other friends or meet with others?"

"Got a ranch north of the Humboldt, and I've seen her eat at the Heritage House from time to time. They might know something. Sorry, Corcoran but I just don't know much about the lady."

"You've been a big help, Tiny. Let's take a walk, Mr. O'Keefe."

———

"MOST FOUL WHISKEY I've ever had in my life, Terrence. And the strongest, too." Corcoran chuckled. "Man could go blind drinking that stuff. He's been making it and drinking it for twenty years? Wonder he's still alive. What exactly are we looking for?"

"A murderer on the one hand, Sean, and those responsible for the theft and fraud at the Eureka Mine and Mill. It hasn't changed since we got here, just added a second murder to the list." Corcoran was leading the two to the Heritage House, a combination boarding house, saloon, and restaurant. Railroad workers and miners made up most of the residents, and there were often beds available for travelers not wanting the expense of a hotel.

"I'm not sure why Sam Tankersley got himself involved, but Holloway, Jonah, and Lacy are behind the deaths and the fraud. We need evidence and we need someone alive who will talk to us. I would have enjoyed discussing all this with Mr. Holloway."

"Discuss?" Sean almost yelped. "You mean hammer, don't you? You didn't have much confidence in that boy, did you?"

"None," Corcoran said. He stopped after the comment. "We have to get back to his office, Sean. He might just have been stupid enough to have left papers about. Either in the office or in that cabin next door. We'll hit the Heritage House later. Come on."

Palisades' streets were laid out based on the railroad tracks, which were, for the most part, east to west. A main street ran north and south and those streets lettered with the east—west streets numbered, so a simple grid made up the business district and the two men made quick time to the sheriff's office. "Don't look like anyone's been here," Sean O'Keefe said.

Corcoran emptied the desk drawers while Sean built a fire and made coffee. "Maybe the coffee will take the sting of mule piss from my throat," Sean grumbled.

"Just sheriff stuff here," Corcoran said. There was a small cabinet alongside the gun rack and Corcoran opened it. There were four shelves and it looked like Holloway had them set up as a file cabinet. "Might just get lucky here," he muttered.

It was tedious work going through each shelf and a full pot of coffee was drank before Corcoran came up with anything. "Look at this, Sean," he said, handing a sheet of paper across the desk.

"My my," O'Keefe said after giving the paper a quick read. "It seems to be a layout of who could sign for purchases and ask for payments to be made. Am I reading this right?"

"That's what I think," Corcoran said. "Even with copies of how each person signed his name."

The various divisions in the mine and the mill were outlined with who could order and sign for goods and who could authorize payments. Alongside each name was an example of each person's signature. "This little gang wasn't stopping at the first twenty thousand dollars, Sean. This was to be an ongoing deception."

Corcoran stood up and stretched, gathering the evidence into its own little pile. "What made them quit? Why did Holloway leave the mine?" Corcoran asked the questions as he paced around the small office. He sat down at the desk and looked at the list of names again.

"How did they cash the checks, Terrence?" Sean O'Keefe was building another pot of coffee. "I think you said they couldn't just walk into a bank and cash them. They were made out to specific companies. Companies that don't exist. I still say they would have been better off just robbing a bank."

"Maybe so, Sean. I want to go through Holloway's stuff in the cabin next door and then we need to start looking for Lacy and Jonah. Latch the door when I go out. Jonah could return."

The resident deputy's cabin was not kept up and

Corcoran found clothing tossed about, dirty dishes stacked on the single table, and crusty food in pans on the stove. "For being such a strutting fool with the way he dressed, the man was a slob." Corcoran chuckled. He found a few cartridge boxes, some tins of food but not what he was hoping for.

There has to be a tin box somewhere in the room. His share of twenty thousand dollars must be kept somewhere and I know he didn't have a bank account. He got down on his hands and knees to search under the bed, under boxes that doubled as chests of drawers and finally got back on his feet.

He pulled the blankets back on the bed and then lifted the mattress. "There we are," he said seeing a manila envelope on the springs. Inside was two thousand dollars in paper money inside its own little envelope. "This is what I wanted."

The inside envelope had been mailed to Jack Nichols, Mgr. YL Ranch, Palisades, Nevada. The return address was from a counting house in Chicago, Illinois. "Well, Sean will be glad to know how they were able to get their checks cashed." Corcoran chuckled. "I wonder who this Nichols character is?"

He was putting things back into order when he heard footsteps coming to the cabin door. *That's not Sean,* he thought and eased his big Colt from its holster. The one-room cabin didn't give Corcoran much room so he slipped alongside the door so that when it opened he would be behind it.

Whoever was outside was fumbling with the latch, got it lifted, and pushed the door open. Corcoran waited until whoever was there took his first step inside and slammed his body hard against the door. The person was shoved across the empty floor from the weight of the push and fell onto the table. Corcoran leaped onto the man, whipping his pistol hard against the intruder's head, rendering him helpless.

Corcoran let the body slump to the floor, grabbed the revolver still in the man's hand, and took a quick look outside. A buggy with a single horse stood alone in front of the cabin. Corcoran closed the door and stepped up to who had to be Jonah Samuels, still unconscious. Corcoran lifted the hefty gentleman up and flopped him down on the bed and pulled the single chair over to the bedside to wait for the man to come to.

There was a rap at the door and Sean hollered out, "You okay in there, Terrence?"

"Come in, Sean. Come in. We have a visitor. See if there's any rope in the buggy or the office."

Sean pushed the door open in minutes carrying a lariat he found in the carriage. "That'll do. Let's get this fine feller all wrapped up so he can talk to us."

"You hit him pretty hard, Terrence. Lot of blood pouring out of that gash."

"Yes, I did," Corcoran said. "Why don't you run and get the doc and I'll lash Mr. Samuels to the bed and clean him up some. Take the buggy."

Sean O'Keefe slipped out of the cabin and Corcoran heard him drive the carriage off. "Wonder why I didn't hear Samuels drive up to the place? Glad I heard him walking to the door." Corcoran was muttering to himself as he tied Jonah to the metal bedstead. "Might get some answers to our questions yet."

He went through all of Jonah's pockets, and besides a pocket knife, a watch, and a few coins, found nothing. "Didn't carry much money, no notes or slips. I wonder if that buggy he's driving is one he and Lacy had? Where's Lacy?" His mind was busy but he also kept close watch on the door and heard everything that passed in front of the cabin.

CHAPTER FOURTEEN

"WE CAN'T DO a whole lot more investigating if we have to babysit all these criminals you've got locked up, Terrence." Corcoran and O'Keefe were in the sheriff's office having some hot coffee, laced a bit with some good bourbon. "You're gonna have to appoint a jailer to watch over them critters."

"I think I know just the man, too," Corcoran said. "Tiny Lawson and his jug of mule piss will keep these jaspers under control."

The doctor brought Spider Watson with him and Corcoran booked him into the Palisades jail. After some doctoring, Jonah Samuels joined him. Corcoran put them in separate cells in the back and saw to it they had small jugs of water.

"We need to have a talk, Mr. Samuels. The charges are piling up; murder of a deputy sheriff, attempted murder of a deputy sheriff, and conspiracy to commit fraud, that is, the theft of twenty thousand dollars from the Eureka Mine and Mill."

Samuels sat quiet, holding his aching head and scowl-ing. "There are other crimes that we'll probably tie you to, which means you'll either hang or be in prison for the rest of your life. Think about that. Never taking a free breath for the rest of your life. Never eating a good meal."

"Go to hell, Corcoran."

"No, Mr. Samuels, that's probably where you'll end up. How did this concept of a fraud, selling items that don't exist, come about?"

Samuels just sat on the edge of his bunk holding his head. "How did Holloway get himself involved?" No answer. "All of this your big sister's idea? She's the one with the brains, eh? You're just some needed muscle. No thinking involved?" Still no answers. Corcoran didn't even get a harrumph out of the man.

"What do you think, Sean? This Mr. Samuels just a big chunk of muscle? No thoughts of his own? Not enough brains to lead a cow to water?"

"Hang the bastard," Sean O'Keefe said. "Right along-side his sister. She don't seem that bright, either. I think it was Holloway who put this all together." Sean had the slightest grin splashed across his mug and Corcoran tried to hide his.

"You think so? Holloway was obviously far smarter that Jonah here, but his sister too?"

"Oh, yes," Sean said. "Think about it, Terrence. We have Jonah in custody and Lacy will be in irons within the hour. They had to get rid of Holloway because he saw the light and was going to rat on them."

"You're wrong!" Jonah Samuels shouted. "My sister

planned all this." He shut up quick realizing too late what he'd said.

Corcoran stood up, pushed the chair back against the wall, smiled, and said, "Gotcha."

———

THEY KEPT the buggy that Jonah had and Sean did the driving. "After we talk with Tiny and convince him to take the job, I'll take one of the horses at the livery and ride out to this YL ranch, Sean. I'd like you to talk with some of the people at the Heritage House about Lacy. She might even be there, so be cautious."

Corcoran stepped down from the buggy and was confronted by a young boy holding a letter. "Are you Chief Deputy Corcoran, sir? This telegram came in for you."

Corcoran found a dime and handed it to the boy. "Thank you, son. Stick around a minute. Might have you take an answer back with you." It was a quick read and he handed it to Sean. "Looks like Lou Foster's been a busy boy in Eureka."

"Stands to reason though," Sean said.

The short wire from Sheriff Ed Connor said that following a talk with mine manager Sherman, he talked with and arrested an office worker named Rory Tibbetts. The man had records of purchases, records of signatures, and dates still in a drawer at his workstation.

"Does," Corcoran said. "I'm thinking Holloway and Samuels created the orders for the merchandise, then Holloway forged authorization to pay for the merchandise, and this Rory Tibbets fool wrote out the checks. Nothing went through regular channels, apparently." He fumbled in his coat pockets for a minute.

"Got some paper, son?" He took the offered sheets and a pencil and wrote a quick reply back to the sheriff telling of Holloway's demise and Samuel's arrest. "A quarter cover that?" The boy nodded and Corcoran handed him thirty-five cents. "See to it this gets sent off."

The boy just made a quick twenty cents and scampered back toward the telegraph office. Corcoran watched him go, chuckled, had a big smile on his face. "Bet he turns those two dimes into ice cream within the hour, Sean."

"My money's on hard candy, Terrence. At that age, hard candy, particularly the red ones, were always my choice. Didn't see a dime very often, though."

They walked through the gates to the stables and found Tiny Lawson pounding some wrought iron at his forge. "Whatcha making, Tiny? Nice work."

"These are fancy wrought iron hinges for Miz Daniel's barn. They'll hold the front door in place. Like to do this kind of work. These are kind of hefty, but she'll not be replacing them in her lifetime." Bold lightning strikes hammered into hinges were still glowing from the forge and hammer when Tiny dropped the intricate piece of iron in a bucket of water and pulled his gloves off.

"Brought my horse and buggy back, did you? Thanks."

"Need to have a little sit-down chat, Tiny. No mule piss on this go around." Corcoran chuckled. "I'm short a good man. Got two men behind bars, about to put more people in jail, and I don't have a resident deputy or a jailer."

"If you're looking for a resident deputy, you're looking in the wrong closet, my friend. I've got a livery and blacksmith business that keeps me out of saloons and off the streets. Sure you don't want a shot of mule piss? It'll cure what ails you."

"I'll take one," Sean said, giving Corcoran a quick glance and turning his face away just as quickly.

"These animals need feed and water twice a day, and cleaning up after them is a lifelong project." Tiny was cackling as he produced the jug for Sean. He put some in his tin cup first.

"Weren't interested in taking you away from your business, Tiny. What I need most is a jailer and what that means is bringing the prisoners food and water twice a day, taking care of their more personal needs, and not letting them escape. Maybe an hour or so in the morning and the same in the evening. You'd be well compensated." Corcoran was having some fun with Tiny comparing taking care of prisoners wasn't any different than caring for his stock.

"Wouldn't have to wear one of them badges, would I? Wouldn't want that. Most people I know that wear them things get shot at. Just feed and water 'em just like I do with all my animals, eh?" Sean gave him a thumbs up and Corcoran nodded. "Well, hell's bells, boys, I'm gonna lose my partner so I'd best make a little extra money while I can. Let's have a drink."

It didn't take a half hour to get Tiny lined out on his duties, where to pick up the food for the prisoners, and warnings about getting too close to them. "Don't pack a gun and don't carry the keys when you're near the cell area unless you're planning to let one out and I don't want you to ever do that," Corcoran said.

"There are places along the bottom of the bars. Have the prisoner stand back and slide the food tray in. Never get close or let the prisoner get close to you. They'll smile and get all friendly like and slit your throat, Tiny."

"Kinda like the mules if they think they ain't gettin' their full share." Tiny cackled. "You said a dollar a day? Dang, that's good money."

Corcoran had to push hard but managed to get a swallow or two of the mule piss to stay down, made arrangements for a horse, and was ready to ride out to the YL, north of town alongside the Humboldt River. "You're sure of these directions, Tiny?"

"Been in that country many times, Corcoran. The main road follows the tracks as if you're heading for Elko, but before you get to Carlin take the West Fork Road north, across the river, and the YL headquarters is about five miles on."

"Do what you can to keep track of Lacy, Sean. I'll be back."

CHAPTER FIFTEEN

LACY SAMUELS WAS STEAMING ANGRY, sitting alone at a table near a window in the café at the Cattlemen's Hotel. She sent Jonah back to the sheriff's office to kill Corcoran more than an hour ago. He was supposed to pick her up there and they were supposed to take the buggy north to the ranch. It was bug-out time.

Catch the Western Pacific to Denver and begin all over again. How many times had the brother-sister gang done that? It started in Missouri when their pa returned from prison and began teaching them the fine art of fraud and scam, conspiracy and theft. The two little scabs learned fast and as they grew older, some say bolder, they moved to greener pastures, ending up in Chicago.

Lacy had never been what would be considered an attractive woman. Short, slightly overweight, slumped shoulders, stubby legs, and hair that just hung about, no life, no bright or shiny color. What she had was a quick and devious mind. She could create a wonderful idea of riches if only the mark would follow through. Many did and many ended up broke or dead.

She had pondered the problem of how to get out without leaving a trail to follow. Nichols had been a good part of their plans, had helped get the money transferred, even helped with the killing of Sam Tankersley. She knew, deep in her heart that she had to eliminate the man, knew, too, that her brother might have to go at some point too. From the time of her first real score, when she was twelve, she was a loner and the thought of eliminating those who helped wasn't difficult.

Lacy Samuels had thoughts of returning to Chicago but knew they would not welcome the lady. She finally decided it would have to be Denver. She'd miss her brother, but he just wasn't smart enough to help with her various plans. They had only been caught in one of their efforts and it was because of Jonah. *Yes,* she thought, *he has to go.*

It wasn't Jonah who gave away the secrets of the Eureka Mine and Mill fraud, it was the fine work of the accountant, but Lacy would rather put the blame on her brother. That made it easier to justify his upcoming death.

Shooting John Nichols wasn't going to be difficult at all. *God, I hate that man. So damned arrogant, so sure of himself. Never once had eyes for me, always the young ones. Never ever told any of us what good jobs we were doing. Only reminded us of how important he was to the organization. I'll remind him how important, just before I pull the trigger.*

Movement on the street caught her attention. "That's our buggy," she said right out, watching Sean O'Keefe driving the carriage on his way to pick up the doctor. "Something's wrong," she muttered. She drained her coffee cup and walked out of the café. There was no chance of getting another buggy at the livery. She knew Tiny would throw a fit if she asked and she was deep in thought, trying to figure out how to get to her ranch.

Something went wrong when Jonah went to kill Corcoran and I've got to get out of here. Got to get to the ranch. Got to kill John Nichols and make my way to Denver. It wasn't panic. Lacy had never panicked in her life but she could feel a strong necessity to get moving. The walls were closing in, and the biggest wall was named Corcoran. *He knows too much. Jonah should have been able to kill Holloway. Why didn't he?*

Two drunk cowboys walked their horses up to the tie rack, clambered down and Lacy stepped forward with a smile. "Let me help you, there, buckaroo. Ha ha, I've been in your spot more than once."

The tall thin one stumbled, staggered some trying to stand up straight, and doffed his well-worn sombrero. "Thankee, pretty lady. Tie my horse off and then come on in. We got our bonus pay and I'll buy you a happy drink."

"I'd be honored," Lacy said, taking the reins from the drunk. She stood quiet and watched the two wend their way into the saloon, bouncing off a post or two. She fought her way onto the horse quickly, let the other horse just stand loose, and rode out of town at a gentle lope. Lacy Samuels wore a broad smile on her face. *Oh, hell yes, boys, I'm always glad to help.*

The stirrups were set for a long, tall Nevada bucka-roo, far too long for her short, somewhat heavy legs, and she stopped about a mile out of town to make the adjust-ments. Being raised in Missouri, Lacy Samuels learned to ride on the family's mules and was an accomplished rider, unlike her brother, who always looked sloppy on an animal.

She wasn't kind to animals, didn't much care whether they liked it or not, about the same way she felt about those she was forced to live and work with. Back in the saddle, she kicked the horse furiously and it responded immediately, showing its thoughts with a series of bucks, almost unseating the woman.

The main road east followed the railroad and when she got to the river crossing turned north. *Don't want to get John Nichols upset showing up like this. gotta ride in calm, nice and slow, and tell him we need to talk. Don't want to give him a chance to think something's wrong.* She realized she was getting upset, getting angry, and forced herself to calm down.

She hadn't paid much attention when she stole the horse but with a long ride like this, she took stock of her current situation. She had her carpet bag, almost a set-piece with her. She carried it, as bulky as it was, in favor of a purse. Didn't go anywhere without it because it contained every dime she had.

Her little two-shot pocket pistol was tucked neatly in her jacket pocket and she noticed there was a fine rifle in a saddle scabbard along with a braided lariat. She glanced around and was delighted to find hand-tooled saddlebags and a bedroll tied off behind the saddle.

I might not have to take the train right away. Her mind was working fast knowing she could ride for two or three days, doing her best not to leave an obvious trail before boarding a train for Denver. If someone was looking for her, they would have a hard time finding a trail.

Nichols prided himself on his marksmanship, his quickness with a gun, and Lacy was working out how to get the man to simply walk away from her, offering his broad back as a target. *I ain't no match for that man, face to face. Pa was right, never go face to face. Shoot 'em in the back is always best. Never give your mark any kind of break.*

Once across the Humboldt River the road north was through some fine range land, across hillsides full of grass and brush. Stands of piñon pine and stunted cedar graced the hillsides, and cottonwood trees often marked where there just might be water. A rancher would ask, "Where's the stock?" There wasn't a head of cattle to be seen and Lacy was inside the YL range.

Owning the ranch was a way of setting herself up as someone involved in legitimate business as was her partnership with Tiny Lawson. She didn't have to answer questions about her trips out of town, about some of the mail she sent and received, nor any of those who might come to town to visit. Some in Palisades would discover they have missing funds in their business accounts in the months to come. She was good at learning personal information and very good at putting that knowledge to work.

I'll be well on my way to Denver, maybe already in business there by then. There was never a negative thought to her plans. Lacy Samuels was well aware that she could work a scam on just about any business when she put her mind to it. Her pa went to jail often because he didn't work out the plan in his head before engaging. *He was dumb and taught me not to be,* she thought and had to laugh at the memory.

As it was late in the fall, the rabbit brush was bright yellow dotting the landscape. She made the five miles through a blaze of color and walked the horse through the YL gates and into the barnyard.

John Nichols was on the porch watching her ride in. "Is there a problem?" He called it out, stepping down to take the reins from her. "This is one fine-looking stock horse, Lacy. Sure there's no problem?"

"No, John, we just need to talk some. The mine job was a good one, of course it's gone now, but I've been working on some ideas concerning the Palisades Bank. I think you'll like 'em."

"Good, Lacy. Come on in and I'll get the coffee heated." He turned and walked into the kitchen. He only made the third step before two large chunks of lead ripped through his back. Lacy closed the door and tucked the little pocket pistol back into her coat pocket. *Sorry, John, but it has to be my way.*

She remembered him saying that there was to be more money coming from Chicago and wondered if it had already arrived. She spent the next several hours going through everything in the main house, discovering that John Nichols had been holding out on her and her brother. That he had been dealing with more than one of the money exchanges in Chicago and she thought there was only the one.

"So, you arrogant bastard, you got what was coming to you, after all. I don't feel the least bit bad about shooting your ugly hide." She was talking loud and mean, after finding several thousand dollars tucked away in a bureau drawer. *Wonder what else I might find.* She took the ranch house apart over the next hour and found letters to money houses that should have been burned, found names and addresses of people they had used in various frauds that needed to be burned, and her anger built with each discovery.

"Damn fool, John. You are a damn fool," she almost shouted, stuffing papers in the hot cookstove. Her next chore would be to get rid of the body and that would be difficult. *Can't bury him. Stuff him under something or burn the place around him?* She opted for stuffing him under loose hay, rocks, and other material near the corrals.

It was quick work, using the horse. She used the lariat to hold his feet, had the horse drag him out of the house, then around to the corrals. She laid him out near a fence post and brought loads of straw over with a pitchfork to bury him. "Goodbye, John. It's a shame you had to be a bastard. We could have continued making a lot of money." There were no tears flushing her cheeks, nor was her nose running.

This was business, no time for emotions, no time for remorse, only thoughts of tomorrow's profits, and where to find the next sucker. She would ride off, probably east, and have no more thoughts of John Nichols, just as she had no more thoughts of brother Jonah.

She tied the lariat back on the saddle horn and clambered on board. In the saddlebags were bundles of notes totaling several thousand dollars. An equal amount was in her carpet bag, and the saddlebags also held enough smoked meat, flour, sugar, and coffee to last her several days.

I gotta stay off the main roads until I get on the east side of Elko, then ride to a station and buy a ticket to Salt Lake City and spend the night. Then I'll take the train from Salt Lake to Cheyenne. Don't want to book straight through. I'll stay overnight in Cheyenne and book another train to someplace well east of Denver. I'll get off in Denver, but no one will know that. She chuckled, putting her plans in order. *I'll be fine. Gotta remember to use different names for each leg of my ride.*

How many times over the yeas had this little scene played out? How many partners, like John Nichols stuffed in straw back there, had been left to rot? New territory, new marks, new opportunity, that's what life was all about. Lacy Samuels laughed, thinking that along with all of that she had enough money to do anything she wanted.

Lacy Samuels felt the thrill again, felt alive and ready for her next chance to score. It was a game, after all, this adventure called life. Tired old men like Sam Tankersley couldn't see what real adventure was. He was offered a large share and was too slow to understand the thrill of creating a masterpiece, and that's what the Eureka Mine and Mill fraud was. A masterpiece.

"I'll let Denver direct me, but there's always Santa Fe, that dazzling little encampment of several cultures."

CHAPTER SIXTEEN

THE RIDE OUT of town was an easy one on a not-so-warm fall afternoon and Corcoran was trying to get a handle on what had happened since he and Sean O'Keefe arrived in Palisades. His resident deputy was dead, murdered by the man he had worked with to defraud the Eureka Mine and Mill. That murder, committed by Jonah Samuels, all but cinched the closure on his sister's involvement. Lacy Samuels was probably the brains behind the scam. Still, there was something missing.

Who killed Sam Tankersley? Jonah tried to use a knife on me, but it was just a hunting knife. not like that fancy one used on Sam. He slowed the horse to an easy walk. "The knife that was used on Sam Tankersley was owned by his daughter," he muttered. He kicked the horse back into a trot. Corcoran was an active man, had an active mind, and periods like this frustrated him, and right now, the horse he was riding would have to deal with that frustration.

They went back and forth from a walk to a trot to a

lope and back to a trot, eating up miles but not helping the frustration level. He simply could not slow his mind down and what was worse, he kept thinking he was close to finding an end to this case of fraud and murder.

Sam of course would have known Jonah from the mine, maybe not have been too upset about being caught with no clothes on. Might be why there was no fight. Have to remember this, old man. Check with the mine to see if Jonah left work early that day.

He remembered what Barbara said about that knife, how it was hers, and had disappeared some time back. If it was Jonah who killed Sam, how did he get the knife? Was Barbara seeing Jonah? But she called the man she was seeing John. *The man who runs the ranch Lacy owns is John Nichols.*

The logic in that thought almost made Corcoran laugh right out. *A fancy dude of a gambler is what people have called this John who infatuated Barbara Tankersley. Yes, that type of man might catch that girl's attention but not a fop like Jonah Samuels. I wonder what John Nichols looks like. I wonder what his background is?*

"Let's step it up, boy," he said, kicking the horse into a comfortable lope, actually giving of a bit of a smile. There was something though that made Corcoran believe that Jonah killed Sam, and that Jonah had stolen the knife well before the killing, and he couldn't get it put together. "Ah," he said, letting his breath out, slowly. "I wonder if Jonah had accompanied Lacy on a visit to Tankersley's and while Lacy and Sam talked, Jonah found and stole the knife?"

Nonsense, he thought. That would make one think that

he knew about the fancy knife. "There would be no reason for Jonah to know about that knife unless he had some kind of relationship with Barbara," he grumbled. "Maybe it wasn't Jonah. The man who had a relationship with Barbara was a man named John," Corcoran muttered. "Stay on target, Terrence, old boy. Stay on target."

He went over the attack on Resident Deputy Sheriff Holloway by Jonah and came to the same conclusion. He and Jonah worked the fraud together, so he wasn't afraid of the man, and didn't put up any kind of fight when Jonah attacked him. Again, he thought, with a run-of-the-mill hunting knife.

"I have Jonah in custody," he muttered. Corcoran, as so many do, always talked to his horse when they were riding alone like this. "Have no idea where Lacy is, and that's worrisome. She could run off and I don't want that to happen. A long talk with this John Nichols feller might clear up questions."

Nichols had received that letter from a Chicago money exchange and Corcoran was well aware that those businesses were notorious for working with the underworld and cleaning up dirty money. "The little puzzle is fitting together nicely. Interesting that Holloway got himself involved but as much as he liked the good life I'm not surprised. Lacy got her brother inserted in the mine's office, and he in turn enlisted the egotistical and vain Holloway and this other feller that Lou Foster picked up. Rory Tibbets was an office worker just as Holloway and Jonah were. Not that many people, really. Wonder how the split went?"

He had to chuckle remembering that Tiny told him how Lacy was trying to edge more money from their livery stables business. "She would have taken the queen's share first and left crumbs for the knaves."

The few miles were eaten up and Corcoran topped a spiny ridge to look down on the YL ranch headquarters. The road he was on led through the main gate and up to the ranch house. Corcoran stepped down from the horse and walked behind one of the rocks along the ridge top. He hadn't seen anyone and hoped he hadn't been seen.

"Let's give this place a good looking over," he muttered.

He tied the livery stable horse to a bush and got down low behind the rock, before pulling his looking glass from a coat pocket. The main house stood off to the east and the large barn to the west. In between were a couple of corrals. Corcoran figured he was probably no more than a quarter mile from the main house.

"Smoke coming from a stove, no horses tied at the rack, and no movement." He shook his head. "What kind of ranch is this? No horses in the corrals. No chickens or dogs running around. No cattle to be seen. And not a single buckaroo spinnin' a lasso." He had ridden through miles of fine open range without seeing a single head of stock and now found himself looking down on a cattle ranch that had no stock. "Amazing," he said right out.

Using rocks as cover, Corcoran left the horse and made his way down the hillside and angled toward the main barn that stood well away from the ranch house. "This sure as hell ain't a working ranch." He was sure that he hadn't been seen—knew he hadn't seen anyone—and sidled up to the westernmost end of the barn.

He eased himself into a crouch as near to an open door as he dared get and listened for activity. There was no noise of any kind and after long moments, he edged his way through the doorway and into the darkness of the barn. It only took a short while for his eyes to get used to the gloom and he put order to the scene.

Not a soul moved, and there was one horse in a stall but no other animals inside. It appeared there hadn't been any for some time. "There's more to this than what I'm seeing," Corcoran muttered. A large ranch with fine grazing, plenty of water, and access to the railroad and there aren't any cattle or horses?

"Ain't logical," Corcoran muttered. "Lacy and her little gang don't need a place like this for a headquarters or a hideout. They've got the whole of Palisades for that. They aren't actually running a ranch, which could make them more money than their schemes." He chuckled at the thought.

"I wonder whose tracks I was following if they ain't at the house? Tiny never mentioned Lacy using one of the stable's horses. Only the buggy." He was quick to notice the horse in the stall was a stock horse, one that would be used by buckaroos on the open range. It hadn't been saddled in a long time, certainly hadn't just made the ride in from town.

He moved to the end of the barn facing the main house and using the natural darkness of the barn, and looked out toward the house. Smoke was coming from what was probably the kitchen stove chimney. The main rock chimney was on the other side of the house.

Corcoran used an old wagon near the doorway as a blind and eased his way out of the barn. From the wagon to the corral fences, and the plan was to get behind the privy. An impressive stack of straw up against a corral post caught his attention. *That ain't right,* he thought and kicked some of the straw loose from the pile, uncovering a leg and boot.

"Gotta clear the house first then see who the dead man is," he muttered and stepped away. "Looks like he was dragged over to the fence." He saw the drag marks, the horse prints and the picture came into view.

"I don't need to clear that house, I need to follow that horse." Corcoran turned and made a fast lope back to the rocky ridge and his horse. It was a matter of time now. He knew whoever did this couldn't be too far in front of him and the sooner he got on the trail, the better. With smoke from the chimney and the fact that rigor hadn't set in on the body, whoever is running away can't be too far ahead.

"Whoever it is I'll be following won't figure anyone would be following. My edge and I always like that."

The day was wearing on, it was cold and a wind was blowing out of the north. He would follow that rail, and would find whoever left the body, no matter how long it took. Time for Corcoran to take a quick inventory of his situation as he followed the obvious prints in the soft earth.

He had saddlebags with smoked meat and coffee, a pot, and that's about it. There was no bedroll or blanket.

"Weren't thinkin' of trailin' an outlaw," he muttered. "This might not be much fun." He always carried a flint and striker, and always carried extra ammunition, but did not ride out of Palisades with the thought of spending the night in the great open Nevada rangeland.

———

LACY SAMUELS HAD BEEN in the area long enough to know her way around and decided her best bet would be to follow the Humboldt River to Carlin then take the main road; they called it the emigrant road, which pretty much followed the Western Pacific tracks into Elko.

"Won't be nobody visiting John Nichols that I know of. Don't got to worry about somebody following me. I'll ride right to the railway station, tie off the horse, grab the saddlebags and my carpet bag, and buy a ticket." She was more than muttering, actually talking right out as she laid her plans.

"Just leave this old horse. Somebody'll claim him." She chuckled.

She rode to where the road to the ranch forded the river to get on the Humboldt River Trail which followed along on the north banks of the ever-twisting river. There were more twists and turns to the Humboldt than one would want to follow and the trail was off by as much as half a mile in places.

Lacy Samuels was riding at a comfortable walk. Figured she would find a place to camp somewhere near the railroad village of Carlin well before dark, which this late in the year came rather early. There were no indications of storms, no high winds, but it was cold. "There's always plenty of wood along the riverbank, and I'll be plenty warm."

There wasn't a care in the world, saddlebags full of money, blankets to keep warm, and no partners. All her partners were either dead or locked up, she thought, and even if one might talk to a copper, what would he say? Only Lacy knew where she was, where she was going, what she would be doing.

Lacy Samuels wasn't the kind of person who could enjoy this kind of ride on a fine fall afternoon. She didn't enjoy the brilliant colors of the rabbit brush, never saw the small herds of antelope stop whatever they were doing to watch her ride by, wasn't aware of the golden eagle fighting off an angry raven a thousand feet above the plain. She was happy in her thoughts, and got somewhat sleepy as the day wore on, lulled by the constant plodding of the horse.

With Lacy sound asleep in the saddle, the horse meandered off the trail since there was no pressure on the reins, and dropped down to the river's edge for a nice drink of cool water. There was plenty of grass under a cottonwood tree for him, and he was quite comfortable when the other horse, bearing a man, rode up alongside.

Corcoran had a smile on his face as he stepped down from the saddle. He took the loose reins of Lacy's horse and led the two horses to some brush near the cottonwood tree and tied them off. He checked around the saddle and saw that Lacy didn't have a pistol strapped on but there was a rifle in a scabbard.

"Bet she's got a gun tucked away somewhere," he

mumbled. He reached up and grabbed her by the shoulder and pulled her from the saddle, hard. She landed in a swirl of dust, her split skirt riding britches showing a bit of calf. Lacy came awake screaming and Corcoran had to slap her hard. She stopped screaming immediately and went for the pocket pistol in her jacket.

Corcoran saw the move and held her by the wrist while he reached in and took the gun away. "That would not have been nice, Miss Samuels," he said. "Let's get you on your feet now." He helped her up and tucked her pistol in his waistband. He was a bit rough checking for other weapons and marched her to his horse.

"Gonna have to tie you tight, lady. We got a ride to finish." She hadn't uttered a sound after the screaming episode and just stood glaring at Corcoran. He smiled and pulled a length of cord from his saddlebag. She started to move off and he grabbed her and pulled her back, wrenched her arms behind her back and tied her wrists together.

"Now just where were you gonna go?" he asked. There was no answer and he pushed to her horse. "Up you go, lady," he said, throwing her up like a sack of potatoes. "Get comfortable." He chuckled. He had simply grabbed her around the waist, leaned way back, and and threw her into the saddle. It was up to her to get seated properly, find the stirrups as best she could.

"Time to go," he said, then jumped in the saddle and led them back up from the river and onto the trail. They hadn't gone a mile before running into a traveler heading for Palisades and stopped him. Corcoran showed his badge, identified himself, and asked the man to find Sean O'Keefe and tell him to come to the YL ranch.

The man was a distributor of gadgets and kitchen-ware from Elko who had business with several merchants in Palisades and said he would do so. He was leading a mule with full packs. "I've heard of you, Corcoran. I've been to Eureka. Sold some goods to a couple of stores there. Nice little town," he said.

"Thanks, friend. Next time you're up Eureka way, look me up and we'll have a beer or two," Corcoran said, waving as the man rode off. "Now, Miss Samuels, we'll ride on back to the ranch and see who it is you buried under the straw, eh?"

It was an easy ride on a late autumn afternoon and they pulled into the ranch headquarters with plenty of sunshine left in the day. He pulled her down from the horse after tying them off and ushered her into the main house. "Looks like you were busy trying to find things, eh?" Corcoran untied her hands and pushed her down into a chair at the kitchen table. Again, he wrenched her hands behind the chair and, first, tied them to the chair, then tied her to the chair.

He got the fire in the wood cook stove going, built a pot of coffee, and got it started. "We'll be talking when I get back," he said. She hadn't uttered a word since leaving the gentleman on the trail, and Corcoran chuckled, walking out the door. "Wants to be a tough old lady, eh? That's fine with me. I've got a lot of time, ma'am."

He wasn't chuckling when he kicked the straw away from John Nichols's body. "Shot him in the back. She's a nasty one." He had a lineup of questions for the nasty lady, such as, how did you get him to walk away from you? Why did you shoot the man who was able to trade those mine checks for cash? How are you, your brother, and maybe this man connected to Sam Tankersley's death?

He was looking at a man who most definitely was not a working cattleman. "This must be John Nichols. He looks like he'd fit right in at a gambling table not a chuck wagon." The thought struck Corcoran like a bolt of lightning. Gambler, fast talker, catch Barbara Tankersley's eye. Fancy knife. "Were you in Sam Tankersley's bedroom?" he chuckled, asking the dead man.

CHAPTER SEVENTEEN

SEAN O'KEEFE WAS SITTING across the desk from Tiny Lawson in the Palisades sheriff's office listening to two cowboys describe the woman who stole one of their horses. Tiny had the barest of grins on his face and tried hard not to chuckle.

"You think that's funny, old man?" the young cowpuncher who lost his horse said. He started to make a move toward Tiny but changed his mind when he found himself looking down the barrel of a thirty-two Remington.

"I guess that, rightly, I do find this a bit funny, sonny." It didn't take a whole lot to get Tiny's ardor up and ready. "Give Mr. O'Keefe there a good description of this missing horse and the woman who allegedly stole it, and we'll see what we can do about that. Don't mind tellin' you there ain't a whole lot of short, chubby women in Palisades go around stealing horses from big ol' tough hombres, though."

Embarrassment was more than evident on the young

cow poke's face and he wrote a quick description of the horse and Lacy Samuels and both men got out the door before Tiny Lawson could have more fun with them.

"Won't live that down for a long time, Sean. They don't know how lucky they are, though. Lacy packs a fine little pistol in that purse of hers or in her jacket pocket. Where do you suppose she lit off to?"

"Not Eureka, I would venture to guess. You told Corcoran about that ranch of hers. I think I'll take a little ride out that way. Corcoran might need some backup."

As he started to get up a man walked through the door. "Looking for someone named Sean O'Keefe," the man said. "Got a message from Deputy Sheriff Corcoran."

"I'm O'Keefe. Let's hear it."

"Wants you to meet him at the YL ranch. Said it was important." The peddler nodded to Tiny, turned and walked out the door.

"You got everything under control here, Tiny? Good. I'll take good care of the buggy and horses," Sean said. "Probably might not be back for a day or two."

———

"WHEN THAT OLD man brings the food in, get him to come close to you, and make a quick move on him. He'll jump back and I'll grab him and get the keys," Spider Watson said. "Dumb old man won't know what hit him."

Jonah's head was throbbing from the hit he took but he nodded. "He won't get out of your grip? You still hurtin' from being shot? You sure he'll be carrying them keys? Ain't seen 'em when he comes in."

"Has to, is what I've been told. Has to be able to save us if a fire gets started or we get sick." Spider Watson was always the blow-hard, the man who knows it all but in fact knew nothing. "It's the law," he said.

Jonah Samuels nodded as if he too had heard of that law, and sat down on his cot, trying to ease the pain. The doctor had been in earlier and given him some powders but they didn't do much. His head throbbed and the pain actually made him sick to his stomach. He didn't know if Spider knew what he was talking about or not, but did know that he had to get out of this jail, had to find his sister, had to get away from this part of the country.

She's probably out at that ranch with Nichols. Get out of here, gather as much of our money as we can, and make for Texas. That's where I'd like to be. She'll pick somewhere else, but I'll run for Texas.

It was getting dark fast when the prisoners heard noises from the office out front. "Must be the old man bringing our food, Jonah. Remember now, make a move on him."

"I know," Jonah said, getting up from the bunk. "You ain't got to tell me what to do over and over." *Just like Lacy. Got to tell me what to do, over and over, like I'm a dimwit or something. Better be careful, Spider, I'm about twice as tough as you are, and a bit smarter, too.*

Tiny got the doors to the cell area open and brought two trays in, each covered with a cloth napkin. Tiny wasn't the type of man who didn't follow direction. He knew he shouldn't get close to the cell bars and wouldn't allow one of the men inside to grab him. He knew he had to put the trays on the floor and slide them into the cells. He also was aware that both men suffered serious wounds and a little kindness might do both of them some good.

"Fried chicken tonight, boys. Stand back now, you know the routine." He took a step toward Jonah who immediately lunged for the jailer. Tiny didn't leap back as Spider said he would, instead, he turned one of the trays sideways and slammed it through the iron bars, splashing fried chicken, mashed potatoes, and gravy into Jonah's face, ending the attack.

"Well, no supper for you two. It's all over the floor now. I'll see you boys in the morning. Have a nice sleep."

Tiny Lawson was a man with a determined mind, one which once made up wouldn't be changed. "Ain't gonna clean that up, neither," he grumbled. "They gonna live in that mess as far as I'm concerned." He was grumbling all the way back to the livery stables where he pulled his jug of mule piss out and settled in for a long night of drinking. He had two swallows when he knew that that wasn't what Tiny Lawson was known for.

"All right, all right," he mumbled to himself. It took a short walk for his anger to dissipate and about half an hour to clean up the mess outside the cells. "What's inside is for you boys to clean up. Ain't allowed in there, you know. That was damn stupid of you. Of course, bein' criminals and all, you are stupid to begin with."

Spider and Jonah simply sat on the edges of their bunks and watched the proceedings. It was Spider who finally spoke up. "Weren't me what got you mad. Why ain't I gettin' no food?"

"You really ain't very bright, are you?" His cackle could be heard all the way out on the street, and his walk back to the livery was filled with cackles, guffaws, and lively talk. "One more good swallow of some mule piss and I'll sleep like a baby."

———

CORCORAN SAT down at the kitchen table across from Lacy Samuels and gave the woman a long hard look. It was returned in spades. Her eyes were piercing, and they bored into him, filled with hate. "You ain't got much call to hate me, Lacy. Shooting a partner in the back? Well, me wearing a badge and all..." He drawled it out, long and slow, hoping to anger the woman even more than she already was.

Corcoran learned years ago as a baby-faced peace officer, that if you can get a suspect angry, they're liable to say just about anything. Most often enough to prove their guilt. "It's my duty, my beck and call, to arrest you and bring you before a judge. Before all that, though, maybe you can tell me some about what brought on that man's death. He arranged for those mine checks to be turned into cash, didn't he? Hell's bells, woman, I'd want to keep that man alive. Might be more checks coming. Whooie." He was putting on quite a show for the dumpy old woman and knew his jests and probes were paying off.

He could see jaw muscles working, knew she was about to start screaming again or worse. "All my life I've lived with the thought that a woman should be treated like a lady until she gives the impression that she isn't one. I've killed men who beat up women while I've had to knock a few women who weren't ladies on their ample butts. Tell me about this John Nichols, the man you killed."

She sat still and quiet, her hands tied tight, her face contorted in anger and hate, her eyes almost gleaming. Corcoran chuckled seeing her jaw muscles working so hard he feared she might even break a tooth soon.

"Well, then, maybe I'll help some," Corcoran said. He walked to the stove and poured himself a cup of boiling coffee. Didn't offer her any, and returned to the table.

"You tried to get Sam Tankersley involved in your little game of chance with the Eureka Mine and Mill's money, and when he wouldn't, you knew he had to be done away with. The man knew too much. Am I right, so far?" She just continued staring, glaring at the big man.

"So, you brought Nichols in to kill Tankersley. Got to get rid of old Sam. He knew too much. He knew about your scheme. So Nichols, the false stockman came on strong to the Tankersley filly, Barbara, to get close to Sam, and even used Barbara's fine little Persian knife to kill the man." He saw enough movement in her eyes, a slight cock of her head, a dip in a shoulder to know he was right.

How many times over the years has he seen this? How many times has he needed to follow through and get the suspect really angry, upset enough to yell at him, spilling guilt in his lap. This was not the time to hold back. This one thing he knew for a fact. Go for the throat.

"He did all that for you and you thanked him by

shooting him in the back." He chuckled. "Remind me not to ever do you a favor."

"You don't know what you're talking about. Tankersley was a fool." She jerked hard at the ropes knowing she should never have said that.

"A fool for turning down the offer of being a partner in your scheme? No, you are the fool, woman. You killed one partner and your brother killed your other partner." Corcoran was standing, both hands flat on the table, bent over the table, his face just inches from hers. "You're gonna hang from a high old tree, Lacy. You and your brother."

He stood up straight, drained his coffee cup and walked to the stove. As he filled his cup, he heard whimpers followed by sobs and turned slowly to see Lacy Samuels crying like a baby, sobbing, but unable to bring her hands to her face. *Something wrong in what I'm seeing,* Corcoran thought.

He walked around the table slowly, watching the performance, and chuckled. "Ain't never seen a woman cry like that and not produce a single teardrop. Good work, Lacy, but you're still gonna hang. We got a special tree in Eureka that we use. It's an ancient old cottonwood, and we got a fine rope, too."

The sobbing continued for another few minutes but it became obvious even to Lacy that it wasn't going to change things. "Go to hell, Corcoran," she said softly, letting her head fall forward, her chin resting on her bosom.

Corcoran heard horses trotting up to the house and went to the door, his pistol drawn. "You expecting someone, Lacy?" She sat upright thinking maybe it was her brother come to save her, forgetting Corcoran told her Jonah was in jail, and slumped back down.

"Hello the house," Sean O'Keefe yelled out. "It's Sean."

Corcoran walked out onto the porch and waved him in. "Got my message, eh? Come on in, coffee's hot, and we got work to do. How is it in town?" He took the lead rope and tied the horses off as Sean O'Keefe climbed down from the small wagon.

"A couple of cowpokes are upset. That horse right there was stole earlier today. They gave a pretty good description of Lacy Samuels."

"One more charge on her ticket, I guess. We got a big fraud, a couple of dead men, and now horse thieving. Might have to hang her twice," Corcoran said, holding the door for Sean and saying it loud enough for Lacy to hear.

"She don't look good," Sean said, taking a seat at the table. "Kinda dull around the edges. What did you mean when you said a couple of dead men?"

"She killed her partner, John Nichols, the man who made the arrangements to have those checks cashed. Ain't a very nice person, Sean. Have a cup of coffee and then we'll get her packed up in the wagon for the ride back to town."

"Good, I could use a good night's sleep," Sean said. "This has been one long day."

"It's gonna get a lot longer, I'm afraid. We've got three prisoners that have to be transported back to

Eureka and the morning express pulls out at six o'clock sharp."

"Lordy, lordy," is all Sean could say. "Unless I'm mistaken, we've got a storm coming our way, as well, Terrence, me boy." They were standing on the porch looking out at a long line of dark clouds off to the north-west. "She'll be blowin' and snowin' before long."

"I expect," is all Corcoran said. "Best keep moving."

CHAPTER EIGHTEEN

THEY LEFT Lacy tied up in the kitchen while they dug a grave and buried Nichols. "The way you describe it, this fool must have gotten himself close enough to the Tankersley's that he could walk into the house or even into Tankersley's bedroom." Sean shook his head. "Some kind of fast talker."

"Sugar-coated and covered in slime," Corcoran agreed. He thought about Barbara. *That girl is even more naive than most. He must have come to town with the express purpose of killing Tankersley and used that girl. Well, he won't get his day in court.*

"I can understand him pulling the blanket over Barbara's eyes, but not Sam's. Tankersley was a hard-boiled mining man not some easy pickin's for a gambler. I wonder if Nichols might have had some mining in his background? Been able to talk the talk, so to speak."

"Some fair questions to ask Lacy on the ride back to town. We ain't gonna get much sleep, Terrence."

"Sleep on the train, Sean. You for a couple of hours,

then me for a couple of hours. We'll put the prisoners in irons connected to the carriage benches."

"Think we should bring Tiny along? And his jug of mule piss?"

Corcoran was still chuckling when they walked back to the main house. "You really like that horrid stuff, don't you?"

"Grows on you," Sean said. "I remember when I was a wee tad, coming through Nebraska it was, and our wagons were stopped near a big corn farm. Dad bought a jug of what was called shine from the farmer. Ain't never had nothing better, Terrence."

"Give me old-fashioned Irish whiskey or give me Kentucky bourbon, and you can have all the shine and mule piss you want," Corcoran said. "This talk is making me thirsty, Sean. Let's keep moving."

As they walked to the house, O'Keefe kept looking over his shoulder as the clouds moved closed, got bigger and blacker, and he would have sworn he could feel the wind cool off and get stronger.

Corcoran had a length of rope he found in the barn, had a set of handcuffs in the saddlebags, and got Lacy out the door and up into the back of the wagon. Her hands were tied behind her back and Corcoran used the cuffs to latch her to the buggy, then tied her feet together. "All comfy, are you? Only a few miles, so just relax and enjoy the ride." No response and he noticed she wouldn't even look at him.

The sun had gone down along with the temperature and Lacy was wrapped in a couple of blankets. Corcoran tied the stolen stock horse to the back of the buggy, stepped into his saddle, and motioned Sean to lead out. "I'll ride back here for a spell," he said.

Stars were bright in the cold air but before the sun had settled in for the night, Corcoran could see massive clouds building up to the northwest. So far there was no wind but the old lawman knew it wouldn't be long and one of the first big storms of late fall would be spreading its cold white blanket on the land.

"Let's put that courser in a trot, Sean. The sooner we get back to town, the sooner we get something to eat."

"That jail ain't got facilities for a woman, Terrence. Where you gonna put her up until the train leaves?"

Corcoran was riding alongside the buggy and looked down at Lacy, wrapped and warm in the back. "Gonna have to bed-up with you, I guess."

Lacy's scream could have been heard fifty miles away in Elko, and the follow-up from Sean O'Keefe was almost as loud. "Oh, no," he howled. "No, sir, Terrence. I ain't sharing no bed with that woman. No, sir."

Corcoran was having a fine time, laughing at the two of them. "You wouldn't shoot him, now, would you, ma'am?"

She was screaming, her squirming about had knocked the blankets off, and Corcoran was afraid she might hurt herself. "Well, all right, then," he said. "We'll make other accommodations. Better pull up, Sean, and get that woman covered up."

The rest of the ride into Palisades was uneventful, and they arrived just as the breeze began to pick up. "Hope they have those stoves lit up in the coaches," Sean said. "It's gonna be a cold ride into Eureka if they ain't."

Sean drove the buggy straight to the livery while Corcoran rode to the restaurant that provided meals for prisoners. "We'll be leaving with the prisoners on the early train so we'll need their food ready by four. Make it simple and box up something simple for dinner on the train. We'll be in Eureka in plenty of time for them to get supper at the main jail."

Roxanne gave Corcoran a big smile and wrote the order down. "What about you, Terrence? Ain't you eatin' too?"

"We'll grab something at the hotel," he said, turning to get out of there as quickly as possible. Roxanne always wanted hugs and kisses. "Gotta get back. Thanks, darlin'," he said, moving toward the door.

The wind was blowing strong by the time he made it to the livery. "Gonna need all your help in the morning, Tiny. You all right with that?"

"Tiny had a conflict with our prisoners," Sean said. "They'll be a testy bunch in the morning."

Tiny spent a quick five minutes telling Corcoran what happened and how the food ended up on the floor and in faces instead of in stomachs. "I guess I've pretty much lost my job, eh?"

"Yes, you have, Tiny, but not because of this incident. You did good. But there won't be any prisoners for you to take care of when we leave. First thing Sheriff Connor will have to do is find a new resident deputy."

"Won't be me," Tiny said. "My mules and horses behave themselves like ladies and gentlemen, not outlaws and thugs. I'll stick with being a liveryman and smithy, thank you." He cackled.

"Food will be ready at four. How about bedding Lacy in the straw in one of your empty stalls?" He looked over at the woman sitting in the dirt with her back against a stall post. "Don't have a cell open at the jail. We'll all meet at the jail when Sean, you, and Tiny bring her and I bring the food. Then we all three of us escort the prisoners to the train station and get boarded."

"I ain't goin' to Eureka," Tiny said.

"No, you ain't." Corcoran chuckled. "We just need you to help get everybody on board. Questions?"

"I ain't sleeping here," Lacy said.

"Why not, you own half the place, don't you? Not good enough for you? Too bad." Corcoran said. "Let's hit the hotel, Sean. Big steak, glass of whiskey, and bed. Been a day."

Tiny looked at Lacy and moved to help her up. With her feet tied together, she could just hobble into the stall. Tiny kicked some straw into a makeshift bed and got Lacy down. "I'll bring your blankets," he said. "No oats, though. Not good for sleeping." Corcoran and Sean could hear his cackle as they walked onto the street.

"Think he'll feed her some mule piss?" Sean asked, laughing and poking Corcoran. "With her going to jail maybe even hanging, it will be interesting to see how that partnership ends," Sean said. "Tiny's one sharp little feller and she's a con man from the word go. I'd love to hear the negotiations."

"We'll probably have to, come morning."

CHAPTER NINETEEN

THE BANGING on the hotel door was loud enough to wake the dead, and Corcoran came out of a sound sleep, his big Colt solidly in hand. It was just moments and the voice said, "Three o'clock, Sheriff."

"Thanks," Corcoran mumbled, shoving the pistol back in the holster and climbing out of bed. It took a few moments for the big lawman to remember where he was, slowly letting the hotel room come into focus. *Feels like that storm's got here. Cold.*

"Up, Sean," he said, poking the man snoring under a load of covers in the adjoining bed. "Up."

"Dead, don't have to get up." He tried to roll over but Corcoran poked him harder.

"Dead men don't talk. If you're not up in one minute, I'll bring the water pitcher over."

Sean O'Keefe slowly pushed the blankets aside, felt the wave of cold air move in, and tried to reclaim the blankets. "Cold," he said. One more poke and Sean was up and getting pants and shirt on. "You're a hard man, Corcoran. Hard."

Coffee and some hot side meat in the hotel dining room helped the men fight off their long hours the day before. There was at least six inches of snow on the ground with more coming down, almost shutting off any view of the street scene. "Usually I look forward to this first big storm of the season, Sean. Maybe not quite so, today."

The only light was from oil lamps inside windows, but it was enough to offer a serious winter's view of downtown Palisades. It was too early for there to be many people out and about, the snow lay pristine, almost glowing in the muted light of the lamps where the wind couldn't attack it. It was the wind that distorted the view. Swirling snow blew haphazardly about, piling up along the boardwalks, filling in depressions in the ground, and drifting where the wind allowed it to.

"We could be having to move these prisoners of yours back to Eureka on horseback, Terrence. Think of that. We'll be riding in a nice warm railroad coach, sipping some fine whiskey, and gnawing on smoked elk. Yep, I've always enjoyed the first really big storm of the season."

Sean went to help Tiny harness a team and get the wagon ready. They would use it to move Lacy up to the jail and then bring all the prisoners to the train station. Corcoran picked up the prisoner's food and brought it to the jail. It was nearing four thirty when Jonah Samuels and Spider Watson were told to back away from the bars and their breakfast was shoved through the slots. Lacy was securely tied to a chair and her hands were untied so she could eat.

Corcoran snickered seeing that Tiny had cleaned up the areas outside the cells, but there was old, cold food splashed about inside the cells. "Ought to make them clean their cells before we leave. Too little time, I'm afraid."

"Not so testy this morning, eh?" Tiny said. "Good decision boys. Eat that food instead of wearing it." Both men glared at Tiny who answered back with a loud cackle. "Glad I'm done with you boys. Won't be seeing you again."

Corcoran had his eyes on Lacy when she recognized her brother. "I thought you were dead," she said. She turned to Corcoran. "You didn't say he was alive." She turned back to Jonah. "What happened to your head?" She twisted back around to face Corcoran. "What did you do to him?"

"Gave him a quick lesson in proper behavior around a man who wears a badge, Lacy. It ain't nice to try and shoot me." Corcoran nodded and finished his coffee. "Let's get this show on the road."

One at a time, the prisoners were brought out of their cells, hands cuffed behind their back and legs fitted in irons making it difficult to walk, more or less try to run away. Again, one at a time they were put in the back of the wagon, already carrying a mantel of cold snow. The short trip to the train station and the scene was repeated in reverse.

The grumbling, cussing, and berating got a little

louder with each move and the three prisoners were also carrying a fine dusting of snow and ice as they were hauled from the wagon. At that early hour there weren't too many spectators but those that were there got a good show for their time. "Gonna be a hangin' in Eureka, Corcoran?" one of the spectators yelled it out and Spider cussed him out.

"Has to be near zero," Sean O'Keefe said. "Ain't never gonna go outlaw hunting with you again, Terrence. Nope, ain't never." O'Keefe had a bear skin long-coat wrapped around a wool shirt covered by a wool coat, and seemed to be shivering from head to toe. "Could use a belt of the mule piss about now."

"We'll be warm soon enough," Corcoran answered. The big lawman had to agree that it was cold but he also had to laugh remembering how, on camping trips into the high mountains it was always Sean who was up first giving Corcoran hell for complaining about the cold.

"You only get cold when you're in town, old man? Or maybe it is that there might be a wee tad of whiskey nearby?" Corcoran got a wry smile from the big man and almost expected the wild call of a wolf to reverberate up and down the streets of Palisades.

That was the extent of talk from the jail to the train station. Was it the cold that limited conversation or was their planning already discussed? What Corcoran found most unusual was the lack of talk among the prisoners. Were each planning something? Had the men already discussed some kind of plan?

"We'd best keep a close watch on Jonah and Spider,

Sean. They just might have discussed a plan of some kind. Don't much care for it when the prisoners get all quiet like." He'd transported many outlaws during his long career as a lawman and the noisy, braggarts seldom gave him problems, but the quiet, sneaky ones were often problems. *Spider might start a problem, but Jonah, ah Jonah, he'll work out a plan. Gotta watch both those boys.*

Corcoran looked at Sean and again felt he had made the right decision to bring his big friend along. Trust wasn't an easy thing to have with casual friends, but then again, Sean O'Keefe was far more than a casual friend. When one hunts and fishes with another, the friendship is far deeper than casual. *We'll be fine,* Corcoran thought. *I can trust Sean regardless of what might happen.*

With the help of train conductor Sparky Mulroon, Spider, Jonah, and Lacy were lifted into a coach, seated, and cuffed to the permanent bench. "Thanks Sparky." Corcoran pointed at Jonah Samuels. "That the man you saw draw the buggy up to the sheriff's office?" Corcoran asked.

"Never forget that," Sparky said. "It's him." He pulled his nicely engraved railroad watch from his vest. "We'll be pulling out shortly. Once we get moving, I'll build a pot of coffee on the stove for us. Only other passengers are at the other end of the coach."

"Good," Corcoran said. "We'll be calling you to testify at his trial. Ain't nice trying to shoot a deputy sheriff."

Mulroon laughed right out. "Can't imagine anyone daft enough to try and shoot you, Corcoran. You can bet I'll testify."

"Time to say so long, Tiny. Thank you. You've been

more than a help and you'll be receiving some money from the county in the next week or so. You and Lacy work out a fair break up of your partnership?"

"More than fair, Corcoran. And in writing, too. Been interesting working with you." Tiny turned to Sean and smiled as he reached deep into a coat pocket. He handed Sean a small earthen jug. "Some mule piss to get you home safe, Sean O'Keefe. You know where there's more. Just come on up and say hello." He cackled. He was still cackling as he climbed down from the coach and headed for his team.

"Your own private source, eh?" Corcoran laughed. Sean just sat in his seat, wrapped in that heavy bearskin coat, a slight smile on his broad face. "I'll be warm soon, Terrence. Warm soon."

Corcoran looked around their end of the long coach and thought about the many hours they would be there. *If there's going to be trouble it will happen right away,* he thought. *It ain't that there's a book to tell 'em how to act but prisoners will try to make their break at the beginning of a journey rather than later.*

"Tell you what, Sean, let's make this journey as comfortable as possible for the both of us. If something's gonna happen it'll be Spider kicking it off. Jonah's got too big a headache to start something."

"What about that old woman? I wouldn't trust her to wash my shirt."

"She'd be an instigator but not a performer, old man. She'll talk 'em into action then sit back and watch 'em die."

The three prisoners were all pretending they couldn't

hear what was being said and Corcoran had to chuckle at their play-acting. "All right, you three, now you know where we stand. Don't be stupid on me and you'll arrive in Eureka alive." He gave 'em a big smile. "That's right, Spider, I'm talking to you."

CHAPTER TWENTY

"INTERESTING," Sheriff Ed Connor said after reading the long wire from Corcoran. "Looks like Corcoran thinks he's got this wrapped up and they'll leave for Eureka first thing in the morning." Connor handed the wire to Deputy Lou Foster and poured some coffee into his tin cup. "Still something a bit strange to me," he mused. "If this Lacy woman came to Sam Tankersley with this plot to defraud the mine, and Sam got all upset by it, why didn't he come to us? Or why didn't he go to Bill Sherman?"

Foster put the wire down, shaking his head. "Barbara Tankersley was involved with this Nichols jerk? I remember him coming to town a time or two, all flashy in his 'look at me I'm a rancher' outfits. Got laughed at by many who could see right through the man."

"Bill Sherman needs to know all about this," Connor said. "Let's ride out to the mine and pay the man a visit. It seems strange that if Tankersley would not get involved in the scheme why did he not alert anyone at the mine about the plot?"

Cold winds and driving snow made the ride out to the mine more than uncomfortable for the sheriff and his deputy. "Those boys working underground are the lucky ones today." Foster laughed. "I tried that once and went back to the ranch and almost kissed the cows. Scared me to death."

"Ain't never had no desire to work underground," Connor agreed. "Takes a special breed of man, I think. They treat that dynamite like we treat coffee beans. Just something to work with. Only blasting I want to hear comes from the end of my Colt. Hope Sherman has that stove of his lit."

"Always glad to see the law come calling," Bill Sherman said, welcoming Connor and Foster to his office. "Have any more news on Tankersley's killing?" Connor shucked his heavy coat and made a beeline for the wood stove.

"We bring news, Bill, but I'm not sure how you're going to take it." Connor warmed his hands at the stove and moved to one of the chairs opposite the mine manager and Foster stood off to the side. "Terrence Corcoran is in Palisades and has just about wrapped up the case of fraudulent purchases but there's far more to it. It appears that this Lacy Samuels may have been in contact with Sam Tankersley as she was developing the scheme and offered to let Sam in for a cut."

"My god," Sherman exploded. "No. Not Sam. He would never do that."

"You may be right. It seems that Sam threw her out,

wanted nothing to do with the idea. That's when this gambler type, John Nichols was brought in, by way of Barbara Tankersley, to kill Sam because he probably knew too much."

Connor saw Sherman's face change from one who simply didn't believe that Tankersley might be involved to something closer to believing the man was involved. "That damn fool," Sherman said softly, quietly, and Connor wondered if there was to be an explosion. "All he had to do was come to me or Gerald McKinnon and none of this would have happened."

"No, Bill, all he had to do was come to me," Connor said. "This group was able to infiltrate your operation. Jonah Samuels and Rory Tibbets in your main office along with Duane Holloway and all your signatures could be duplicated, all purchase orders were cut and accepted by the finance people, and checks were cut and sent off."

"Not one bit of it had to happen if Sam had said something to someone," Sherman said. "Why didn't he? What was it that kept him quiet? Not like the man, Sheriff."

"Can't answer that," Connor said. "Was he planning to? Who knows? Corcoran will be leaving Palisades with the prisoners first thing in the morning so we'll know a lot more when he gets here."

"Sam Tankersley looked on the mines where we worked as holy ground, Sheriff. He held the property and its valuables in high respect and for him not to come to someone was as far out of character as he could get. If there is an answer, I hope you find it and pass it on to me."

———

"That is one sad man we're leaving back there, Lou," Sheriff Connor said as he and Deputy Foster rode out from the Eureka Mine and Mill Company property. "I wonder if there is an answer as to why Sam Tankersley acted the way he did. He felt what Lacy was talking about was illegal but didn't follow through, just told her to leave and not come back."

"Think there might have been a threat involved?" Foster asked.

"From what I know about Tankersley, he wouldn't take a threat without some kind of response. No, neither he nor his children were under any threats. That came later but not as a threat. Nichols came to town to kill the man and used Barbara in order to get close to him. No, but something kept him from saying anything about the scheme to defraud his own company."

They rode right up to the front of the Bonanza Club and tied off. "Maybe a cold beer will loosen up my old brain," Connor joked, pushing the bat-wings open. "Were you watching those clouds as we rode in? We're in for it, Lou."

"The wind is already picking up and I could feel the cold. Corcoran will be glad they're coming on a train and not riding in with those prisoners."

"How many times Corcoran and I have had to do that," Connor said. He got a long cold look in his eyes, the smile disappeared as he continued. "Lost good friends bringing criminals in during storms. Seen hard men cry out in pain, seen men just roll over and go to sleep, knowing they'd be dead by morning."

Foster hadn't seen this side of the sheriff, almost had a change of heart about the way the sheriff seemed to want Foster to chase something down in a hard storm. "Never get used to it, eh Sheriff?" Connor nodded as they made their way to the long oaken bar.

"Hello, Sheriff, Foster, what can I get you fellers?" Jimmy Henderson was behind the bar on this cold afternoon. "Understand Corcoran will be bringing in a load of prisoners tomorrow."

Connor looked at Foster and shook his head. "Doesn't take long for the word to spread, does it? Telegrams and wires are supposed to be private, Jimmy. How is it you know this?"

"Hell, Sheriff, half the town's talking about it. Corcoran even named the man who killed Sam Tankersley is what I heard. That dude who pretty talked his way into Barbara Tankersley's knickers did it, right?"

"Gonna have to have a chin-to-chin meeting with that telegraph operator, Lou. When we leave here, run him down and bring him into the office, eh?" Foster nodded and smiled at the thought. "In the meantime, Jimmy, give me a shot of bourbon and back it up with a glass of beer. It's already been one hell of a day. Give my fine, upstanding deputy the same."

———

"HERE HE IS, Sheriff. Didn't want to come. Said he couldn't leave the key unattended." Foster pushed Lawerence Peterson through the office door.

"Sit down, Peterson," Connor snarled. He looked at Foster. "You know how to run that key?"

"I learned it some time ago, Sheriff. I thought it would be a great job. that is until I met Corcoran."

"Go back to the telegraph office and send a note to the company that they need a new agent in Eureka and shut the place down." Connor looked at Peterson. "You, sir, are under arrest for spreading what is supposed to be, by law, private information. Those laws are in place for a reason, Mr. Peterson. The judge will be here next week. Let's go," he said, standing the telegraph clerk up and marching him into the cell area behind the office.

"You can't do this. that office must be maintained and open, available."

"Yup, and everything's supposed to be private, too." Connor chuckled. "In you go. Supper's at six," he said, closing the cell door with a clang and turning back to the office. "You'll be checked on from time to time. Anyone need to be notified of your being locked up?"

Peterson didn't say anything, just stood behind the bars with a dumb look on his face and watched the door being closed as the sheriff walked out.

It took Foster a little extra time to get the word out to the company since he hadn't tried to work a wire key in several years, but they answered and he turned the power off and locked the doors. "Sending and receiving wires is supposed to be sacred, I thought," he mumbled, heading back to the office. "I wonder how much of what

Corcoran sent us was spread all over town? How many people know about Corcoran's plans?"

There was another wire for the sheriff waiting for him when he got there and carried it back with him. "Too many people know what's going on." The thought bothered him more than he realized and he stepped his pace up some. "What if that bunch has friends and they try to do something about it. Break the prisoners free. Sheriff ain't gonna like what I tell him."

The wind was blowing hard by the time Foster made it back to the office and he could feel the sting of ice hitting his cheeks. "This is gonna be a full-blown blizzard by morning, I'm afraid."

CHAPTER TWENTY-ONE

"WE'LL WANT to be at the train station when they pull in," Sheriff Connor said. He put the telegram down and grabbed his coffee cup. There was a hint of a smile on the older lawman's face, as if he was thinking of something. "Two wires in two days and both of them with good news," he mused, looking up at the ceiling. He shook his head, forcing himself to come back to reality, to find himself in his office chair, not out on the ride with Corcoran.

"You wanted to make that train ride to Palisades with Corcoran, didn't you?" Deputy Sheriff Lou Foster refilled his and the sheriff's coffee cups. "You miss the action that you had as a deputy instead of office work of a sheriff?"

Connor chuckled, took a sip of coffee, and sat back in his chair. "I've been lucky over the years, Lou. Worked for a fine bunch of range riders along the New Mexico-Texas border country. Lots of cattle rustling on both sides of the border in those days. And then I got even luckier being elected sheriff here and inheriting Terrence Corcoran." Connor's eyes almost misted up thinking of his early years as a lawman.

Foster had heard stories of Corcoran's escapades and was hoping the sheriff would tell some tall tales of his earlier life. "Carrying a badge for all these years," Foster said. "Doesn't it get awfully heavy? So much responsibility."

"We all bend the law just a tad once in a while, but not Corcoran. He'll work right up to that thin edge and not go over it. But god help the man who flaunts the law or who hurts a woman. Guess that's why I'm not surprised that Nichols is the man who killed Tankersley."

"How's that, Sheriff?"

Connor smiled. "Corcoran took an immediate dislike of the gentleman. He could almost smell out someone destined to be an outlaw. Never did like that feller myself, either, I guess. Talked a good story about having a ranch and all but he had gambler written all over him. Corcoran told me it was his hands that gave him away."

"His hands?" Foster asked. "How's that?"

"Working with animals all day every day, one's hands get rough, gnarly, not smooth and soft as a gambler's would. Corcoran spotted that right off. I wonder if Sam Tankersley also saw that?" Connor looked around the small office, as if trying to remember something. "Did Sam try to break up the romance Barbara was building with Nichols? How did that all fit together?"

"Those are questions we'll surely have to ask, Sheriff." Foster poured some more coffee for the two of them.

"Well, it looks like we'll need a wagon when the train pulls in."

"I'll take care of it," Deputy Lou Foster said. "The wire said Jonah Samuels was hurt bad. Should we bring the doctor along?"

"Good idea, yes. Did you have a chance to talk with Rory Tibbets? He must have been a fair-sized part of the plot to defraud the mine."

"Knew how to get the checks authorized and signed. He's given me a good set of statements. I think he's afraid of being tied to Sam Tankersley's murder. Looking at a long rope," Foster said. "He ain't afraid of prison, but don't want to hang. He'll cooperate. He isn't very smart, Sheriff, but once he learns something, it stays with him. He knew the money flow at the mine. We'll want to keep him separated from the others. They'll want to silence him for sure."

"You ever thought of living in Palisades, Lou?"

"Oh, now, Sheriff," Foster said, slowly enunciating each word. "I'm very happy working with you and Corcoran. He's been teaching me a lot about this job. I don't think I'm ready to be the resident deputy up there."

Connor looked at the young man. *He's born and raised in Eureka, knows the county, knows the people, and is comfortable wearing that tin badge.* "It would be a big step, Lou, but you're the kind of man we need up there. Duane Holloway was a weak man, easily turned, took the easy way out, becoming a criminal."

"Only met him once, Sheriff," Foster said. "Seemed rather proud of himself."

Sheriff Connor almost spit his coffee out, coughing

and laughing at the same time. "I wish Corcoran were here to have heard that. He'd slap you on the back so hard."

Foster chuckled at the thought and brought the coffeepot to refill the sheriff's cup. "Won't be nice having Spider Watson back in our jail. He is one dedicated troublemaker. I met Jonah Samuels once on a visit to the mine. He's a big strong fella."

"He is, but Corcoran's wire says he's hurt bad. At least we now have separate facilities for women prisoners. The district attorney will meet with everyone, one at a time, tomorrow and we'll decide on how to charge these people." Connor shook his shaggy head slowly back and forth. "Sam's murderer, that Nichols chap, is dead, but were Lacy and her brother connected? Corcoran's sure they are and says he has more than enough proof to send 'em off for a long time."

Foster slipped into his jacket. "I'll go get the wagon and let Dr. Whidby know he should be there. Storm is really howling out there." He took a step or two to the door and turned.

"I don't like it that so many people in town know about Corcoran coming back, know about this John Nichols fellow, and know that he and Barbara Tankersley were seeing each other. Might give somebody ideas."

"Between the telegraph operator and our friend Jimmy Henderson at the Bonanza Club, the whole damn county knows about it. Two telegrams in two days is like an avalanche of news flowing through the canyon, Lou. People love bad news." He chewed on a knuckle for a minute. "You're right, though. We'll need to be on our toes. Spider has friends, don't know about the others."

––––––––––

"You're as much responsible for Dad's murder as the man who did it," Junior Tanksersley yelled at his older sister. They were leaving the Eureka cemetery following a brief ceremony and burial. Wrapped in coats, scarves, gloves, and hats, the screaming could not be heard by others because of the high wind. A raging late fall blizzard hampered the ceremony and had a lot to do with those attending wanting to get back somewhere warm. The mining crowd had turned out, many friends from town were there, and Betty Johansen was walking several feet behind the Tankersley children.

Betty couldn't hear what was being said but there was no doubt a lot of anger was involved. She wanted to say something during the burial but Sam seemed to be in charge of the event and wanted it over with as soon as possible. Was it because of the weather or was whatever the two siblings were arguing about the problem?

"What a horrible thing to say," Barbara said. "How dare you. How dare you, Junior, to say such a thing. John and father never got along. I'm the one who broke up with the man and told him to leave me alone."

"You flung yourself at him. Made a fool of yourself and invited him into our house." Junior was crying, sadness being set aside by anger. "You're the one who took great pleasure in showing that man your pretty little knife, along with other things. You need to change your ways, Barbara, or you're going to become nothing more than a working girl, a floozy," he almost shouted into her face.

The snow was driven by strong and bone-chilling winds and despite the noise of the storm, those standing within ten feet of the two Tankersley children could hear the slap and see Junior reel from the blow.

"How dare you," Barbara screamed and tried to hit her younger brother again.

Betty Johansen quickly made her way to the two. "Stop that," she said, and Barbara glared at her. "Whatever the problem, this isn't the time nor the place for such behavior. Now stop that."

Barbara was in tears, Sam Junior was boiling angry, and Aunt Betty tried to step between the two. "Calm down, you two. That's your father we just buried, this isn't a rot-gut whiskey saloon we're walking in, it's a cemetery filled with the remains of loved ones. Show some respect."

Her words seemed angry but her face told another story as she looked back and forth at the two. Betty had never been a mother but seemed to be the perfect one at the moment. What she had said was filled with love, not anger, and the children, all but grown, responded immediately.

"Let's go up to the house, I'll fix a pot of coffee and you can tell me what this is all about." She tried to smile, but she hadn't had a dry eye since Lou Foster told her of Sam's dreadful death. "Think of your father and what he would think of your behavior."

There was a lot of love in what Betty said but both

Junior and Barbara recognized what the intent of the words were as well. "You're right, Aunt Betty," Junior said. "We'll discuss this at the house."

His face was reddened by the slap and he felt humiliated as well, but of the two, even being the youngest, Sam Junior was the more grown up. He had seen his sister flaunt her beauty and a little too much of her body, teasing men unmercifully, and watched the sleazy gambler called John Nichols take advantage of her. She in turn welcomed his advances, thrilled that an older, successful rancher was so interested.

At the rather elegant maple dining room table, fitted out with wrought iron flanges and corner decorations, Barbara sat across from Junior. Betty got a pot of coffee boiling, found some fresh biscuits from that morning, a tub of spring-cooled butter, and a bowl of strawberry jam.

She sat down and folded her hands in her lap. "Emotions are not to be spread across this table as we work out whatever problems we have," Aunt Betty said. Her voice was quiet, her eyes were warm, but it was known immediately, these were the rules. "Now, let's be adults and discuss the problem."

Both Junior and Barbara started talking at once and Betty rapped her knuckles on the table. "Again, we're adults." Betty wasn't frustrated but she wasn't that far from it either. "Junior, you make your say and Barbara, wait your turn." Every kid in Eureka County had heard this before, including these two. Aunt Betty, the Eureka goat lady, refereed problems among those growing up in such a manner that every kid loved her to death. It was her way, a soft voice, a strong will, and spread evenly with love.

Betty looked at the two, fully understood their loss, after all, it was hers as well. These two could very well have ended up her stepchildren. The loss of a father as loved as Sam Tankersley was devastating and when it came by way of violence, it was worse. Why did Junior think Barbara was behind it all? Or was there something else at play?

Junior washed down his last bite of biscuit and jam with a sip of coffee and looked at Betty. "Because of the way Barbara was with that rotten John Nichols, I believe she's as much responsible for Dad's death as Nichols," he said. "She even gave that knife to the man."

"I did not." Barbara belted it right out, stopped, gave Betty a quick look before continuing. "He must have taken it. I did show it to him." She was crying, tears running down both cheeks, and took a moment to blow her nose and wipe her eyes. "I'm not responsible for Dad's death. That's a horrible thing to say. I'm not." She was adamant, almost thumping the table. "I loved Dad. I'd never hurt him. Never." She was crying still, sobbing, her nose running again. It was a soft sobbing, and Barbara laid her head on the table.

Betty Johansen sat looking at the two Tankersley children thinking of Sam, their father, her lover. "This is a most difficult time, children. Emotions are raging, and anger is too often a part of their rampage." She took a sip of coffee, working to get her thoughts in order. "No, Sam, I don't think Barbara is any more responsible for your father's death than I would be or you would be.

"John Nichols knew what he was doing, from what I gather. Everything we know is nothing more than gossip at this point, brought to us by a pair of telegrams sent to the sheriff by Corcoran, so we're not dealing with actual knowledge. Nichols was a sleazy gambler, Sam, you're right there, and Barbara, you are so young and, I'm afraid, rather naive. You flirted and then fell for his gambling man's tales."

Barbara tensed up at the comment but didn't say anything. She didn't like criticism from anyone. Betty smiled at her and took another sip of coffee. "You're young, most attractive, and, honestly, darling, a flirt. You tease the boys, but John Nichols wasn't a boy. He was a man who lived by never dealing in the truth, and he played you. Take this as a learning experience, understanding that people often aren't who they appear to be. Who they want you to believe who they appear to be."

It's a fine line, isn't it? Is he who he appears to be? Or is who he appears to be a fiction in order to take something from you? Betty Johansen wondered if Barbara was adult enough to grasp the difference, to understand that she had been leading on a man who was depending on her to do just that. Nichols needed to be able to be close to Sam Tankersley without frightening the man. Barbara provided that.

"Being naive is one thing, Barbara, but when it comes to flirting, to exposing too much of your body, when it comes to a confidence man, a gambling man, a man set on murdering, your actions led him right to Sam."

She looked hard at the young girl and wasn't sure Barbara was aware of how she had acted. "Corcoran's telegram to the sheriff, if you can believe what the gossip is, since none of us has seen the wire, says Nichols was sent here to kill your father. He recognized your youth, beauty, and naiveté, and used you. Even a much older, wiser person might have been taken in. That's what sleazy gamblers and confidence men hope for. The easy mark, my dear."

Betty's kind but weathered face looked so sad that Barbara just started bawling and sobbing, then she got up from the table and walked around to get on her knees and wrapped her arms around the strong, slight woman. "I'm so sorry," she whispered. Betty let her hold on for a moment or two and then eased her back.

"Junior, do you have a slightly different picture of the situation now? Yes, Barbara brought the man into the family, so to speak, but is not the one responsible for Sam's murder. Becoming an adult is so difficult, discovering that there are people who will say or do anything to get their way, even if it means death to someone, is the most difficult part of growing up."

Junior hadn't said a word since his initial thrust and Betty saw during the conversations a teenage boy become a young man, saw in his eyes that he recognized the truth of what was being said, and the set of his jaw told her that he knew Barbara had not done the right thing but was also not responsible for their father's death.

"I think I understand," Sam Junior said. "I don't like what happened. I wish Barbara had never met the man, but I was wrong. Barbara, I'm sorry I said what I did and I hope you accept that."

Barbara's sobbing started all over again and she

rushed to Sam's side of the table and threw her arms around her brother. "I should grow up, shouldn't I?" She hugged him tight for another few moments and stood back from the table. "It was so exciting to be accepted as a woman by this fancy man." She looked at Betty. "He made me feel so special, a rancher and all, spending money, telling me stories. I'm so sorry." She fell into her chair and laid her head on the table.

"What do I do now?" she asked, looking as deep into Aunt Betty's eyes as anyone ever had. "What?"

"I think you just have, little darling," Betty smiled. "I think you just grew up." Betty got up and walked to the stove. "This is a beautiful house your father has put together and the two of you are going to have to make some serious decisions in the next few weeks. There is money and property that needs to be taken care of, and I'm reasonably sure there will be bills to be paid.

"You know where I live and you know that you will always be welcome. Any time you have questions, any time you want to just sit and talk, I'll be there. I came close to being a part of this wonderful family, I want to remain close."

Betty Johansen slipped into her heavy canvas work coat, pulled a scarf tight around her face and neck, slammed a slouch hat on her head and headed for the door and the long ride through the blizzard to her hungry goats. Sam and Barbara sat across the table, tears in their eyes and noses running wild, and stared at each other.

CHAPTER TWENTY-TWO

Sparky Mulroon was spending as much time at the potbelly stove in the railroad coach as he was tending to his passengers. Snow was falling heavier now than when they left the station an hour ago, and the wind was driving it at gale forces, strong enough, it seemed to rock the coach.

Terrence Corcoran had his thoughts on how much longer this trip would be. "We're not running on time, are we Sparky?"

"I'm afraid not, Terrence. We'll be making that long climb soon and it will slow us down even more. If you have people waiting for you in Eureka, they're in for a long wait, I'm afraid. I'm sure those boys up front are pouring the wood to the boiler, though. We're pushing tons of snow aside and it's gonna get worse."

Thoughts and memories of railroad disasters in winter storms were in both men's minds. Engines on their sides, passenger trains unable to move, no food, and eventually no heat. Would rescue even be possible in a wild storm like this one?

Corcoran motioned for Sean to move a little closer so they could talk without the prisoners hearing them. "We need to think about what we'll need to do if this train gets stuck in the snow, old man. Those three are already making their plans, I'm afraid."

"I've been watching that Spider feller. He's an instigator, Terrence. Sparky has us pretty much separated from the few other passengers, maybe we can split Spider and Jonah up. Put one at a window seat on one side of the coach and one at the opposite window seat. They'd have to talk pretty loud to do any planning."

"Damn good, Sean. I'm going to put a pistol to Spider's head, you unlock Jonah and move him across to the other side. Then we'll move Lacy to the seat behind Spider. They'll have to do some loud yelling to make any plans." He chuckled, sat back and looked at the three. "Let's move Lacy first. Get her out of the way, so to speak. Be as careful as if you were dealing with a boar hog, Sean. She's feisty mean, and strong, too."

She had her eyes on the two men, scowling, seeming to understand what they were discussing. "You touch me wrong, buster, I'll have your hide."

"I almost married a woman like her, once. Did I ever tell you about that?"

"Another time, Sean." Corcoran laughed. He loved Sean's stories, told many of his own, but there was a time and a place and this wasn't it. "Get in the seats behind her and unlock her feet first then her hands."

He did and his bulk made it difficult. He had to get

down on his hands and knees behind the seat to reach under and unlock her feet. She was thrashing, trying to move her feet away from him, kicking out and Sean O'Keefe was glad he was behind her, not in front. Corcoran, standing in front of the woman pushed her back hard and put a big boot on top of her feet, stepping down hard.

"That hurts," she cried out.

"Gonna hurt a lot worse if you keep trying to kick away," Corcoran said, putting even more pressure on her feet. She was screaming obscenities at the top of her lungs and even Sparky came down the aisle to see if Corcoran needed help.

"Got 'em," Sean said, pulling the leg irons away and trying to get back on his feet. "They need to make a little more room between these seats."

"I'll mention that to the bosses," Mulroon said.

Corcoran laughed. "Now, her hands. Loosen one cuff and free it from the seat, then re-clamp it to her wrist." Corcoran leaned forward, leaving his foot on Lacy's feet, and put both hands on her shoulders. "One wrong move and I'll drive my fist all the way down your throat, woman."

"You ain't no gentleman." Lacy started to wrench away and saw the fist coming. She stopped immediately and Sean got her one hand free, slipped the cuff free of the seat and hooked it back up.

She was marched across the aisle to the other side of the coach and locked back in place with no further nonsense. "Think she learned something back there?" Sean asked.

"Not a chance, Sean. Same thing now with her brother." Corcoran pulled his revolver and placed the end of the barrel squarely between Spider's eyes. Sean moved behind Jonah's seat and got down to loosen the leg irons. Corcoran slowly pulled the hammer back until it clicked into readiness.

"Won't take much of your stupidity to make this thing go off, Spider. All right, loosen the leg iron and then re-connect. Let me know when you're done."

It was just moments and Sean grunted his answer. "His feet are free."

"Good. Now the hands, same as with Lacy."

When Jonah Samuels felt his hand cone free he tried to jump to his feet, swinging the free handcuff at Sean's head. Sean O'Keefe was a big man, wrestled large wagon wheels on a daily basis, forged wagon axels, and used heavy four-pound single-jack hammers and draw knives often. One driving right hand came straight out of his shoulder and Jonah's nose exploded in a shower of blood.

The man crumpled to the floor and Spider tensed up expecting to die the next second. Corcoran eased the hammer on the big iron back down, holstered the weapon, grabbed Jonah, and flung him onto the bench across the coach. Jonah was unconscious and just flopped down as Sean moved over and got the man all hooked back up.

"Hated to have to do that, Terrence, what with his head already a bloody mess. He was gonna whip me with that iron cuff."

"I know, Sean. You did what had to be done. Better get a rag and some water. You gave him a pretty good wallop. On top of the one I gave him, his head ain't gonna be the same ever again." Corcoran checked to make sure the man was breathing and got him more in a sitting position. "Hope the sheriff has the doc at the station when we get there."

Samuels regained consciousness as Sean was cleaning up the mess he made of the man's nose. Blood flow was reduced to a dribble and the area was wiped clean. "Don't never swing on me again, youngster. I ain't like Corcoran there. I don't take kindly to it. You hear me? Answer me or I'll rip your tongue out."

Jonah Samuels was also a big man, strong and mean, but he was hurt bad. The fight was gone out of him and he wheezed ever so softly, "I hear you."

"That's better. You really look like hell." Sean turned to Corcoran who was back on their bench seat. "Makes me hungry moving around like that. How about we eat some of that roast elk they made for us."

"You're thinking of a draught of mule piss, ain't you?" Corcoran laughed. "We're gonna have to get them fed, too. Be almost like what we just went through."

"Then I really need some of Tiny's best," Sean said.

"For a man raised on the finest Irish whiskey, I don't know how you can drink that stuff." Corcoran got up and walked up to the potbelly stove, then back to the end of the coach. He opened the door and stepped out onto the coach's porch. "Damn," he muttered, seeing snow coming in great waves, cascading, blowing, tumbling down. He stepped back in. "It's worse now than when we left Palisades."

The coach was not moving along smartly, was making

some jerks and it felt like it was hitting bumps in the road as well. "Having a hard time getting up this hill," Corcoran said. "Pushing as much snow as the cow catcher is bumping it aside. Chunks of ice are falling back on the tracks, too." He wiped fog off the window and tried to look out, maybe have an idea of how much more climbing they'll have to do.

"Can't see nothin'," he barked.

All he could see was a visual cacophony of snow, blowing in every direction at the same time. Snow dust from being blown aside by the engine made it worse and Corcoran settled back on the bench. *This old train comes to a halt and we're gonna be here for a while.* He knew there was wood for the stove, there was plenty of water, what with all that snow, but food would be limited.

He got up and walked to where Sparky Mulroon was standing near the potbelly stove. "Tried to see how close we are to the summit. Can't see nothing."

"We'll go over the top in less than five minutes, Corcoran, if they don't jump the tracks. Cow catcher ain't a plow. Snow gets under it and builds up and just lifts that big engine right off the tracks."

"Love a man who's full of good news," Corcoran said. "We didn't bring much food with us. How are you fixed?"

"I got my lunch bucket and that's it. Yup, Corcoran, I'm full of good news." He shoved another split log into the stove. "If we make this hill we're only ten miles or so from Eureka. Ten long, slow miles at that. All we can do is try to stay warm and think good thoughts."

"Thanks, Sparky."

———

Lou Foster was driving one wagon with two up and Dr. Whidby was driving his single horse buggy as they made their way down from Eureka to the train station. Snow was not falling, it was moving sideways at more than forty miles per hour and the horses were having a difficult time going down the slight hill. There was a covering of ice under the snow. "This is how horses break legs, Sheriff. They lose their footing in the ice and down they go."

"They won't be doing much better when we head back to town," Sheriff Ed Connor said. The icy wind was cutting right through the man. He was dressed in wool shirt, wool pants, and a long bearskin coat. He wrapped a Hudson Bay point blanket around him watching Lou trying to keep the horses moving down a road they couldn't see.

"You remember saying something about how much you liked these first storms of the season?" Connor asked.

"Weren't me, Sheriff. That was Corcoran. He's all snug in a rail car with a hot stove and a bottle of bourbon. He can like something like this. I don't." The two men were almost yelling at each other in order to be heard above the storm's noise.

Connor laughed as they drew up to the train station, all lit up and the station master out on the platform looking down the tracks. "He can't see any more than about fifty feet at the most."

"Train's late, Sheriff. Storm like this ain't good for

trains. Come on in, I got the stove lit and there's coffee boilin'."

"Thanks, Pardee. You said storms like this ain't good for trains. What does that mean?"

"Means snow and ice can pile up and lift the train right off the tracks. Means avalanches can come crashing down the mountainside and wipe out the tracks or worse, hit the train. Lots can go wrong for trains in a storm like this."

Connor seemed to be visibly taken with that account and walked slowly into the station. Benches lined the walls but no one was sitting, photographs and murals of engines, coaches, and tracks of the Eureka and Palisades line were hanging from or painted on the walls, but the scenes were all spring and summer, not winter's reality. The feeling though, was generally one of hospitality. Connor didn't see any of that. He wrapped that point blanket tighter and made for the stove.

This ain't good. If that train ain't here in half an hour I'm going to have to put together a rescue posse. People die in storms like this. Corcoran and O'Keefe bringing three dangerous outlaws in. Connor's mind was going a mile a minute as he tried to put together the rescue. Getting good men out in a raging blizzard, having extra animals, would he even think of bringing wagons? He would need the doctor, lots of blankets, and more than anything else, food.

He motioned Foster over. "If that rain ain't here in half an hour we gotta go find it. Here's what I want you to do. Go to the firehouse and ring the bells. It won't be easy but we'll need to put together a rescue posse."

"We'll need horses and mules, Sheriff. I don't think we could drive wagons through this mess."

"That's right, and after you get the men for the posse, line up extra riding horses and pack mules. There'll be regular passengers on that train, the crew, too, not just Corcoran, O'Keefe, and the prisoners."

Connor looked at the young deputy and was mighty glad that Corcoran brought him into the department. "Then, go to the Bonanza Club and get food and blankets. We'll need meat and bread mostly, and get that packed on some mules. Food for our posse and what might be on the train. Pardee doesn't have a count, so plan on maybe at least another twenty-five people."

"This'll be a circus, Sheriff. Doesn't the railroad have wires strung for communications? He should be able to get information if they're stuck somewhere."

"If they're stuck, maybe the lines are down. Maybe they aren't stuck. None of that matters. Our job is to save every sumbitch on that train."

"I'm be ready to leave, Sheriff." Lou Foster watched as Ed Connor paced around the station. "Man's got the whole world on his shoulders right now. Don't know if I'd want that kind of responsibility." Foster found Pardee, the stationmaster. "Do you ride to work or bring a buggy?"

"I ride, Lou. What kind of question is that?"

"We brought wagons down and I have to go back to town to organize a rescue. Those wagons are useless in this kind of weather. Can I borrow your horse?"

"Oh, hell, yeah. I'll get it saddled for you."

CHAPTER TWENTY-THREE

"We just cleared the summit, Corcoran. Won't be going that much faster but it will sure be a lot easier on the engine." Sparky Mulroon went to work for the Eureka and Palisades Railroad from the day it was conceived, knew the road better even than the engineers who drove the trains. "Still a real good chance of jumping the tracks, but those boys up front are pretty good at what they do. Won't be high-ballin' down this grade."

It would be a steady downhill ride into the great Diamond Valley and then flat going into the Eureka station. Corcoran was sure there was at least between one and two feet of snow on the ground with more still falling. Every lurch of the coach, every grinding, rasping howl from iron and steel joints was a cause of concern and Corcoran kept trying to put together some kind of plan to keep everyone alive if this train jumped the tracks.

"What's the chance of an avalanche knocking us off the side of the mountain?" Sean asked.

"It's happened before," Sparky said. "Usually later in the season when the snow's built up high and we get some really heavy wet storms come through."

"Like I said." Corcoran laughed. "You're just full of good thoughts. Can you get word to Eureka that we've cleared the summit?"

Sparky shook his head. "No, not without stopping and tapping into the lines and we ain't stopping. We're late and they know it, Corcoran. We're warm and dry, the train's moving forward with a good head of steam." Sparky stopped and took a long look at the big deputy.

"I've known you a long time, Corcoran, heard stories told about you, even been involved in some of them. You're gettin' yourself riled. Need to stop and look around you for a minute or so. You're worrying yourself over something you have no control of."

Corcoran laughed right out and it felt good. "Thank you, Sparky. I needed that." He reached into the wood box and handed the conductor a split log for the fire. "I'll worry about my prisoners, you worry about the train."

He walked back to where Sean was seated and sat down, pulling a blanket around his legs. "How about a chunk of that elk, old man?" He looked around at the prisoners and saw that Sean had spread blankets over them. "They'll be warm at least. Gotta be uncomfortable as hell with their hands cuffed behind their backs."

"Lacy's complaining about being hungry and cold."

"When I'm through with mine we'll feed 'em one at a time. Cut the meat into bite-sized pieces and we'll let them have one hand free. Even that's gonna be danger-ous. Gotta watch Spider and Lacy most carefully."

The chunk of elk was almost frozen but a sharp knife solved that problem and Corcoran was surprised at how hungry he was. "Been one long day, Sean, and it ain't half over." Cold meat, cold bread, and cold water made for his dinner and his mood was equally cold as he got ready to feed the prisoners.

Sean had three plates of nicely cut-up slices of roasted elk and some cold biscuits set up. "Who's first?"

"I ain't eatin' frozen meat," Lacy exclaimed. "It ain't good for my system. Gotta heat it up. Won't eat cold meat."

"Suit yourself," Sean said. "How about you, Spider? Your system up for some frozen meat>"

"Go to hell," Spider said. He turned in his seat and stared out the window.

"And you? Jonah, you up for some vittles?" Sean lifted a plate.

Jonah Samuels didn't respond and Corcoran moved over to sit next to the severely injured outlaw. He tried to find his pulse and wasn't able to. He leaned as close as he dared and couldn't find that the man was breathing either. "I'm afraid we've lost him, Sean. His head took too much of a beating, I'm afraid."

The information sent Lacy into a screaming fit. "My brother. Oh, my dear, dear brother. You've killed my brother," she howled, shaking her head violently back and forth. Corcoran sat quietly next to the dead man watching the show. *That's some of the best play-acting I've seen in a long time.*

"Ain't nobody left but you to face the music, Lacy. From fraud to murder is a big jump. From five years' hard time to the gallows in one jump. You might want to remember that it was you who ran off and left your dear, dear brother to face the music."

Corcoran unbuckled the dead man and covered him with the blanket and moved back to sit next to Sean. "Ain't nobody eating? Good. Makes our job that much easier. We'll be pulling into Eureka within the hour, I imagine." He grabbed a piece of meat and a biscuit and headed for the warmth of the stove.

———

JUNIOR TANKERSLEY and Barbara were standing near the huge desk that their father had had built. It had visible drawers, and Junior remembered, hidden drawers. The slatted cover moved with ease opening and closing, and the two looked at each other. The blizzard was howling outside the tightly fitted windows in the Tankersley home and the fireplace was sending waves of gentle heat through the room.

"I feel like we're invading his privacy," Barbara said.

"I know but it's something that has to be done. Banker McKinley said we need to look for property deeds and bank accounts. It was all Dad's private business but, now, mostly all ours. I wish we could hand this off to someone."

It was the banker, Tobias McKinley who had called the two in earlier that morning. Despite the storm they trooped through knee-high snow to the bank and their meeting with McKinley. He was a slight man, balding and pale, and a three-piece wool suit hung on his spare frame.

McKinley's eyes were warm and friendly as he ushered the two into his office and had them sit across the desk from him. The massive desk accentuated the smallness of the banker. "Your father left this with me several years ago," he said, handing Barbara a manila envelope, she being the older of the two. "I wasn't to open it until his death."

Barbara found a letter addressed to her and Sam Junior that outlined what property the family owned, what bank accounts were available to them, and other vital family information. "Didn't know any of this existed," she said. She handed all the papers to Junior and pulled some more papers from the envelope. They were bank account records and she showed them to McKinley.

"Yes, your father left everything to the two of you. You will have to make your own decisions on how or if you split it up. Along with your home, there are two parcels of property in the heart of town, currently leased to successful businesses. Your father was an astute businessman who understood the value of the dollar."

"I don't see property deeds in that bunch of papers," Junior said. "Nor lease or rent papers."

"Did your father maintain an office at home?" the banker asked, and the children nodded. "Probably find all that in his desk. If the Bank of Eureka can help with anything, you be sure to come straight to me," McKinley said. "Your father and I have had a most pleasant relationship."

The two fought their way back to a warm home and went to where Sam Tankersley had that large desk and began looking through it. "Papa was not telling the truth when he said he didn't have any money to invest in my theater project," Barbara said, after going over some of the bank records. "We're rather well-off, Junior."

"Along with all that, we have interests in mining projects, too." Sam Junior sat back and stared into the dark recesses of the large desk. "I wonder why none of this ever came up in our supper conversations?" He chuckled. "Yes, Dad," he said as if answering a question, "I'm going to continue working with Mr. Taylor at the cabinet shop." Barbara laughed, poking him lightly in the shoulder.

"And I'm going to have my theater troupe," she said. The problems of hours just past were gone from the scene as they continued going through their father's desk.

Junior was reading something and almost fell to the floor, gasping for air. "What? What is it?" Barbara cried out, slipping the single sheet of paper from his fingers. He was staring at the ceiling as she read the note.

My god." She too gasped. "We've got to get this to the sheriff. Oh, no," she cried out. "This is horrible."

She helped Junior to his feet and they scrambled into their heavy winter coats and boots for the long walk to the sheriff's office. "This must have been devastating for Betty and Papa," Barbara said. "That bastard," she said and turned crimson after saying it.

"Just proves what a foul person that Lacy woman was. Maybe that's why Nichols was able to just walk in on Dad without Dad fighting him off."

"I'm so ashamed," Barbara whimpered. "I brought him in."

"Aunt Betty said it best," Junior said. "Nichols had every intent on getting as close to Dad as he could. You just helped him along. He would have done it with or without your help. Dad was protecting us and Aunt Betty." He stopped before reaching for the door handle. "I wonder if Aunt Betty knew any of this?"

Barbara stopped and looked at Junior. They were on the porch, the wind was fearful and the snow was piling up as they watched. "He was going to kill us, Junior. What if he had someone working for him. What if someone is stalking us right now?"

It wasn't theatrics that Junior Tankersley was looking at. Barbara was frightened to her soul and reached out for him. "Let's hurry," she said. Tears were forming and her eyes wildly looked all around the two.

Slogging their way through drifts, fighting raging winds and horizontal snow, the siblings reached the sheriff's office to find it closed up. the note read, "At the train station."

"What do we do now?" Junior asked.

"Let's go to the Bonanza Club. Mr. Henderson might have an answer or two. We'll be safe. Oh, Junior, I'm so sorry I brought that evil man in."

CHAPTER TWENTY-FOUR

"I'M ONLY GOING to wait another two or three minutes," Sheriff Connor said, "and then we're going to get that posse put together. This storm isn't letting up and people are going to die if we don't move in to help."

"I'm ready, Sheriff. Just say the word." Lou Foster shivered just thinking about what it was he would be doing right in the middle of a major early blizzard. Men, horses, mules were huddled around fires waiting for the word from Sheriff Connor to start their terrible trek to find a wrecked train.

There was little grumbling from the group. They knew they had an opportunity to save lives, to help friends and neighbors, and at the same time put their lives in danger. Food and blankets were packed on mules, extra horses, saddled and bridled were standing ready. They'd be riderless going, and have riders coming back.

Deputy Sheriff Lou Foster hadn't taken two steps out the door when he turned and rushed back in. "They're coming! They're coming!" he shouted at the top of his lungs. "I can hear the whistle. They made it."

Connor joined Foster and they rushed to the open door and could hear the strained and plaintive call of the whistle fighting its way through blinding snowfall. "My god, they made it," Connor muttered, turning back to find his heavy coat. He motioned for Dr. Whidby to get ready. Doc was wrapped in a wool blanket nursing a cup of coffee, sitting almost too close to the wood stove.

Outside the men who were to make up the rescue posse started yelling, almost dancing in celebration. The train was safe. The people on the train were safe. They didn't have to make that terrible ride and the train and its occupants were safe. Jubilation could be heard for half a mile at least.

It was many minutes before the snow and ice-covered engine pulled slowly to a stop, sounding one last, long blast of its whistle. Lou Foster said he could almost see the steam turning to ice. Great ice sculptures covered the cow catcher, hung from every available scrap of iron or wood on the engine and coaches, and windows were covered in fog and ice as well.

Pardee rushed to get steps in position for the coaches, helped along by the sheriff, his deputy, and Sparky Mulroon. Members of the posse were helping, almost getting in the way. Connor called the fire chief over. "Better send these men home, Shorty. Tell them they were heroes just for showing up. We'll get the food and blankets taken care of sometime tomorrow, eh?"

Conner didn't wait and fought his way into the last coach, finding Corcoran and O'Keefe getting Jonah

Samuels's body wrapped in a blanket. "Hope you brought the doc with you, Sheriff," Corcoran called out. "Lacy and Spider need looking at. This one died on us."

"Just glad you made it at all, Terrence." Ed Connor rarely showed his emotions and Corcoran was surprised when the man grasped his hand and shook it solidly. "We were just moments from putting together a rescue party." Connor let go of Corcoran's hand and stood up straight, looking about. "What the hell am I smelling?"

Sean O'Keefe quickly shoved a cork in the flask and tucked it in his coat. "It's called mule piss." Corcoran laughed. "And our favorite wheel-wright thinks it's good for fighting off anything that ails you." Corcoran was still laughing as he said the doc would need to check on Sean as well. "I think he's lost his mind."

Connor just shook his head moving aside as Doc Whidby came down the aisle. "These two are more than dangerous than anyone you've treated in a long time, Doc, so let's be careful now." Corcoran eased the sheriff aside to let the doc in and pointed specifically at Spider Watson. "Don't need you to get hurt in all this, too."

"I'll just take a quick look at 'em here, Corcoran, then we'll bundle 'em off to the jail where I can give 'em a full check-up." Whidby looked at Spider Lawson. "Yes, son, I remember you and you'll never get another chance to hurt me." Spider grinned at the doc remembering how he had kicked the elderly man hard enough to knock the air right out of him. Lawson also remembered Corcoran slamming him up against the iron bars of the cell, breaking two ribs.

"Young people today don't even know how to spell respect, Corcoran, more or less show some."

"This one's headed for the big house in Carson City, Doc. He's carrying a bullet wound after trying to kill me. Be as careful as you've ever been around this outlaw." Corcoran stood just off to the side of Spider and the wounded prisoner saw the doubled up fist ready to slam into his head.

Dr. Whidby checked Jonah Samuels first, and determined that he was, for certain, dead. Then moved to check on Lacy Samuels. Her wrists were bloody from all the twisting and turning the woman did constantly during the trip.

"I'm getting mighty tired of having to patch you up, Spider Watson. Looks like you've managed to get that bullet wound opened up. Let's get these people behind bars first. Ain't nothing I can do for them here."

———

IF IT WAS a circus getting them on board the train it was full fledged theater getting them off and into the wagon for the trip into town. Lacy Samuels cried, wept, screamed, kicked, and spit at anyone who got near. It was Corcoran who finally put an end to the theatrics, grabbing her cuffed wrists pulling up on her hands and arms, which were cuffed behind her back, almost lifting the woman off her feet.

The hurt was intense enough that Lacy actually shut up and Corcoran hustled her over to the wagon and he and Lou Foster lifted and not so gently shoved her into the back of the wagon. She went in face first and floundered about in the accumulated snow. "Get comfortable 'cuz you're about to get company," Corcoran snarled.

He and Foster descended on Spider Watson who decided it would be best to cooperate. He too, was literally thrown into the wagon and Doc Whidby watched Lou Foster, Terrence Corcoran, and Sheriff Ed Connor drive off into the continuing blizzard. He found his buggy, stepped in and followed at a discrete distance. Sean O'Keefe sat next to him, and the two sipped on mule piss enjoying the ride back to town.

"Ain't medically approved but Corcoran does get the job done," he snickered, flicking his horse gently with the reins.

"This stuff is good for you," Sean said.

———

BARBARA AND JUNIOR had just walked up to the doors of the Bonanza Club when Foster and the team passed. "There's the sheriff now," Junior said. "Let's go back." They trudged back across the main street and up to the brick courthouse with the sheriff's facilities next door. Junior caught Lou Foster's attention and called him over.

"Might not be the right time, Junior. Just got these prisoners in from Palisades."

"I think it's just the right time, Deputy. That Lacy woman was going to kill Aunt Betty," Junior said, pointing at Lacy Samuels. He held the paper out and Foster took a quick look before tucking it under his coat.

"Sheriff," he called out. "Important." Foster and

Connor stepped into the office, out of the screaming winds and icy snow. Connor read the letter quickly and called Corcoran in.

"It just got worse, Terrence."

Corcoran stood close to the wood stove and read the short note. It was written in a fine hand. He motioned those in the office to gather around and read the missive out loud. "Listen to this. 'You've made a terrible mistake, Sam Tankersley, throwing me out like you did. If you mention what my proposition was, your daughter, Barbara, will die a slow and agonizing death. If that doesn't compel you to be quiet about our plans, your friend Betty Johansen will be next.'" Corcoran's anger could be seen plainly in his eyes and the set of his mouth.

He looked at the sheriff and simply shook his head. It was Barbara who held his gaze the longest. No one spoke but it was obvious that everyone in the room had their minds on Barbara and the Goat Lady of Eureka.

"Do you suppose she has someone besides her brother and that John Nichols working for her?" Corcoran spoke directly to the sheriff.

"It wasn't signed," Connor said. "But there's no doubt where it came from. When Nichols showed up Tankersley must have had some idea who he was and why he was there."

"That answers why Tankersley never said anything to Bill Sherman or to Gerald McKinnon. He must have been terrified when he got to his home to change clothes and found Nichols there. He died not knowing if his daughter was alive, if Betty was alive."

Corcoran's mind went in a different direction. *I would*

have fought him instantly but even after, when the man showed up in his bedroom, I would have fought him. The lean, hard-muscled chief deputy looked about the office, particularly at Barbara and Junior Tankersley. "And we don't know if there might be another killer working for Lacy."

"We'll have to have twenty-four-hour guard on Lacy Samuels," the sheriff said. Connor turned to the Tankersley children. "Did you know anything at all about any of this?"

They said no in unison and Barbara actually shivered. "I need to sit down," she said. Junior grabbed a chair and the girl sat quickly. "I never knew any of this until Junior found that letter earlier. Poor Daddy. Poor Betty." The tears were flowing, and Corcoran turned to help Lou Foster get Lacy Samuels in the door.

"We'll have somebody assigned to be with you two until this is finished," Connor said.

Corcoran and Foster had pulled their weapons and slipped them into the sheriff's desk before attempting to move the woman. Her screaming epithets echoed through the small office along with kicking and spitting. Lacy Samuels stood just over five feet tall but weighed a hefty one hundred eighty pounds and was using every ounce to make it difficult to get her in the back and into a cell.

Corcoran held her face down on the cell cot while Lou Foster unlocked her leg irons first and then her handcuffs. He tossed them out the cell door and held the door open while Corcoran let go of the woman and made haste through the door. Foster slammed it shut as Lacy came across the cell in a rage.

"Damn," Foster said. "How would you like to face that every morning?" Corcoran had to laugh right out.

"Let's get Spider tucked away and find some hot brandy, Lou. I've had it with this woman. Sean's still outside in the snow with Spider."

"She ain't gonna let Doc Whidby anywhere near her," Foster said.

"We'll have to chain her to the iron bars, I'm afraid. Two of us hold her and the third or fourth connect the irons. There's more than just conniving and fraud in her background to come up with that much strength."

Sean O'Keefe was standing alongside the wagon, a mostly empty clay jug in his hand. "Well, Spider Lawson, I've just about finished my mule piss. Time to get you in a cell. Stand up, boy," he said, watching Corcoran and Foster come out of the office.

"Go to hell," Spider said. He was sprawled in the snow in the back of the wagon and didn't move. Corcoran walked up in time to hear Sean's command and Lawson's answer and reached in and grabbed the chains holding Spider's legs together, jerked it hard. He had a slight smile and watched the young outlaw slide across the wagon on a field of ice, and tumble onto the snow-covered street.

"Don't never take back-talk from outlaws, Sean. It ain't good for the stomach." Corcoran reached down and grabbed Spider by the shoulders and jerked him onto his feet. "In the office, Spider. March," he commanded, and Lawson tried to walk on the ice with his legs chained together.

"He's goin' down," Lou Foster said, and grabbed him

just before Spider did a face plant in the ice. "Best learn to walk in those things, boy. You're gonna be wearing them for a long time now."

"Get him in a cell, will you, Corcoran?" Doc Whidby crawled down from his buggy. "He's managed to get that wound bleeding again. In fact, chain him to a chair in front of the wood stove. I'm half froze."

Foster was chuckling all the way into the office, keeping Spider as close to upright as he could fighting the ice and the ankle chains. Connor put a chair near the stove and they got Spider solidly in place for the doctor. With his feet chained together and his hands in cuffs behind his back, Whidby was able to work on the open and bleeding wound.

Lawson saw Corcoran off to his right and Lou Foster off to his left and knew just how much it would hurt if he made some kind of play against the doctor. Whidby opened his black leather satchel and pulled a bottle out.

"That's whiskey," Sean O'Keefe said watching the doctor pull the cork.

"Of course it is," Whidby said. "Best way to clean a wound that I know."

"My throat could use some cleaning," O'Keefe said and Corcoran stepped forward and took the wheel-wright by the shoulder and walked him outside to the wagon.

"Let's get Mr. Samuel's body moved over to the doctor's buggy, shall we, Sean?" The both of them were chuckling getting the near-frozen Samuels tucked in the back of the buggy. "No more mule piss for you, old man."

"Taste kinda grows on you, Corcoran. Makes me want

to howl with the wolves, sing songs of the auld home, dance with fair maidens."

"Next you'll be inviting Tiny to move to Eureka." Corcoran laughed.

It was another hour or more before the assembled group made their way to the Bonanza Club. Fill my cup about a third full of coffee, Jimmy, and the rest should be brandy. And, just keep 'em coming. Ain't had a day like this in a long time." Corcoran almost fell into one of the chairs near the fireplace.

It was a noisy group in the bar as many of the men who were part of the rescue posse were there as well. The party didn't break up for hours. Sean led some old Irish songs, and Corcoran proved that he could do an Irish jig better than any man in Eureka.

CHAPTER TWENTY-FIVE

IT WAS AT LEAST another hour before calm returned to the sheriff's office. Barbara and Junior were in chairs across from Ed Connor, the letter opened and on the desk. "Are we still in danger?" Barbara had calmed herself some, the tears were under control and the hands weren't shaking quite as bad.

"I heard you and Mr. Corcoran talking about another killer," she said.

"That's something we don't know, miss," Connor said. "With the Samuels woman locked up, her brother and Mr. Nichols dead, it would appear that you and your brother are probably out of danger." Connor sat back in his chair and looked up at the ceiling. "We don't know of anyone else in the organization."

"Nichols always talked about one of the men who worked for him at the ranch. He called him Dusty," Barbara said.

"Dusty, eh? Did he have the second half of a name?" Connor motioned for Corcoran to grab the coffee pot and join the discussion. "Heard of anyone called Dusty while you were in Palisades?"

Corcoran looked over at Sean O'Keefe. "Didn't Tiny tell us about a cowboy who hung out at Nichols ranch? Nasty tempered feller who was more than mean to his horses?"

"Dusty Loper," Sean said. "Bad sumbitch, Terrence." He turned toward Barbara and gave a slight nod, as if apologizing for the language. "Tiny wouldn't let him anywhere near his mules."

"That's him," Corcoran said. "Forgot all about that gentleman. Ran into him that one time, at the hotel." Corcoran looked over at the Tankersley children. "Did you ever run into him, Barbara, in your dealings with John Nichols?"

"No, but John did talk about a man who worked at the ranch called Dusty," she said.

"You remember what this Dusty Loper looked like?" Connor took a sip of coffee and sat back up in his chair. "We need to get word to Betty Johansen, too."

"I'll take care of that," Lou Foster said. "She needs to know what all has been happening, too. She ain't alone out there, with the Mexican herders and those big dogs, but it's best if she knows what's going on."

Corcoran was gazing at the walls trying to picture Dusty Loper. "He's not a big man, wiry, I'd say. He isn't quite six feet, thin but strong, as I remember."

"Strong enough to straighten you up when he pasted you in the jaw," Sean said. "He's got sneaky eyes, doesn't know how to smile, and a bad scar on his left cheek. Knife scar."

"I have seen a man who looks like that," Barbara said. "He was working for the carpenters, building the theater. He left right after you told me about Papa being killed," she said to Corcoran.

"Have you seen him in the last day or two?"

"No, but all work has stopped because of this storm. And..." She paused, holding back the tears, "I haven't been around the theater, because of Papa's funeral, and everything that's been happening."

"We need more people," Sheriff Connor said. He poured the last of the coffee and motioned that maybe they should move to the Bonanza Club for other types of liquid refreshment. "Foster, you ride out to the Johansen place. Try to talk Betty into coming to town for a few days."

"She can stay with us," Junior said immediately.

"Good," Connor said. "Corcoran, you and I are going to find those carpenters and find out where our Dusty Loper might be. First, though, some hot brandy might be in order."

"I'll join you for something hot," Sean O'Keefe said, "and then I've got to get back to my business. Forge hasn't been lit for several days."

"ONE OF THESE days the sheriff is gonna have me riding off and it won't be in the middle of a storm," Lou Foster grumbled, stepping into the saddle. The leather was as hard as cold iron, stirrups wouldn't move, reins wouldn't bend, and the horse didn't like any of it. A dance to the right, another to the left brought spurs into play along with strong words.

"All right now, 'cause, it's you and me and I'm gonna win. Let's get it on, and I mean right now." A touch of spurs and Lou Foster had the horse in a comfortable trot heading out of town.

Foster and his horse came to a mutual agreement, but it was a grueling five-mile ride to the Johansen goat ranch and Foster was covered in snow and ice when he rode up to the kitchen porch. The two big white dogs were ready to take one of his legs off when Betty came to the door to call them off.

"My goodness sakes alive, Mr. Foster. You come in here right this minute, young man, and get yourself warmed up. Why, my goodness, you'll catch your death being out in this weather."

"Hello, Aunt Betty. I'm afraid I'm the bearer of bad news once again," the young deputy said, shaking as much snow and ice off as he could. He stomped his boots a couple of times, shook himself, and doffed his hat before walking into the toasty warm kitchen. "Something smells mighty good in here."

"Fresh bread, Lou. Sit, boy, and tell me what would bring you out in a storm like this."

It took a few minutes for Deputy Foster to explain, first the letter, then its contents. "This whole business has been strange, Aunt Betty, but you need to know the danger of the situation. The Tankersley children would like it very much if you could move into town until this is all over and done with."

"Oh, no, I couldn't do that, not with this storm. No,

the goats come first around here."

"I know that's the way it's always been, Aunt Betty, but we're talking about a man looking to do you harm. You're more important. Your dogs, those Mexicans who work for you, they can care for the goats, let us care for you."

Betty was busy around the kitchen, adding wood to the firebox, slicing bread straight from the oven, finding a tub of fresh strawberry jam, anything to keep her from having to face the truth of what Foster had said.

Finally the thin, wiry little goat lady of Eureka sat down at the table, staring at one of the boys she had helped raise. "You and just about every child in Eureka have always called me Aunt Betty. I've been here for you any time you needed me." She smiled at the young deputy. "You know, I've needed you, too."

She covered a slice of fresh bread in strawberry jam and shoved it across the table to Foster and reached for the coffee pot. "We've had a hard time these last few days keeping the goats alive and well. Wolves and coyotes have come-a-hunting, lions, too. My boys have killed at least three wolves, and the dogs have fought off coyotes and lions."

She shook her head slowly, took a big bite of her own slice of bread and jam, and tried to smile. "My goats are my life, Lou. I wouldn't feel right running off to be safe in the Tankersley home and leaving them to whatever fate nature may have in store. No, Mr. Foster, my dear friend, I'll stay right here and if somebody tries to do me in, my dogs will take care of the problem."

"The sheriff ain't gonna like it when I tell him, Aunt

Betty, but I more than understand how you feel." Memories of having to leave his home after his parents died still brought an ache to his heart. Home, he thought is something so dear. It's not a dwelling or walls and a roof. Home isn't a place, it's a feeling, a feeling of warmth and love, of memories and people.

Foster looked across the table at Betty Johansen, and smiled. *This is home,* he thought and reached across to take the lady's hand. "I'll check on you regularly, Aunt Betty. The men who work for you, those monster dogs that love you, and this deputy sheriff ain't gonna let anybody mess with you."

Foster finished his slice of bread and jam and smiled at his longtime friend. He also knew that he would be making that five-mile ride to see to it that Eureka's goat lady was safe regularly.

She stood at the kitchen door and watched Lou Foster climb in the saddle, wave, and ride off back to town. She also saw two young Mexicans, rifles in hand standing near the barn doors with two massive white dogs nearby. "So kind of the Tankersley children to ask, and so kind of Lou Foster to ride out in this terrible storm, but I'll be fine and so will my goats."

She called the two men to come over and ushered them into the house. "There might be some men looking to hurt me, boys. We aren't gonna let that happen, are we."

They ate their slices of bread and jam, patted their rifles and laughed right out. "Nobody will hurt you as long as I'm alive," Juan deSoto said. His companion just smiled. "Nobody."

CHAPTER TWENTY-SIX

"A LITTLE SNOW blowing about and the bunch of 'em walked off," Jimmy Henderson groused when Sheriff Ed Connor asked about the carpenters. "Three big strong men, working inside, mind you, and a storm chases 'em off. I tell you, Sheriff, today's young people aren't like the way we were."

Connor chuckled and turned to Corcoran. "He's right, you know. Why, when I was a young man just starting out in life, I'd work extra hours if there was a blizzard, I'd walk five miles through four-foot drifts just to get to the job."

"Broke horses in blizzards, too." Corcoran laughed. "Cut timber after the storms started, not before, and..."

He was cut off by Henderson. "Have your fun, boys. What are you drinking?" the businessman returned.

"I want a half cup of hot coffee, the other half brandy," Corcoran said.

Connor nodded and motioned he'd have the same.

"We're asking about the carpenters because one of

them just might be connected to John Nichols, the man who killed Sam Tankersley." Corcoran pulled a sheet of paper from his coat pocket. "Named Dusty, maybe Dusty Loper. Slim, strong, knife scar on his face, and has a bad temper."

"One of 'em was called Dusty," Jimmy Henderson said. "But he quit the job the day Tankersley was killed. Do you think he did it, not Nichols?"

"No. John Nichols is the one who killed Sam but this fellow Loper, worked with him and may have been hired to kill others. You say he quit?" Corcoran took a long drink of hot brandy. "Just right, Jimmy. Learned how to drink these when I lived in Virginia City."

"Before or after you shot the sheriff?" Ed Connor laughed.

"Both," Corcoran said. "Those were good times." He smiled and turned to Henderson. "He quit or just isn't working." Corcoran had to keep the conversation going in the right direction or they'd end up giving him a ration about shooting the sheriff. It never ends, he thought.

"He's still in town, but quit the job." Henderson got a second pot of coffee put together, hoping the storm would keep these gentlemen inside the warm Bonanza Club. "Not sure where he's been living but I did see him at the grocers. His eyes were always a bit scary to me and coupled with the scar on his face, made me certain that I wanted to stay away from him."

"Molly Malloy might know more about where we can find this Dusty fellow," Corcoran said. "Let's have another round of hot brandy, Jimmy, and then I'll take a walk over."

Molly Malloy arrived in Eureka a few years ago but her name was Molly McGuire back in those days. She was in her early twenties, more than attractive with bright red hair, flashing green eyes, and had the immediate attention of Terrence Corcoran and Dennis Malloy.

Terrence was busy chasing crooks and Dennis took advantage of the situation, getting the lovely Molly to say yes to his proposal. Malloy's Market became Molly Malloy's Market soon after the wedding. Dennis Malloy was not a good husband, tried one time too many to rough up Molly, and she beat him half to death. He never fully recovered and passed away a bitter man.

"You going to ask about Dusty Loper or ask a lovely lady to dinner?" Sheriff Ed Connor joked. "Dennis is out of the picture, Terrence."

"So he is." Sean O'Keefe laughed. "From what I've seen a certain Benedict Sloan has been spending considerable time around that grocery store."

"Bless his soul," Corcoran said, almost as a snarl. He finished his hot brandy. "Mr. Sloan will do fine stacking peach cans on a shelf. I'm not looking for romance." Corcoran had a grim look on his face and those present realized that Sean had touched something very tender and it would be best not to continue the conversation.

Connor watched his chief deputy slip into his heavy buffalo robe long-coat and walk out of the saloon. "Man has deep feelings and it isn't often we're included, Sean." He turned to Jimmy Henderson. "Anything you can think of about this Dusty Loper that we might want to know?"

"Like I said, I considered him scary. I'd be mighty careful around him." He watched as Corcoran walked past the front windows, his head bent against the flying snow. "Corcoran still has thoughts about Molly, I'm afraid. He put his job before himself and he's paying for it right now."

"It's not the first time, either," Connor said. "He's still nursing that loss of Crazy Hair a few years ago. To lose her in such a tragic way, and then to lose Molly because he's a good lawman weighs heavily on that man."

———————

CORCORAN WAS STILL HALF a block from the grocers when he spotted Lou Foster riding into town and hailed him. He had to chuckle seeing Foster covered in a cake of ice and snow. "How did it go with Betty Johansen?"

"She's going to stay at the ranch, feels safe with her Mexican herders and those dogs. She doesn't recall Dusty by name or otherwise. Has a great dislike for John Nichols, of course."

"Tie that iced-up horse off and come with me. Henderson says he's seen Loper at the grocers, and I'm going to see if Molly knows anything about the man. Maybe where he lives." He almost laughed, watching Foster try to step down from the saddle. He was covered in ice and snow and his coat and pants simply wouldn't bend. Ice shattered when he tried to bend his knees, and ice broke from his shoulders when he tried to tie his horse off.

"You're a mess, my friend."

"Do you have any idea how much time I've spent riding in storms since I took this job? When I was riding herd on cows with my father and uncles, I didn't ride in this many storms. I don't think the sheriff likes me."

"It's because he does like you that you get these assignments. It's called trust, youngster."

They walked the half block to Molly's and stepped into a wonderfully warm grocery store. The potbelly stove close to the middle of the store was cherry red, a coffee pot was boiling away, and three people were sitting in chairs around the stove. The aroma of vegetables and fruit filled the store.

"Terrence," Molly called out, jumping to her feet. "Oh, my. You must be half frozen. Come, stand by the fire."

Corcoran and Foster slipped out of their heavy coats and hung them on a coat tree close by. They walked to the stove and Molly wrapped her arms around the big chief deputy and hugged him tight. "It's so good to see you." She hung on for a little longer and finally eased back. "You know Karen Thompson and Benedict Sloan, I think."

"Yes, of course. Mrs. Thompson, it's good to see you up and around. How's that leg feeling?"

"I'll be more careful getting off my horse in the future, Mr. Corcoran. The bone is healed according to Dr. Whidby but I know when a storm is coming." She laughed and motioned for Corcoran to sit by her, which he did. Corcoran had to chuckle at her comment. Her saying she'd be more careful getting off her horse could also be, I'll try not to get thrown by a nasty old mare in the future.

Was it intentional or did Corcoran just not take the

time to recognize Sloan? Benny Sloan got to his feet before Corcoran sat down. "Hello, Terrence. How was the trip to Palisades?"

"Sloan," Corcoran said, offering his hand. "That's why Deputy Foster and I are here." Everyone was in their seats, the fire was nice and hot, and Corcoran continued. "We've become aware of possibly another person who might be involved in this Tankersley conspiracy. Does the name Dusty Loper ring a bell with any of you?"

"I know a man named Dusty, Terrence," Molly said. "He comes in once or twice a week. I don't know if it's the one you're looking for."

"The man we're looking for carries a nasty knife scar across his face, has a bad temper, and may have worked for or with John Nichols, the man who killed Sam Tankersley. Ring a bell, anyone?" Corcoran was having a hard time taking his eyes off Molly Malone. She was even more attractive than just a couple of years ago.

I think it's her eyes that smack me so hard. Come on, Corcoran, shape up, old man, and get your nose back on the business at hand.

"That's the man," Molly said. "Not sure but I think he lives in one of the cabins along the gulch. When he comes in, he'll usually buy a can or two of meat and a can or two of fruit, and that's it."

"With the good hunting we have around here, why would anyone want to eat canned meat?" Benny Sloan said. "Why, I shot a beautiful deer just yesterday, Molly. I'll have to roast some for us. Would you like that?"

"We can talk about that, maybe, Ben." Molly looked Corcoran right in the eye and he was sure she winked.

"What has this Dusty man done, Terrence? Should we be a bit worried about something?"

"No, I don't think so. I need to talk to him about John Nichols. He may have worked for the man, and Nichols may have given him orders about a job before he was killed. It wouldn't have anything to do with any of you."

"I'm glad to hear that," Molly said. Her eyes were twinkling and she ran her fingers through her long red curls. Was she remembering the exciting days and nights with Corcoran? Did she make a mistake by not being willing to share the big man with his job as a lawman?

Corcoran couldn't take his eyes off her and it became more than apparent to Benedict Sloan who most definitely had his eyes on the lovely widow Malloy. "Well, then, you'd best be getting on with your search for this Dusty fellow, shouldn't you, Deputy Corcoran?"

"Now why didn't I think of that? Thank you, Mr. Sloan. We'd best get right on it, eh, Deputy Foster?"

Molly Malloy burst into laughter, along with Mrs. Thompson. Benny Sloan either didn't catch the slur or wasn't able to. He just sat next to the fire and nodded. "Terrence," Molly said through her laughter, "your humor is going to get you in trouble one day. I love it. Please drop in more often, will you? We do have some catching up to do."

"I'd like that," Corcoran said. He wanted to look over at Sloan but didn't. "Before we go, do you have any idea which of the cabins in the gulch Loper might be staying in?"

"It's one of those on the east end of the gulch, I

think. He's mentioned a couple of times that he's had trouble with the stove. It might be the cabin with the bent stove pipe, the one that smokes so bad."

Mrs. Thompson chuckled. "My late husband, Harold, is the one who accidentally bent that stove pipe. He was a chimney sweep, you know, and slipped while driving a brush into the pipe. He grabbed the pipe and got it all twisted before falling off the roof. That stove pipe's been a mess ever since."

"Poor Harold," Molly gasped. "Was he hurt bad?"

"Broke his arm is all. Hurt his feelings more than anything. Chimney sweeps aren't supposed to fall off roofs."

"Thank you," Terrence said, trying to hold back a laugh. "Let's take a walk down the gulch, Lou."

He was surprised when Molly walked him to the door and gave him a long hug. "Be careful, Terrence," she said, kissing him lightly on the cheek. He had his arms around the warm and inviting lady and promised she'd be seeing more of him.

CHAPTER TWENTY-SEVEN

LOU FOSTER WALKED BACK to get his horse while Corcoran walked to the sheriff's corrals and saddled Dude. There was no let-up in the storm as the two met up already half covered in snow. It would not be a long ride, maybe half a mile or so and the chances of seeing anyone foolish enough to be out in this melee was slim.

"If this wasn't so important, Terrence, I'd be home wrapped in a blanket hunkered up by the fire, listening to the pine logs popping and hissing." Lou Foster wanted to chuckle and couldn't get it started.

"Well, youngster, it is important, but I do understand what you're saying. If this Dusty feller is connected to Nichols, we got to root him out. You read the note that was left."

"We'll get him, I just hope it's before they find me caked in ice and frozen solid.".

The gulch, as those in Eureka called it, was the actual bottom of Eureka Canyon where a small stream emptied into the Diamond Valley. It ran along the north side of the canyon and the town sat on a ledge that extended back into the southernmost hills of the Diamond Range. The east-west road along the gulch was stream-side with cabins lining the roadway.

"If there's smoke coming from the cabin with the bent stove pipe, we'll just ride on by and try to see what we can," Corcoran said when the two started off. "That cabin has entrances both north and south and the front entrance, just off the road, has a window on each side of the doorway."

"Other than what you know about the man, what might we see?" Foster asked.

"If he has company, if others might also live there, things like that." Because of previous traffic, Corcoran and Foster were riding through trenches of snow, and more was falling. Off the roadway the snow was anywhere from one to three feet deep, depending on how the wind blew, and the wind was blowing snow in every direction.

Smoke was coming from all the chimneys along Gulch Road, even the bent-up one. Corcoran and Foster were at a walk as they went by and turned back up toward Eureka's main street. "I saw three horses," Terrence said. "Two near the barn and one in the corral. Looked like several sets of boot prints, too."

"There was movement inside the cabin. Couldn't tell if it was one person or more," Foster said. "How do we get inside?"

"By invitation, Mr. Foster. We need a solid reason for stopping and then an invite in."

"Jimmy Henderson told you the carpenters just

walked off the job? Checking on their welfare wouldn't be a good one."

"No, it wouldn't," Corcoran said. They rode back toward the center of Eureka, thinking of a good reason for stopping off at the cabin. "That chimney has been smoking for a long time so that wouldn't be a good reason, either."

"I checked the creek a couple of times," Foster said. "It's not running high, either."

"No, but it will be." Corcoran smiled and nodded at the deputy. "Good thinking, Mr. Foster. We'll stop at the cabin next to where we think Loper might be and suggest those people keep an eye on the creek. Follow my play on this," he said.

They rode back down the Gulch Road and stopped in front of the cabin next to the one with the bent chimney and tied their horses off. Jacob Somerset, an elderly and retired miner answered their knock.

"Corcoran. This is unexpected. How is it you know that I shot a bear and need a little help getting him cut up. Lots of fat for gun-grease for a year, too." He swung the door wide and motioned for the two deputies to come in. The cabin was more than warm with a wood stove burning hot in the front room and a cook stove burning hot in the kitchen.

There was a rifle rack filled with three rifles and two shotguns mounted on the wall opposite the living room stove and heads of antelope and mule deer mounted on the wall on either side of the stove. A rocking chair sat near the stove and a buffalo robe was folded nearby. It was the living room of a man who lived off the country-side and was more than comfortable doing so.

"We have our ways, Mr. Somerset," Corcoran said, giving Foster a big wink. "Be glad to help. Just want to let you know that if we get a quick warm-up, following this storm that creek might go over the banks."

"Planning on it." Somerset laughed. He was a big man, heavy in the shoulders and with long strong arms. Lou Foster thought he would be someone fierce to go up against. "Bear's a big one. Got him ready to hang on the back porch. Should get some good roasts off that bruiser, too."

They walked toward the back door of the cabin, just off the kitchen, and Corcoran asked him about his neighbors. "That bunch of drunks?" Somerset said. "Supposed to be carpenters. Well, at least they do have the right tools. Spend more time arguing and drinking than they do building anything."

"One of 'em named Dusty by chance?"

"Yeah, Terrence, there is one named Dusty. A mean sumbitch, I'll tell you." He opened the back door and stepped out onto the enclosed porch. "Just look at that big old bear."

Corcoran saw the heavy limb attached to the hind feet and ready to hang on hooks near the ceiling. The bear, fully skinned, seemed to be slouched on a divan.

Foster took in a deep breath and Corcoran realized the young man had never seen a bear skinned out. "Looks more like a heavy-set man, eh Mr. Foster?"

"If you hadn't told us it was a bear, Mr. Somerset, I'd think about arresting you for murder."

Both Somerset and Corcoran laughed at the comment. "Tell me what you know about the men next door, Jacob," Terrence said. He wrestled the bear so that it was hanging from its back legs and Corcoran took a butchering knife from Jacob and started separating a front shoulder. "You want this on that table?"

"Do indeed, Terrence. Those fellers drink more than I've ever thought about and then fight. Ain't been no gun play that I know of, but they've broke just about every piece of furniture in the place." He followed Corcoran to a large table and began boning out the shoulder.

"Dogs'll love these bones," he said. Jacob had three what he called red-bone coon dogs, and they loved treeing bears and lions. Jacob was an expert with that knife and separated the boned meat into good sized roasts, setting aside the smaller pieces and cutting them into even smaller chunks. "Bear stew coming up for tonight. You boys stay for supper?"

"Sure would like to, Jacob, but we'll have to move on. Making sure everyone knows there might be a flood coming this way. You have this under control now?"

"I do and I thank you. Hanging like this makes it easier but I couldn't lift that big boy onto the hooks." He wrapped a roast in a feed sack and handed it to Terrence. "It'll freeze solid in your saddlebags, Terrence. Thank you again." He wrapped about three pounds of the stew meat and handed it to Lou Foster. "You boys saved me and my old back a lot of grief. Come by any time."

"Will do," Corcoran said. He was wearing a big smile as he and Lou tucked their bear meat away and walked the horses to the cabin with the bent stove pipe.

"How old is he?" Lou Foster asked. "Gotta be ancient and still full of it."

"He'll be talking hunting and eating off the land during his funeral, Lou. That I'm sure of," Corcoran said, laughing loud. "Jacob is nearing ninety if he's a day. President Jefferson sent Louis and Clark to find a trail to the Pacific Ocean a little more than fifty years ago, Lou, and Jacob followed along the next year as a full grown man."

"My god in heaven," Foster said. "He was a mountain man, for real?" Foster moved to tie his and Corcoran's horses off at the cabin with the bent stove pipe. "I'd like to get to know him."

CHAPTER TWENTY-EIGHT

"STAY SHARP, Mr. Foster. If these men are drunk, we might find ourselves in a mess."

"Should have brought that beautiful knife you were using," Foster said. That was a special knife indeed. Would I like one like that," he said. "I've got a good collection of knives, but that one, it was special."

"Jacob makes his own knives, Lou. You'll have to get a little more acquainted with the man. He's a master at the art of knife making." They walked up to the cabin door and stood listening for a moment before knocking and hearing heavy boots coming to the door.

"What do ya want?" The big man's slurred speech told Corcoran that the day's drinking was well underway. Corcoran was looking at a big man, probably nearing forty or so, a belly showing through an unbuttoned shirt. He wore a full beard with streaks of gray threaded through. His eyes didn't seem to be well focused.

"I'm Deputy Sheriff Terrence Corcoran and this is Deputy Sheriff Lou Foster. Just letting everyone along

Gulch Road know that when this storm ends, there might be some flooding from the creek." Corcoran did what he could to seem friendly.

"Yeah, big deal. What makes you think I'd be afraid of a little water. I ain't scared of nothin'." He sneered, spit some tobacco juice out the door, just missing Lou Foster. "I ain't even scared of that badge you seem to be mighty proud of, showin' it off like that." He turned and hollered into the room. "Sheriff thinks we should be scared of that creek down there. Ever heard of anything that dumb?"

"Take it easy, Lefty. Here, I'll talk to him," someone said, and the two lawmen could hear movement toward the door. The cabin was about the same as Jacob's next door. A fair-sized living room with a wood stove, not burning well, and a kitchen warmed by a wood cookstove. The bent stove pipe wouldn't allow the living room stove to breathe properly.

The man coming in from the kitchen was a smaller version of the first man, shirt untucked and open, a full beard, but bald. He too was in his cups and walked with a limp. "What is it about the creek?"

"Just wanted you to know it might flood when this storm lets up." Corcoran looked around the untidy room, saw bottles and jugs laying about, dirty clothes spread around, saw that the floor hadn't been swept in some time. "Been known to get deep here in the gulch more than once."

"Don't much matter. Be movin' out soon anyway." He stood aside and nodded. "Come on in. Ain't got nothin' to offer. Creek flood some, does it?"

"You tell 'em, Butch. Like I said, we ain't scared of nothin'. You hear me, Deputy? We ain't scared of you or nothin'." He moved up close to Corcoran, shoved his chin out, daring the big lawman. "Why don't you just walk on out of here before you gets yourself all hurt."

"Threats aren't your best choice, Lefty," Corcoran said. He gave the smallest of a nod at Lou Foster, telling him not to do anything until either of these two men made their move. He turned to the second man.

"Butch, is it? Best ease this man off. We came to offer a warning. Don't much care to be threatened by a drunk." Corcoran saw a third man ease his way into the living room.

"I didn't hear no threat," the third man said and Corcoran knew he was looking at Dusty Loper again.

"Hello, Dusty. Name's Corcoran, Terrence Corcoran. Remember me?"

"Don't matter none if he remembers you or not, Deputy. You called me a drunk and I don't like that. You better take them words back. I ain't scared of you or your badge. Now, take them words back." Lefty moved hard into Corcoran, trying to shove him with his fat belly.

Corcoran took about a half step back and swung a massive right fist, up from his knees, and deep into Lefty's fat belly, knocking the man back into Butch. "Wrong move, Lefty. Now you've made the wrong move." He grabbed the half-bent-over man and shoved him into the wall.

Corcoran slammed his face into the wall, had one of his hands behind his back, and a cuff slapped on and was reaching for his other hand when he felt something move past his head, close enough for him to feel the air move.

He had Lefty's other handcuffed and whirled the man around, slamming him a second time in the belly. "What was that, Lou?"

"Knife," Lou said, showing Corcoran a large Bowie knife. Foster had his revolver in his other hand, pointed at Dusty Loper. "I think Dusty remembers you, Terrence."

"Walk over here nice and slow, Dusty. Come on, nice and slow. Walk over here right now or Deputy Foster will shoot you dead. Slow now."

The tension was obvious on every face in the room. It would take the slightest of mistakes to set off a firestorm of death. Foster had his gun aimed in the middle of Dusty's body, Corcoran was holding the Bowie knife that was thrown at him. Lefty was out of it, and Butch simply stood in the middle of the room, quiet and respectful. Corcoran wondered how he even fit in with these other yahoos.

Lefty was on the floor, trying to catch his breath. His hands cuffed behind his back, and Corcoran stepped back, waiting for Dusty. "Turn around," Corcoran said, pulling his revolver. "Cuff him, Lou."

Corcoran didn't put the gun away but instead turned to Butch. "Where's the fourth man?"

"Sleeping. On his bunk in the back. Don't be pointing that gun at me. I ain't done nothing."

"No, you haven't, Butch," Corcoran said. He tucked the big revolver back in its leather and smiled at the man.

"And good for you. Lou, why don't you and Butch wake that man up back there and bring him in here."

"Who are we waking up, Butch?" Foster asked as the two walked from the living room.

"Name's George. Don't know his last name. He's not like Lefty or Dusty. Don't got a mean bone in his body. I want you to know that I nudged Dusty when he threw that knife, or your deputy would be dead right now."

"I know, Butch. I saw that," Foster said. "I'll see to it that Corcoran knows it, too." The room was dark, not a lamp lit. The cook stove was hot but there was no coffeepot visible, no cooking utensils, either.

"That George, on the bunk?" The kitchen had a wood cookstove but no table or chairs. Instead there were four bunks scattered about, clothes spread on the floor, and wooden boxes filled with carpenter's tools. "You boys lived a little rough, I'd say. You don't seem to be the type to run with men like Lefty and Dusty."

"Needed a job and Lefty got the one at the Bonanza Club and hired me and George on. Dusty ain't one of us. He just needed a place to stay. Me and George had to quit when Lefty did or we wouldn't have got paid."

Foster looked at the man and shook his head. "You were paid by Mr. Henderson, weren't you?"

"No. Henderson hired Lefty who then hired me and George. When he quit we were out, too." Butch had a sad look on his face when he shook George awake. "Got company, George. Gotta get up."

George was a long, tall man, thin to the point of being skinny, and slowly came awake. "Why you waking me up, Butch? Damn, I spent most of the night out in this storm fixin' that woman's roof. I need my sleep."

"You'll have plenty of time for sleep, George, but we have visitors and Lefty has again proved he ain't got no brains. Get up now. This man standing with me is a deputy sheriff so come up nice and slow."

"Deputy sheriff? Damn that Lefty. I warned you about him."

"I know," Butch said. "Between Lefty and Dusty, we could end up in jail. Come out to the living room and we'll get things straightened up." Butch turned to Lou, almost asking if things would be made right. Lou turned and walked back into the living room.

"We have an interesting situation, Corcoran." Foster saw Lefty sitting along the wall, his hands cuffed behind his back and Dusty Loper sitting alongside, trussed up as well. "When Dusty threw that knife at you, Butch gave him a shove. That's why it missed. I think Butch and George have got themselves mixed up with a couple of fools."

George and Butch walked in and George had his mouth open seeing Lefty and Loper cuffed and sitting on the floor. He looked at Butch as if asking a question. "Like I said, George, Lefty's done us in again."

CHAPTER TWENTY-NINE

"MR. FOSTER, will you bring me up to date?" Corcoran walked over to the wood stove and shoved a small log in. "Butch, right now I want to trust you. Don't let me down."

Butch nodded. "Deputy, I feel the same. Me and George are here because we had a job. George even worked all night for a lady in town who had part of her roof blown off. I do drink some, George don't drink hardly at all. Me and George ain't like Lefty, but we did work for him."

"I think I understand," Corcoran said. He had a smile on his face. "Got any coffee? We got a little more talking to do and then some moving."

"You ain't putting us in jail, are you?" George asked. "I ain't done nothing wrong."

"No, George, you aren't going to jail but I am going to ask you to help us get those two down to the jail. Some hot coffee would help," he said, again with a smile.

Butch walked into the kitchen and over to a wooden

box filled with carpenter's tools. He hefted it onto one of the bunks and pulled a tin of coffee beans and a coffee pot from the box. "Gotta keep these hidden from Lefty. Damn fool would drink five pots of coffee before he'd buy a bean."

He ground a goodly amount and within minutes the aroma of freshly ground beans filled the air and mingled with the aroma of boiling coffee. "Changes the whole atmosphere, doesn't it?" George said. "Wish I'd never met that Lefty. We ain't had a decent meal or a good cup of coffee since the day we went to work for the man. Don't like making those kinds of mistakes."

"I'm pretty sure that if you have a nice chat with Jimmy Henderson, you and Butch could get a job finishing that theater. I don't think he knows the situation with you boys and Lefty," Corcoran said. "Tell me what you know about Dusty Loper. How is it he came to be living with you?"

"That's one strange sumbitch," George said. "He dresses like a ranch hand but he ain't one. I'm from Nebraska, raised on a big ranch with cattle and sheep. Loper's a killer through and through, the kind that robs banks and kills women. I seen them in the Dakotas, in Nebraska, in Wyoming. His eyes tell you all you need to know."

Corcoran took a long look at George, feeling good thoughts about the man. *I'd like to take a few days and get to know this man. There's been a whole lot going on in his life.* "How'd Loper come to be here?"

"Lefty brought him in," Butch said. "Something about losing his job at a ranch north of here. The owner being killed or something like that. He didn't buy a piece of food for anyone but himself, didn't do a lick of work around the place, and tried to pick a fight with me or George every damn time Lefty and he got drunk."

"Nice guy," Lou Foster said. He looked at Corcoran and caught a slight smile on the chief deputy's face.

"Did Loper ever mention that rancher's name?" Corcoran asked.

"John something," Butch said. He looked over at George. "Can't remember the last name." George shook his head.

"Does Nichols ring a bell?" Corcoran asked.

"Yup, that's the man. John Nichols." Butch turned to George who nodded. "Don't know too much about the man other than he liked young girls and spent money freely."

"Ever say why he was in Eureka?" Corcoran was getting close to some questions that had been bothering him. Was Nichols here to maybe prod Sam Tankersley into joining the mine fraud? Was he using Barbara to get close to Sam? To kill him if he talked too much? George and Butch just might have some answers.

"He was in town, dancing with that floozie who's going to be putting on shows at the theater," George said. "She did flaunt her stuff for the so-called rancher. Got hisself killed, though. When the little girl wouldn't play one of his games and he went back to his ranch. Don't know what Dusty did for the man but he was paid well."

Corcoran took the coffee offered by Butch and took a long look at Dusty Loper sitting on the floor, scowling right back at the big lawman. *I wonder if he's still on the payroll even if John Nichols is dead? Was he paid in advance to kill the Tankersley girl and her brother? To kill Betty Johansen?* "Other than drinking too much, did Loper ever talk about what he did for Nichols?"

"He rarely talked at all when he was sober but he did enjoy telling stories about his so-called escapades when he was drinking," George said. "Said he was doing secret work for Nichols and others were involved. Big money, he liked to say."

"Damn fool, but he and Lefty got along well," Butch said. "They both drank heavy and I think that Lefty may have known that Nichols feller maybe a little more than me and George. Something in the way they seemed to react to one another."

"You're saying you think that Lefty, Dusty, and Nichols may have all been friends?"

Corcoran saw that Dusty was listening and was angry as all get out over George's descriptions. "Don't like to hear those words, eh, Dusty? Too bad for you," Corcoran joked. "One more question and then we need to get these two down to the jail. Did either Nichols or Loper have any friends here in town?"

"Nichols was hard to get along with," Butch said. "He only had eyes on that filly, Barbara Tankersley."

"But maybe knew Lefty?" Corcoran asked.

"I think so," Butch said. "I'm pretty sure, maybe because of Dusty, that Lefty and Nichols became drinking friends. Nichols was a gambler and so was Lefty."

"Yeah, with our wages," George said.

"Dusty hung around with a couple of the gamblers at

the Bonanza Club," George said. "Don't think he had any friends, though. He and Lefty or he and one of the gamblers, and all they talked about was how good they were at what they did."

Corcoran chuckled. "And just what were they so good at?"

"Lefty believed he was the best carpenter in the world." George laughed. "And Dusty was hired at a high rate to see to it that people didn't live long."

"Actually said that?" Foster asked. "My god, how stupid can you get?"

"That's why they're outlaws, Lou," Corcoran said. "Ain't got smarts one between 'em. Well, let's bundle these two up and get them tucked in cells. Butch, I'd like it if you and George could help, and we'll talk some more when we get them put away."

———

IT WAS an interesting parade with Corcoran in the lead, riding Dude, Lefty and Dusty, their hands cuffed behind their backs and walking through deep snow. Lou Foster rode behind the prisoners with George and Butch bringing up the rear on their horses. Foster chuckled to himself, looking out across the scene, thinking, all they needed was a brass band.

Moving the prisoners from the cabin and onto Gulch Road didn't take much effort, either. They had jackets wrapped around their shoulders and buttoned, hats placed on their heads, and the threat of a good beating if they didn't play the game.

Corcoran used the rope hanging from his saddle to tie the two men together so they would walk side-by-side. "You try something stupid in this deep snow and ice and all you're going to do is get hurt." Corcoran said. "The other end of this rope is tied to my saddle horn. Got it?" He didn't wait for an answer, stepped into the saddle and nudged Dude into a nice walk.

"We ain't going but about half a mile, boys, so just watch where you're stepping and you'll be fine."

Neither prisoner said a word the entire walk into town and because of the storm there were few residents out and about. The few who were out yelled their greetings in sometimes colorful language but Lefty and Dusty stayed quiet.

Getting Lefty and Loper in cells didn't take much effort. The two were half frozen being out in the bitter cold and neither man was willing to take another punch from Corcoran. The rest of the group settled into chairs around the stove, hands as close to the hot iron as they dared.

"We'll need a statement from you, Butch, about giving Loper a push as he threw that knife. You'll be on your way home shortly." Corcoran was standing alongside the stove and smiled at George. "Stop off at the Bonanza Club on your way and talk with Henderson. I'm pretty sure he'll want you two working on that theater when he finds out what happened."

CHAPTER THIRTY

"WE'RE MISSING SOMETHING, SHERIFF," Corcoran said when Butch and George left. "The way George talked, Dusty Loper has already been paid to kill Barbary Tankersley and Betty Johansen."

"Well, they're safe, Terrence. Loper's all locked up back there."

"That's the problem, Ed. I'm just not so sure. I'm going to take a ride up to the Tankersley's place and see if I can get some more from Barbara. Jimmy Henderson said she hasn't been down to check on the theater at all."

"Are you thinking somebody else is involved? I don't see that at all," Ed Connor said. "Nichols brought Loper in to take out the Tankersley children and Betty Johansen if Sam Tankersley decided to come to the law. Even if he was paid in advance by Nichols, he's behind bars."

"I know. Sometimes I really don't much care for logic, Sheriff." Corcoran laughed. He bundled up in his buffalo robe long-coat and walked to the door. "Looks like this storm is finally gonna blow itself out," he muttered, stepping into the saddle. It was a quick ride to the Tankers-ley's and he found Barbara at home, pulling fresh bread from the oven.

"Smells mighty good in here," Corcoran said when she invited him in. "So, you're a dancer, singer, and bread maker, eh?"

She giggled. "Mama taught me a long time ago. Let's go in the kitchen," she said. "Yes. I love making bread and I've got fresh bread out and another loaf to go into the oven. You look like you're worried about something."

"Just a little bit, Barbara. I'm going to get a little personal with some of my questions, I'm afraid. You'll be glad to hear that we have Dusty Loper behind bars but I need to know as much as I can about both he and John Nichols. As far as I'm concerned, that threat is still an open question."

She gave him a quick look at the word threat. "Ask away, Mr. Corcoran. I've embarrassed myself so much already." She was ready to start crying again. "I've really been stupid, haven't I?"

"I wouldn't call it stupid, Barbara. Maybe one of the penalties of youth. You'll grow out of it." He smiled when she poured fresh coffee for him and then sliced still-warm bread and offered it with a bowl of strawberry jam.

"Good," he said, still chewing his first taste. "Tell me about Nichols and Loper, particularly Loper."

"He was a strange man," she said. She looked up toward the ceiling, thinking about how to answer the question. "He scared me just being in the same room with him. Even if there were others around, I felt scared. Something in his eyes said he was planning to do something awful." She sipped some coffee and took a small bite of bread.

"Have you ever walked up on a dog and knew immediately that the dog was going to attack? That's how I felt when I was around the man."

"You ever get the same feelings around Nichols?"

"No. That's why that letter surprised me so. It was John who was doing the threatening and I would never have thought that. He was a smooth talker, I see that now, and I fell for his sugary words and actions. All he wanted was to get near Papa and I led him right in the door."

Corcoran didn't want to sit through another sea of tears and weeping but had to keep getting answers. "Did you see anyone in particular hanging around with either Nichols or Loper? Even if just casually?"

"Dusty didn't have a single friend that I saw, except for one. He was one of the carpenters. I'm sure I heard his name, but can't recall it right now. I think John was also friends with the man. They seemed to all get along."

"Does the name Lefty come to mind?"

"Yes, that's him. Lefty. Never heard a last name. The three seemed close. Even some of the low-lifes that hung around John seemed afraid of Dusty. John tried to be friends with everyone and even the men who were always around the gambling tables saw through him and his smooth talk. Wish I had. Do you think there's someone else who might be after me or Aunt Betty?"

"No, I really don't, Barbara. I think you, Junior, and Betty are safe." Corcoran wouldn't come right out and say he was worried about something because he didn't know what it was he was worried about. *There's something missing and I can't put a handle on it.*

"How soon after your father threw Lacy Samuels out did John Nichols appear in town?"

"Maybe within the week," Barbara said. "I was talking with Mr. Henderson about the theater when he just walked up and joined the conversation."

"Did Henderson know him?" Corcoran asked.

"As I think back on it, Mr. Corcoran, I don't think he did." She blushed and then seemed to get angry. "He seemed to have a great interest in me. Damn," she said and blushed even more. "I'm sorry," she said.

"That's all right. I think I understand. We've all been young."

"And stupid," she said. She walked and got the coffeepot and poured for both of them. "He just joined right in but was most interested in talking with me and I was enchanted by the approach and interest. It had to be just a few days after Papa told Lacy to leave."

Corcoran drained his cup, thanked Barbara for her time and headed back to the sheriff's office. *Whatever it is that's got me riled, I'm not going to find out any more from Barbara.* "When did Dusty Loper appear? Did he come in with Nichols?"

"He wasn't with him that first day but very soon. He showed up within a day or two."

Corcoran sat back and looked at the table, the coffee. *Nichols's backup. Dusty Loper was brought in to make sure Nichols got the job done. Did Lacy pay him, or did John Nichols? Either way, when Nichols died, Loper's job was to kill the Tankersley children and Betty Johansen.*

———

CORCORAN, Sheriff Connor, and Deputy Foster were sitting at a table in the Bonanza Club café having pie and coffee when Henderson came in and joined them. "Nice little parade earlier today, Corcoran. You're getting good at it."

Corcoran grimaced but Connor laughed right out. "Two parades in two days, eh, Jimmy? Remember that on the Fourth of July and we'll see what we can do."

"Did George and Butch come over to see you?" Corcoran asked.

"Did, Terrence. Told me all about how Lefty managed to foul things up. They'll be back at work in the morning. Things'll be peaceful around the job without Lefty there. Think it's all over?"

"I'd sure like to think so," Connor said. Corcoran gave him a look that said otherwise, but Connor didn't catch it. He kept right on. "Let's go have a brandy and talk elk hunting, trout fishing. Anything but murder and mayhem."

I guess that's the difference between us. I don't see this as being over with at all. We think Loper was hired, even paid in advance, to kill Barbara Tankersley and Betty Johansen, but we don't know it for a fact. Worse, we don't know if he had help. Damn.

Corcoran always insisted he never wanted to be sheriff, that his life was best when he served as a deputy, but wasn't he showing signs of being a sheriff with these thoughts? Was he questioning the sheriff? He'd look you in the face and say no right out. Why then did Corcoran have these thoughts that there was yet something that he, they, had missed?

The four men were at a table by the front windows watching a few people out on a cold evening. The wind was strong but wasn't carrying a load of snow. The barman brought glasses and a bottle of brandy over. "Anything else?"

"Want hot coffee with that brandy?" Henderson asked.

"Not this time. Just brandy and talk about anything but crime and outlaws." Connor laughed.

They were on their second round when gunfire erupted across and down the street. "That's mighty close to the jail," Corcoran said, jumping to his feet and grabbing that heavy buffalo long-coat. "Let's go."

He and Lou Foster almost made it a race through the deep snow arriving at the jail in time to see two men ride off. "Who were those men?" Lou yelled.

"One of 'em was Dusty Loper. Saddle our horses, Lou. I'll go see what happened inside." He looked back toward the Bonanza Club and saw Sheriff Connor limping as fast as he could go toward the jail. That bad leg of his just wouldn't let the man run. "He's given more than most men would ever give to keep Eureka safe," he muttered.

Corcoran had his revolver in hand when he burst through the door and into the office. Lefty had a shotgun, still chained to the rack and dropped it when Corcoran aimed that big Colt at his face.

"On the floor, Lefty. Now, dammit." Lefty was half a second from death and dropped to the floor, staring up at the big lawman. "Who else is loose?"

"Just us," Lefty said.

"Us?"

"Loper and me."

"Who brought the gun?"

"Friend of Lopers. Don't know him."

"All right. On your feet and back into the cell area. Move it," Corcoran snarled. He pushed the man into a cell holding Rory Tibbets and slammed the door. The other cell had the door open and no one inside.

So the other man must be Spider Watson. If that's so, how did a gun get involved? Who brought the horses? Where is this third man? How did that door get unlocked. All the gunfire in the world isn't going to get that cell door open, so what was the shooting?

Corcoran looked around the jail and couldn't come up with any answers. "Who set you free, Lefty?"

"Don't know. One of Dusty's friends."

No it wasn't, Corcoran thought. *Dusty doesn't have any friends.* "What was the gunfire?"

"Shot the chain holding a rifle for Dusty. Was supposed to blow the chain off that shotgun for me but it didn't quite come loose. You'll never catch 'em."

Corcoran took a fast look around the cell area and saw Lacy hiding under her cot. "All right, woman, come out of there. Why didn't they set you free?" She eased her bulk from under the cot and sat down on it, never saying a word.

You weren't a part of this, were you. This wasn't your doing. Corcoran was trying to see this escape; he would have been sure that it was Lacy's setup. Nichols worked for

Lacy. In fact the whole mine fraud was Lacy's. *But this escape wasn't her doing.*

Corcoran made sure the door holding Lefty was secure and walked back into the office. He saw the key ring to the cells was not hanging on its hook, and two rifles were missing. He checked the shotgun Lefty was trying to get loose and saw where bullets hit the chain but didn't break it. He found the cell keys on the floor behind the wood stove and walked toward the office door just as Lou Foster came running in. Sheriff Connor was right behind him.

"They went east, Corcoran. Could be toward Aunt Betty's." Connor was breathing hard. "Two men riding hard."

"There's a third man and he's close." Corcoran looked at the two lawmen standing with him. "That was Spider and Dusty riding off but somebody brought them horses and set them free, supposedly a friend of Dusty's."

"Thought Dusty didn't have any friends." Foster was quick to pick up on that.

"Yup," is all Corcoran said. "Ride hard for Betty Johansen's place, Lou. I'm gonna find that third man. He's on foot and in town. Stay with Betty. Sheriff, the rest of the prisoners are back in their cells."

Lou was gone in seconds and Corcoran found the keys to the rifle rack and unlocked a short-barreled shotgun and dumped several rounds in his coat pocket, after shoving one in the gun. Sheriff Connor was rubbing his bad leg after fighting snow drifts and high wind on his way to the office.

"What've we got, Corcoran?"

"That problem that's been bothering me for two days. Someone we know nothing about brought this on." Corcoran went on to describe what he thought took place in the jail, the fact that two horses were brought but it was Spider who took the second horse, not Lefty, and that Tibbets and Lefty were back in their cells.

"Everyone has told us that Dusty Loper didn't have any friends other than Nichols and Lefty." Corcoran stood next to the stove and shook his head. "He obviously damn well does have at least one."

"You thinking George or Butch?"

"No." Corcoran snapped out his answer. "No, but whoever it is is willing to risk his life on this. Must have been watching us, too. Brought two horses to the jail and just walked right in? Knew we weren't home, Sheriff." Corcoran was still wearing that heavy coat and made for the door.

"Gonna do some tracking," he said and walked out.

CHAPTER THIRTY-ONE

No new snow was falling as Corcoran started looking for boot prints leaving the sheriff's office, but the wind was still blowing hard, moving snow about, hiding the prints Corcoran was looking for. Seemed like half a dozen men had walked all over the area in front of the office and Corcoran had to start his search for boot prints further and further out.

When a tracker simply doesn't know which way his prey went, he starts working in a circle from a known point, eventually crossing the track as the circle widens out. It is most helpful if the tracker has a good idea of what his prey's prints look like, and in this case, that third set of boot prints were embedded in Corcoran's mind.

It was a long search with the big lawman letting his circle get wider and wider. *There you are.* There was a line of prints, mostly out of the wind, leading up the hill from the sheriff's office toward the courthouse about a block away. Corcoran stopped at one distinct boot print to give it a good look.

Probably a fair-sized man I'm trying to find. Prints in the snow could be almost like prints in mud and Corcoran was trying his best to pick out something that would distinguish that boot from others. *He's not wearing spurs and these look like heavy work boots. A man working cows from high on a horse doesn't wear these kinds of boots. Neither does someone who sits at a poker table all night.*

He was following the prints, some getting hidden in windy areas, putting together a good idea of the person he was following. *I wonder if this is a friend of Lefty's, not Loper's. Lefty seemed to make friends with ease.* He followed the prints as they turned east at the courthouse and Corcoran's brain turned on full force.

I'm sure I'm right thinking this can't be a friend of Dusty Loper. Whoever I'm following is a friend of Spider Watson. Now we're getting somewhere. He was in a section of town filled with residential housing not businesses, and the wind, mainly because of trees, hedges, even brick and wooden fences wasn't hiding the boot prints, and he slowed down near a large elm tree.

"Randy Skilicorn lives in this neighborhood," he muttered trying to remember where the former resident of the Carson City Prison lived. "Randy went up for robbing and battery on an officer and he and Spider have been accused more than once of robbery. Why didn't I think of that? We just walked out of the jail and left it open for him. Sheriff won't like me telling him what we did, since he was one of us."

There were small homes, some almost cabins along

both sides of the street. Elms, fruit trees, some evergreens and of course the staple of Nevada's hillsides, cottonwood trees grew in profusion and Corcoran knew he could be walking into an ambush. *A man with a rifle could be in any of these building, behind any of these trees, in the shade anywhere. Which of these homes is Randy's?*

Corcoran got his answer the hard way. He was standing next to a large pine tree when a bullet hit the tree just inches from Corcoran's head. He fell to the ground, had the shotgun cocked and hoped there would be a second shot. He thought the first one may have come from one of two houses across the street and down some.

Corcoran was looking for a way to get closer to the cabins and saw elms, but not thick trunks, and a cottonwood, which would be perfect. Lots of trunk to hide behind.

Come on, take a second shot, and the man did. *Okay, mister, you're in the smaller cabin and firing from a window.* Corcoran sprang to his feet and raced across the street where he dove behind the cottonwood, spraying snow about. A third shot was fired but missed and Corcoran used trees, the house he was near, and bushes as he sprinted his way toward the gunfire.

He was under a flowering bush of some kind. The flowers were dead but the leaves still allowed him to hide in their shadows. He was within fifty feet of the window where he was sure the gunfire came from and waited to see if any more was in somebody's plans. It didn't take long and he saw a rifle barrel extend a bit through the open window.

Corcoran put the shotgun down and drew his revolver. *Come on. Show me a part of you I can hit. Come on, now.* The person holding the rifle was apparently looking in all directions trying to find him but not getting close enough to the window for him to spot the man. Corcoran picked up one of the rocks that encircled the bush and tossed it out into the snow and Randy took the bait.

He leaned out the window, the rifle to his shoulder, and Corcoran shot him through the chest. Randy yelped, dropped the rifle, and Corcoran ran and dove through the open window, ripping part of the frame loose, leaving part of that buffalo long-coat hanging on the splintered frame. He rolled across the floor, ending up hard against the man he'd shot.

Randy Skilicorn's blood was pumping from the chest wound and he was dead in just a few seconds. "Wanted you alive, mister. You have created some serious problems for us." Corcoran grabbed the man's rifle and moved quickly from room to room, rifle at the ready, to see if Randy had help. He didn't, and Corcoran made the long walk back to the office. *Damn. My favorite winter coat. Hope it ain't ruined.*

———

"It was Spider's break-out, Not Loper's," Corcoran told the sheriff. "I gotta get out there and help Lou. Tell the doc where Randy's body is." Sheriff Ed Connor nodded.

"Want a coffee warm up before you go?"

"I do but I won't." Corcoran chuckled. "Want the

whole pot half filled with brandy but Lou might be in trouble. Both Spider and Loper have rifles or shotguns. Watch out for that bunch in the back, Ed," Corcoran said and walked out to find Dude, wrapped the buffalo robe and jumped in the saddle to ride off through town. Jimmy Henderson waved from the café window.

No parade today, Jimmy.

Five miles, he rode at a fast trot head-on into the wind but at least the snow had quit. Patches of blue sky could be seen and if the reason for the ride wasn't filled with so much danger, Corcoran would probably have been delighted in the views. It was getting late in the day, and shadows were stark in the sunshine. Every tree, every brush, every rock was its own little statue, some rather exotic, some almost erotic.

Dube's favorite gait was a strong trot and the ride to Betty Johansen's would have been a quick one, but wasn't. Corcoran could see the prints from the two riders trying to get away and Lou Foster's stood out as well. "Where the hell are they going?" Corcoran said as the three riders took a turn at a north fork in the road. "This trail goes north to the Ruby marshes."

He changed Dude's gait to a stronger trot and put some speed on. "It'll be a cold night, Dude. Even if we find 'em, it'll be a cold night." He hadn't gone two miles and heard gunfire in the distance.

"Ease up, boy. Let's make sure we ride up on the right side of this fight." Two more shots rang out and Corcoran was able to come close to pin-pointing their location. He moved off the main trail and slowly made his way through deep snow and drifts around heavy brush and had to watch for ditches and draws that would severely injure his horse. Two days of high winds and snow filled in all the low spots and those kinds of drifts were most dangerous.

He let Dude pick the way, not worrying about running in a straight line. As they came up from a low spot he caught sight of two horses about thirty yards or so off to his left. "Damn," he muttered. "Almost rode up on 'em." He stepped down from his big stud and tied him off to some brush before beginning his stalk.

Can't see Foster's horse. Sure would like for him to know that it's me coming toward Spider and Loper. It was slow work and it wasn't easy trying to be quiet about it. One would think moving through fresh snow would be a quiet adventure but slippery rocks under the snow made one dance some, and dead brush under the snow, looking like a rise, was tripped over, and Corcoran had to keep his eyes roaming the vast area in front of him, looking for something unnatural, like a head or hat, like something making a bush quake.

It had been many long minutes since the last shot was fired and Corcoran feared the worst, afraid that a bullet had taken young Lou Foster, not just out of the fight, but out, all the way. *He has all the makin's of a fine lawman, young, strong, good thinker, almost fearless. Stop it, Terrence. Right this minute, stop it.* Let his mind run away? Can't have that when men with guns are nearby and willing to kill on sight.

Corcoran took a deep breath and continued forward, slowly, small steps toward those horses and two men with rifles. He was behind a large stand of sage when he spotted some movement slightly to the right of the standing horses. *Too far for the shotgun and I don't recognize what made the movement.* Was it a bird lighting on a bush? A rabbit or ground squirrel running away? Or was it a man searching for a target?

He froze in place waiting for whatever made the brush move to make it move again, and it did. *So, Mr. Dusty Loper, we meet again. Where's Spider?* Corcoran eased the Colt from its holster, cocking it on the way out, and took a long sight down cold steel. His finger barely moved before fire erupted from the end of the barrel. A great blanket of white smoke hung in the still air.

Two men screamed out, one seriously wounded and bleeding heavily, the other from the sheer shock of a gun being fired within ten feet of his head, not knowing anyone was nearby. Dusty Loper fell forward, face first into a snow-covered bramble bush and Lou Foster whirled in time to see Terrence Corcoran recock the Colt.

"Holy catfish are flying," Foster said. "Where the hell did you come from?"

"Stay down," Corcoran said. "Where's Spider?"

"Dead. About fifteen feet on the other side of Dusty. I could almost feel the heat of that shot. You are something being able to sneak up on me that way. Never heard you." Foster stood up and moved to Corcoran's side. "Sure glad you're here."

"Don't want to have to spend the night, Lou. Let's get these yahoos tied to their ponies and head back to town. It's gonna be below zero before long. We want to do everything we can to keep Loper alive. I want to know what John Nichols paid him to do."

The two of them got Spider's body sprawled across his saddle and tied in place and started working on Loper. "Lots of bleeding, Corcoran." Lou Foster stuffed some rags down into Dusty's shirt front to try to stem the bleeding. "Sometimes you're just too good of a shot."

Corcoran had to chuckle softly and helped Foster wrap a tight band around the wounded man.

Lifting Loper into the saddle took joint effort and getting him tied onto it made for frozen fingers. "I'll ride close to him in case he tries to fall off," Corcoran said. "You break trail and don't slow down unless I yell loud."

The sun dropped those last couple of degrees quietly and the men headed back toward the village. It was bitter cold and Corcoran was grateful that there was no wind. Stars shone brightly, lighting the trail somewhat. There was no moon, but the trail stood out and they made good time riding up to Dr. Widby's home/office. Light was shining from the windows and Lou handed the reins to Corcoran and ran to the door.

Whidby heard them coming and met Lou at the door. "What now?" he asked.

"Got a man shot bad, Doc." Foster got back to the horses, got both of them tied off while Corcoran started getting Loper untied. Whidby had the door opened wide and the two deputies carried Loper in to the doctor's examining room. "The other one's dead," Foster said.

"Leave the body outside in the cold while I do what I can for this one." Whidby shooed the two out and started undressing the body. Lefty's remains would freeze solid overnight. "Get a fire going, bring me a bowl of warm water, and then go away," he said.

"Is he always so friendly?" Lou Foster asked, trying to hold in a chuckle. He found split logs to stoke the already burning fireplace and got some water while Corcoran untied and moved Spider's body near the porch. The temperature had to be near the zero mark and the body was almost frozen already.

"Do what you can for Loper, Doc. I really want to talk to him," Corcoran said, sticking his head in.

"Quit shooting 'em and you can talk all you want," Whidby shot back. Corcoran just shook his head and he and Foster headed for the sheriff's office, trailing the two riderless horses.

CHAPTER THIRTY-TWO

"NO MORE SURPRISES," Sheriff Ed Connor said, sitting behind his desk with a full cup of hot coffee. "Finding Skilicorn involved in this mess was a real surprise."

"Too much of one," Corcoran said. "It isn't like us to get caught up like that. I should have thought of Spider's friends right up front. Won't happen again, Ed. Won't."

"In the morning, Lou, ride out to Betty Johansen's and let her know she probably isn't in any more danger. Corcoran, you let the Tankersley kids know, too. I'm calling it a day, gentlemen." Connor got up, drained his cup, found his coat, and walked out the door.

"Love that man," Corcoran said. "Best sheriff this town's ever had and I've worked for three of 'em."

Foster wanted to say, "and haven't shot any of therm," but caught himself. There was a time and a place for that kind of humor. Instead he went back into the cell area to make sure the night jailer had everything he needed.

"These people are most dangerous, Leroy. Don't get close. They'll be bringing food in the next hour or so.

Remember not to get tricked by them. That woman is most dangerous." He came back into the office to see that Corcoran was getting into his heavy coat.

"You put a pretty good rip in that coat, Terrence. I've got some good strips of buckskin if you want me to sew it up."

"You do that? Years working cattle as a young man, I learned how to take care of my duds. I'll fix it, but thanks," Corcoran said. "Cocktails and then a steak about this big," he said. His arms were well out to the side and his grin said it all.

"I'm going to check on Barbara and Junior and then head home and get a huge fire in the stove," Lou Foster said. Corcoran gave him a long look and smiled.

Don't know if he's ready for her, but it will be a good learning session if nothing else. "Enjoy," Corcoran said. "If he makes it, we'll want to have a session with Dusty Loper in the morning. I really want to know what Nichols had him paid to do."

————

CORCORAN, Foster, and Sheriff Connor were sitting at a window table in the Bonanza café, waiting for breakfast to be served. The sun was doing its best to chase off the overnight freeze, there was no wind, and streets were icy. More than one person was seen to be doing the world famous Eureka two-step coming down the icy boardwalk.

"You went by Doc's already?" Connor asked.

"Soon as I saw smoke from the chimney." Corcoran

laughed. "Loper's going to make it, he said. He gave me hell again for shooting to kill. How else would I shoot?"

"Keep doing what you do best, Corcoran," Connor said. "Do you think Loper had any friends? Any?"

"After getting caught with my pants down by Skilicorn I've gone through everything Lefty, Butch, and George said and I don't think the man had a friend at all. What bothers me, is did he have anyone working with him on Nichols's dime? He might have access to a hired gun as well."

"Was Nichols a partner with Lacy Samuels or did he work for her?:" Connor asked. "She's the brains behind the mine fraud, and worked to get Tankersley involved. When that didn't work, she knew Tankersley had to go. He knew too much." Connor was shaking his head. "This is what we know."

"Right," Corcoran said. "And we know that Nichols killed Sam, but was it on orders from Lacy, or did he do that on his own? And," he said again, "was he alone?"

"We've been thinking that Dusty Loper worked for Nichols. What if he worked for Lacy and was sent here to see to it that nothing else went wrong? She had time to send someone here in Eureka a wire before she left for the ranch. Our outlaw wire operator didn't say anything about one, though." Connor looked over to Lou Foster.

"Well, young man, what have you got to say about all this. Particularly your visit with the kids."

"Barbara and I talked about that last night," Foster said. "She can't remember anyone meeting or talking with John Nichols other than at the gambling tables or at the bar other than just casual conversation."

"Have a good time, did you?" Connor teased. "Mighty pretty young filly there."

"She's quite well-read, sings beautifully, and, yes, I did enjoy myself." Corcoran looked for a slight blush and didn't see one. *That boy is growing up. Good for him.*

By the way Foster said it, it seemed obvious the young man wasn't going any further in the conversation. "What did Doc say about being able to talk with Loper?"

"Maybe later this afternoon. You riding out to see Betty Johansen?"

"Right after breakfast. Be riding in bright sunshine for a change." Foster gave the sheriff a quick look and turned away, catching a smile from Corcoran. "I enjoy riding in the bright sun."

Connor headed for the office after breakfast, Foster to see Eureka's goat lady, and Corcoran stepped into the bar area hoping Jimmy Henderson might be about. George and Butch were working on the theater and he caught their eye.

"Morning, Corcoran," George said. "Cold enough for you?"

"And then some." Corcoran laughed. "Caught Dusty last night. Wounded, but hopefully will live. Seen Henderson around?"

The two men shook their heads and Corcoran moved off toward the bar and saw Henderson emerge from the counting room of the big club. "How about some coffee, Jimmy?"

"You bet. Brandy?"

"Not yet. Tell me again everything you know about John Nichols."

"I've been thinking about him, seems like every minute since all this started. You know what I know. What's bothering you? I thought you had this pretty much put together."

Corcoran took a seat at one of the tables nearest the rock fireplace and thought about that. *I want to think that Nichols killed Tankersley because Lacy thought he might talk about their mine scheme. I'm just not sure of that. Was Nichols told to kill the children and Aunt Betty because they might know too much? And did he hire Dusty Loper to do it? Why? Why didn't Nichols do it? He already killed one, what would one or two more mean? Why did he return to the ranch and get killed by Lacy?*

Henderson brought the coffee over and sat down. "Nichols was a killer, Terrence. Simple fact. Came to kill Sam Tankersley, which he did."

"Then, oh great thinker, why did he have to hire Dusty Loper to kill the Tankersley children?"

"You're under the impression he did. Nobody's said for a fact that he did. You haven't put the question to Loper, have you?"

Corcoran leaned way back in the chair and stared at the ceiling. "Nichols left town immediately after killing Sam and in turn, Lacy killed Nichols at the ranch, not here in town. Was it Nichols who wrote the notes to Sam saying he and the children along with Betty Johansen would be killed if anyone talked about the mine scheme?"

"What if it wasn't?" Henderson asked.

"Damn," Corcoran said. "I've been chasing shadows ever since I heard about the fraud plan. And I'm still chasing a shadow." Corcoran sat quiet for a couple of minutes, sipping at his coffee, staring off into the barroom. "Lacy sent him to kill Tankersley, and someone else saw opportunity, Jimmy. Not Spider, hell he would have tripped over it. But Loper? Very possibly."

Who else? Corcoran let his mind wander over all the names that have surfaced in this simple plot to rid the Eureka Mine and Mill of several thousand dollars. "The note wasn't designed to get money, it was designed to put fear in someone's mind."

"That's right," Henderson said. "In Sam Tankersley's mind. The children, even Betty Johansen, weren't supposed to know about the threat."

"All the little leads running around in my head end at Dusty Loper. He had to be the one to write the note and there is no reason for him to do so unless he was being paid. He had no other part in the scheme. Nichols was paid by Lacy. Her brother was paid by Lacy. Palisade's resident deputy was paid by Lacy."

"I think you just answered your question," Henderson said.

"I think so, too. A talk with Loper is still on the schedule, but a longer talk is about to happen with Lacy. That mean old woman is about to have a chin-to-chin chat with Corcoran, Terrence Corcoran."

Jimmy Henderson laughed, grabbed the cups and headed for the coffeepot. "Brandy in both of them this time."

———

IT WAS a little later in the morning when Lou Foster rode back into town. He had a small feed bag tied to his saddle horn and grabbed it as he dismounted in front of the sheriff's office. "Brought some gifts from Aunt Betty," he said, easing the sack onto Ed Connor's desk. "Cheeses, smoked elk and goat meat, and some of her good sourdough rolls. She's going to be fine and this is her way of saying thank you."

"Wonderful," Connor said. "That lady got you milking her goats?"

"Oh, I've milked her goats many times, Sheriff. Every kid in Eurekas has milked those goats, eaten pounds of the best cheese in the country, and dunked cookies in the milk, too." His eyes were bright remembering all those times. "If I ever get married, I want a woman like Aunt Betty."

There was genuine laughter in the office for the first time in many days. "What did you learn at the Bonanza after I left?" Connor asked Corcoran.

"I'm about to have a chat with Lacy Samuels, Sheriff. That's the most important thing I learned."

CHAPTER THIRTY-THREE

SHERIFF ED CONNOR listened as Corcoran spelled out what he thought was how the fraud scheme investigation was finally going to play out. "You have it, I think. We all put too much emphasis on John Nichols thinking he was working for Lacy. I think we were right in that he was her hammer, Terrence. The difference, though, is Loper. I'm almost positive, right now, that he was paid by Lacy not Nichols."

"Nichols was a hired killer and Lacy had to get rid of Tankersley," Corcoran said.

"Why?" Lou Foster asked. "He did his job, that's for sure."

"Nichols was sloppy in the killing and Lacy knew if I tracked him down that he would give everything up. She knew the man too well, I think, and knew he had to die. She also feared that Sam Tankersley had told both Junior and Barbara, along with Betty Johansen, why he threw her out. That's when she brought Loper in."

Corcoran nodded to Lou Foster. "Best bring the lady in, Lou."

He headed into the cell area. "Better be two of us," he said.

"Let's bring her out here, sit her near the stove, keep her coffee cup filled, and get some answers. She's wily, Ed, has been questioned by some of the finest lawmen in Chicago, so we won't simply get answers. We'll have to drill and blast to get them."

"Is she a drinker?" Connor asked and Corcoran shook his head. "I was thinking a bottle shared between us might loosen a tongue."

"Tiny never once said anything about her drinking. I don't think so, but she is an eater. We could share a platter of cheese, some good smoked meats, and maybe some sourdough rolls. Her eyes would be bulging, Ed."

Corcoran and Foster were chuckling as they walked into the cell area to bring the feisty woman out. "Morning, Lacy," Corcoran said. "Have a good night, did you? Time for you and me to have a nice little chat."

Lacy fought hard but Corcoran used all the tricks and got her hands behind her back and Lou got the cuffs on and tightened. When a man fights you, Corcoran told Lou more than once, you use what's necessary to subdue the prisoner. If that means a solid punch to the face, so be it. It ain't the same with women prisoners. You might want to beat the hell out of 'em, but the judge will have some sharp words for you if you do.

Lou Foster did what he could to hold the strong woman in place, wanted to smack her a good one, but remembered Corcoran's words. "She needs a good smack to the jaw, Corcoran," he said after Lacy was cuffed.

"Sometimes it's the only way, but it has to be in serious self-defense, youngster." The cuffs gave Corcoran the leverage he needed to guide her out of the cell and into the office. She was quite willing to be seated near the hot wood stove. She scowled at Sheriff Connor and was still cussing Corcoran and Foster.

"Thought you might like to know what happened after those men broke out yesterday. Bet that tooted your horn, eh, Lacy? Those fools just ran out and left you. You ain't got a friend in the world, do you?" Corcoran opened a package of cheese and cut a wedge off, taking a big bite. His eyes were bright, and he had a grand smile, saying how good it was.

"Why did they do that, Lacy?" Ed Connor cut a slice for himself and poured a healthy shot of bourbon from his flask. "Didn't they know you were the honcho of the mine fraud? That you were the one who paid the bills?"

Lacy Samuels had had a bowl of boiled oats and a slice of unbuttered toast for breakfast and that was hours ago. That cheese looked good and she knew she could smell smoked meat close by, too. She didn't say a word, thought, just looked away. Lacy Samuels had no intention of talking with these fools, wasn't going to be bribed with smoked meat and good cheese.

"How much did you pay Dusty Loper, Lacy?" Corcoran asked it right out. "We talked with him earlier, you know."

Connor took a quick look at Corcoran and smiled

gently. *He's got a way about him. Will she bite? It has to be that she brought Loper in to kill the Tankersley kids, not Nichols.* "Dusty got shot real bad, trying to run away, but Doc Whidby's getting him all fixed up." The sheriff took a drink of whiskey.

"He'll be more than well enough to testify at your trial," Corcoran said. "How much did you pay him to kill those children and Betty Johansen?"

Lacy didn't say a word but watched intently as Corcoran opened a package of thin-sliced smoked elk and made a little sandwich of it and another slice of cheese. The sourdough roll, probably baked earlier that morning at the Johansen goat ranch, filled the office with a delightful aroma.

It was Sheriff Connor who broke the ice. "Smells good, doesn't it? How close to dinner are we, Corcoran?"

"Another hour, at least, Ed."

Connor looked at Lacy. "You getting hungry? Like a slice of elk and some of this fresh bread?" He caught her almost saying that she indeed would but she held back. Connor looked at Corcoran. "We ain't bein' very gentlemen like, Terrence. Think Miss Samuels would like a slice of elk?"

Corcoran walked behind the lady outlaw and undid one of the cuffs, brought her arm around and connected her wrists in front. "Maybe a small slice, a chunk of bread, and a slice of cheese, Ed." He looked down at Lacy who had her head turned up to see him. "Think that might help you talk to us a little bit?"

She didn't say anything but did nod her head and

Corcoran in turn nodded his to Connor. The sheriff fixed a small plate and handed it to Corcoran who slowly handed it to Lacy. "Take a nice bite or two Lacy, and then talk to us some. The judge might look favorably on what you have to say."

"Ain't got nothing to say," she said, after stuffing the morsels in her mouth. Corcoran withdrew the plate and looked at her, shaking his head slowly back and forth.

"You killed John Nichols, Lacy, because he was sloppy and brought the law toward you, and you're gonna hang for that. It's a shame we can't hang you twice because others have died also, because of you. What we can do, however, is give the judge a report in which you gave us information that led to saving the life of others. The judge could change that penalty from hanging until dead to life in prison."

"Think about that, Lacy. You could be the queen at the prison for the rest of your life," Sheriff Ed Connor said. Would she bite? Lacy Samuels was always the one in charge. She demanded to be the boss, and with her bulk and strength, she would run the other women prisoners.

Lacy motioned for Corcoran to bring the plate of meat and cheese back. "What do you want to know?" It was almost a whisper and Corcoran held the plate out for her.

It took less than half an hour and the entire mine fraud was discussed along with the killings and threats. "I'll see to it that the judge is fully informed, Lacy. Back to your cell now," Corcoran said, and he and Foster walked her back. She was as quiet as a church mouse the rest of the day.

———

Lou Foster knocked on the front door, which was opened almost immediately. "Mr. Foster. What a nice surprise," Barbara Tankersley said. "Look at you, not covered in ice. Please, come in."

"Thank you." She led him into the warm living room after he shucked his heavy coat and hung it and his hat near the door. "It's for sure, Barbara, that you and Junior are safe. Lacy Samuels just told us that she was the one who wrote the threatening note and hired Dusty Loper to..." He wasn't able to say the words.

"To kill us?" Barbara asked.

"Yes," he said softly.

"I'm glad it's over, Lou. I've learned so much, still feel awful because I was so naive, so young and foolish. Give me a good kick in the rear if I do something stupid like that again." She looked up at him and smiled. "I rode out to see Betty Johansen earlier and we had a long talk. She seems to know so much about life, and I seem to know nothing."

She motioned Lou Foster to sit near the fire and she sat across from him. "I'm going to continue with building the theater, put on shows, but I won't be acting like I have been."

"You're more than just an attractive young woman, Barbara, and I think you know it. What makes you so special is your new attitude toward life. I wish your father was still alive."

"Me, too, Lou, but why do you?"

"Because I would like to have a talk with him. I would

like to sit in this very room, across from Sam Tankersley and ask him, straight out, if I could ask you to have supper with me. To go to the fireman's picnic with me. To go to the Eureka Fair with me."

Barbara Tankersley squealed, jumped to her feet and took the two steps across to Lou's side. She sat next to him and took his hand, bringing it to her face and kissed it. "Father would have a few questions to ask, you know. About intentions and all that."

"Intentions would be obvious, Barbara. I'd like to rope and tie you, drag you to the fire, and burn my brand deep." He was crimson by the time he finished. Lou Foster had never, ever, talked to a woman as he just did. He fully expected to get slapped for the indignity of it. Foster had his head bowed, not willing to look into her eyes but kept right on talking.

"I don't have a cattle ranch, don't own my own business, Barbara. I'm just a deputy sheriff and I want to be one for a long time. I don't make a whole lot of money and don't have very much to offer someone like you, but those would be my intentions."

"Father would invite you to have dinner with us and would have a lot of interesting questions to ask. Since he isn't here at the moment, I will ask you. Deputy Sheriff Lou Faster," she said, almost as a judge might, "Will you have Thanksgiving supper with us? I'm not sure that Junior will be able to make it, though."

Foster was sure his heart stopped, and managed to get a breath or two in, and, still holding her hand, simply nodded his head. They sat in the living room next to each other, holding hands for the rest of the afternoon. There is no indication that they said a single word to each other, just looked into their eyes and smiled.

Lou Foster was unable to tell Corcoran or the sheriff what they had for Thanksgiving supper.

CHAPTER THIRTY-FOUR

"COME IN, Sheriff. Corcoran, good to see you. I hope you're bringing me some good news this time." Eureka Mine and Mill manager Bill Sherman ushered them into his office and slipped behind his massive and cluttered desk. Sit, gentlemen.

"I think you'll like what we've found out since our last visit," Connor said. "Lay it out for him, Terrence."

"I'm aware how close you and Sam Tankersley were and how worried you were that Sam might have been involved in the fraud. Lacy Samuels hired John Nichols to kill Sam because she feared he was going to come to you or us and give her scheme away."

"Yes," Sherman said. "I'm aware of all that. It was his idea that we bring the information to you, though."

"Yes, but he was under intense threat and couldn't talk about it. The woman took one more step, Sherman," Corcoran said. "She sent a note to Tankersley saying that if he went to us or to you, she would have his children killed along with the woman he had been seeing, Betty Johansen. That's why he didn't come to us or to you. He was even more fearful when you planned to come to us."

"The fact that our bookkeeper discovered the fraud that allowed him to want to come to see you," Sherman said, seeing how it all played together. He knew what was happening and didn't dare say anything or Barbara and Junior would die. That woman is a fiend, Corcoran." Sherman sat back in his chair, an ugly scowl on his face.

"I'm glad to know all this, Corcoran. Thank you," Sherman said. "Do you think she would have done that? Killed Barbara and Junior?"

"She hired a man named Dusty Loper and we believe to do exactly that, Sherman. He was in town and we think he was waiting for her word. He didn't get the go-ahead because we took her into custody before she could send the message."

"My god, that close." Sherman sat absolutely still, staring at the walls. "If you hadn't jumped on this case, those children would probably be dead right now. Terrible." He stood up and walked to the window. "I have a bit of good news, too. We've made some big changes here at the mine as far as how we order and pay for material. Orders are centralized and payments can only be made by our finance department. We won't be open to that kind of scheme again. I want to thank you, Sheriff, and you, Corcoran for a fine job. We don't have any of our money back but we know those who took it are either dead or in jail. Good job."

"Thank you," Ed Connor said.

"Remember that at election time," Corcoran joked and they all shook hands.

"Any plans for Thanksgiving?" Sherman asked. "The wife and I are having a mixed table. I captured two squab and shot a turkey day before yesterday. Baked apples and green beans that she raised and canned. I'll not fit in my pants, I'm afraid." Sherman didn't laugh often, but he did at his own comment.

Connor looked at Corcoran before saying anything. "I don't do much at these holidays since I lost my wife. Corcoran wants me to come over but I turned him down. Probably just fry up some meat and maybe make some biscuits. I'm not a holiday kind of person."

Sherman wagged his head. "You're missing out, I'm afraid, Sheriff. How about you, Corcoran? Got plans, do you?"

"Gonna roast up half an elk, Bill. Sean O'Keefe, Buster, and George, the carpenters, are coming over. It'll be a long night with lots of good food, plenty to drink, and I'm sure some fine Irish singing. Maybe one day, I'll talk the sheriff into joining us."

"Not my style, Corcoran." Connor chuckled. "Glad all this is over, Bill. Keep those drills pounding and tap 'er light, my friend."

They rode side by side back to town. "You really should come over, Ed. Good food and friendly people."

"I know, Terrence. Maybe next year."

———

CORCORAN WAS SITTING in front of the fire at his little cabin at the far eastern edge of Eureka when Sean O'Keefe came through the door, walked over and sat down. He had always been like that and Corcoran just accepted the fact the man didn't knock, just walked in. "Sparky Mulroon brought me a package, Terrence. Two packages, actually. One is addressed to you."

"Are you going to tell me they are from Tiny? I see you got my message, though."

"Indeed I did, laddie buck. Indeed I did and I'm looking forward to roast elk and all the trimmin's. One thing I know about you, Terrence me boy, you know how to cook."

"Mother taught me, Sean. Said with my personality it would be a long time before I got settled with a wife, you know, and I'd best learn how to cook for myself. Aye, Sean, it'll be roast elk and a pot of boiled potatoes we'll be enjoying. I've got two apple pies cooling as well. What's in the packages, really?"

"For you, Terrence, a bottle of Irish whiskey straight from the old country. We'll share it, I'm sure." Corcoran laughed and nodded his okay at the thought. "And, for me, my own bottle of mule piss, freshly distilled."

"Not even barrel aged, Sean? Blasphemy, I say." They chuckled and Corcoran stuffed another log on the fire. "I didn't think we'd ever get to the bottom of that mine fraud investigation, but we did. Wish you'd been with us at the mine."

"Bill Sherman glad it's over as well, I imagine."

"Yes, yes, and they've changed the way they do business, so we won't have more of this in the future."

"I'm still confused about this Dusty Loper. He came to Eureka before John Nichols or after?" Sean opened the bottle of Irish whiskey and poured each a godly amount.

"Loper was Lacy Samuels fireman, Sean. When she discovered how close Nichols was to Barbra Tankersley, she sent Loper to keep track of the man. She also gave him standing orders that if anyone in the Tankersley orbit gave indications they would come see either the sheriff or me, they were to be eliminated."

"Nichols's job was to eliminate Sam Tankersley and Loper's was to eliminate the children and Betty Johansen. Lucky you saw all that developing before it could take place."

"It was when Lou Foster and I met up with the carpenters that things started to fall into place. In my mind, there was no reason for Loper to be there. He was not a carpenter, he wasn't even a good man on the ranch, but he was a killer."

Banging on the door interrupted the conversation and Corcoran let the boys in. "Welcome, gentlemen. I'm glad you got my invitation."

Each of the carpenters carried a bottle, and George had his fiddle as well. Sean jumped to his feet and howled to the wolves. "Oh, my, Terrence Corcoran you do know how to set up a party. You do, indeed, laddie buck."

Corcoran had no neighbors so there were no reports on how long the night's festivities went, but Corcoran was found well after sunrise sitting alone at a table in the Bonanza Café, a pot of coffee on the table.

Sean O'Keefe did not open the carriage and wheel

shop the next day, and no work was done on the new theater that was being built at Eureka's leading casino. Sometime after nine o'clock that morning, Lou Foster walked into the sheriff's office wearing a broad smile and not talking.

A LOOK AT: BORDERTOWN TROUBLE

A Snake and the Dog-Man Classic Western

In the early 1870s, from the Rocky Mountains to northern Mexico, a couple of drifters discover their true purpose—in the form of hard-hitting western adventure!

When Snake and Dog-Man are "asked" to leave Deadwood and travel south to what they think will be gold country, the nomadic cowboy pair manages to stir up trouble, help others, and attempt to locate the hard money they set out for in the first place.

And while their adventures are always rollicking fun, they're also incredibly dangerous. But at least they're able to maintain their dignity—most of the time.

Join these daring drifters as they navigate the rugged terrain of the Wild West, where danger lurks around every corner and the pursuit of gold is only surpassed by the bonds of friendship forged in the crucible of adventure.

AVAILABLE NOW

ABOUT THE AUTHOR

Johnny Gunn has worked in print, broadcast, and internet, including a stint as publisher and editor of the Virginia City Legend. These days, Gunn spends most of his time writing novel-length fiction, concentrating on the Western genre. Otherwise, you can find him down by the Truckee River with a fly rod in hand.